The Advocate's Dilemma

Teresa Burrell

Silent Thunder Publishing
San Diego

This book is a work of fiction. References to real people, events, establishments, organizations, or locales are intended only to provide a sense of authenticity and are used fictitiously. All other characters, and all incidents and dialogue are drawn from the author's imagination and are not to be construed as real.

ISBN: 978-1-938680-06-9

DEDICATION

To all the victims of sexual abuse who have suffered the shame only they can know.

ACKNOWLEDGMENTS

I will forever be indebted to my good friend and editor, Marilee Wood. Without her, my books would not be possible.

THE ADVOCATE SERIES

THE ADVOCATE (Book 1)

THE ADVOCATE'S BETRAYAL (Book 2)

THE ADVOCATE'S CONVICTION (Book 3)

THE ADVOCATE'S DILEMMA (Book 4)

Chapter 1

"Why is there a dead man in your office?" Bob asked.

Sabre spun around to face her friend.

"Oh Bob, I'm glad you're here." Sabre shuddered. "The police just arrived."

Several police officers and detectives were checking for evidence. Sirens blared as more police cars arrived. An officer approached Bob and asked, "Who are you?"

Bob reached out to shake the officer's hand but put it back down when he realized the policeman was looking elsewhere. "I'm Attorney Robert Clark, a friend of Ms. Brown's." He nodded his head toward Sabre. He looked around the room and then added, "And her attorney, if I need to be."

"Please step back. Actually, I'd like both of you to wait in there." He pointed to another office next to Sabre's. "And please don't disturb anything."

Bob and Sabre entered David's office. Sabre hadn't been in there in a long time as David seldom came to work. He spent most of his time with his new ice cream business. Sabre walked her new Gucci heels and cobalt blue suit over to David's window. Her brown hair hung just beyond her shoulder. Bob followed her to the window.

Sabre started practicing law when she was twenty-five, just over six years ago. Bob started a few years earlier. They both knew not to touch anything and were very careful. As they gazed out the window, they watched the cops block off the area outside of the building.

Bob put his arm around Sabre's shoulder. "You okay?" he asked.

"It was a bit of a shock to find a body on my desk, but I'm all right. I'm just wondering how and why it's there."

A tall, thin detective with blond hair entered the office. Sabre had spoken earlier with another detective, but she had yet to meet this man. He appeared to be in his mid-thirties, around Bob's age. His hair was just beginning to recede.

He reached out his hand to Sabre and then Bob. "I'm Detective Shane Klakken with the San Diego Police Department."

"Sabre Brown. This is my office. Well, not this office; the office with the body is mine."

"I'm Robert Clark. I'm a friend and colleague of Sabre's."

"Have a seat if you'd like," Klakken said.

Sabre looked at the black powder on the beige chair and decided to remain standing with Bob and the detective.

Klakken looked at Sabre. "I understand you found the body."

"Yes, I did."

"What happened?"

"I don't know. I walked in and found him lying across my desk."

The detective turned to Bob. "Where were you?"

"I wasn't here; Sabre called me. I was on my way to court, so I wasn't far away."

The detective turned back to Sabre. "Come with me and show me exactly what you did." He looked at Bob. "You wait here."

Sabre walked out the door, the detective close behind her. Bob followed. Klakken frowned at Bob but didn't say anything. Sabre walked past her office and into the small entranceway to the back door. The area also functioned as a copy room.

"I came in here through the back door."

"Was the door locked?" the detective asked.

Sabre thought for a second. "Yes, I think so. Yes, it was. I had to put my key in the door and I…I turned the lock."

"You're sure?"

Sabre nodded. "Yes, I'm sure."

"And then?"

"I walked into my office."

"Show me, please."

Sabre walked past a large copy machine that had a sign on it that read, "TEMPORARILY IN ORDER," past a small desk, and through the hallway until she reached her office. A policewoman was leaning over the body, examining him. The dead man was still sprawled across the desk, lying exactly as Sabre had seen him earlier. He appeared to have been standing behind her desk and had fallen forward. His face was turned away from them, his right arm hung partway off the far side of the desk, and his left elbow lay next to his body with his hand on a manila folder. He wore torn jeans and a dirty, black t-shirt. The only other things on the desk were a penholder, a desk lamp, and the key box, all of which set near the corner of the desk closest to the door. Sabre kept her desk very tidy. Two other men were in the room. One was dusting for prints; the other was looking through Sabre's bookshelf.

"What looks different than the way you left it yesterday?" Detective Klakken asked.

Sabre pointed to her desk chair that was now about two feet from her desk. "My chair was pushed in behind my desk, not over there. That photo of my brother on the credenza was standing up. And there was no body on my....Oh no!"

"What is it?"

"Ron's hourglass is gone." Sabre stepped forward and pointed to a spot on the desk near the man's head. "There was a large hourglass sitting right there."

"What did it look like?"

Sabre fought back the tears. She had so few things left that belonged to her brother and couldn't bear the thought of losing one more.

"It was an antique, mahogany, Victorian hourglass. Very solid and heavy, about ten inches tall," Bob said, helping her out.

Klakken noted it on his pad and then walked over and told the man standing near the bookshelf. Bob put his arm around Sabre. She took a deep breath and composed herself. She looked at the man on the desk and muttered. "I guess there are worse things than losing a keepsake."

Klakken returned. "Start from the top and tell me what you did and what you saw when you came into the room."

Sabre took a deep breath and blew it out. "When I came in here, the first thing I saw was him lying on my desk. I dropped the files I was carrying because I was startled."

The detective looked around at the floor. Two manila folders, each at least one inch thick, lay on the floor near the door. A number ten envelope lay just under the desk near the leg, and a single sheet from a yellow legal notepad lay close to the folders. "Is this all you had in your hands?" he asked.

"Yes," she said. Then she shook her head. "No. I also had my keys."

"Where are they?"

"I dropped them in that little box on my desk. That's where I always put them."

"Where is your purse?"

Sabre looked puzzled. "What?"

"Your purse? What did you do with your purse?"

"I don't carry a purse."

"You don't carry a purse?" Klakken asked skeptically.

Bob spoke up. "Nope. She doesn't carry a purse."

The detective shook his head and mumbled. "I've never met a woman who doesn't carry a purse."

"Well, now you have. I have a briefcase that is with me most of the time. That's in the trunk of my car. I don't need another piece of luggage to drag around."

"Okay," the detective said, "so after you came in, you saw the body and dropped your files. Then you put your keys in the box?"

"No. I still had my keys in my hand."

Bob spoke up again. "Does it really matter what she did with her keys?"

"I'm just trying to get a clear picture of exactly what happened and what may or may not have been disturbed."

"It's okay, Bob." Sabre said. "I remember yelling, 'Hello,' but he didn't say anything. I said something else like, 'What are you doing here?' Still nothing. I pulled my phone out of my pocket."

"With which hand?" the detective asked.

"With my left. My keys were still in my right hand. He didn't move. That's when I reached over to try to awaken him."

"You didn't know he was dead yet?"

"He looked dead, but I thought he might be drunk."

"You weren't afraid?"

"A little, but I didn't really think about it. I just wanted the man off my desk, so I touched him on the arm. He felt cold, so I called 9-1-1."

"What did you do before the police came?"

"I stepped out of the room and I called Bob."

"Do you know the dead man?" the detective asked.

"No, I don't think so," Sabre said. "I walked around the desk and looked at him, but I didn't stand there studying his face. I'm pretty sure he's not anyone I know. At least I didn't recognize him."

"Well, let's take another look." He led her around the side of the desk. Bob followed.

"Do you know him?"

Sabre shook her head. "No. I've never seen him before."

Bob ran his hand through his prematurely gray hair and said, "I recognize him." He looked up at Sabre and Klakken. "He's the husband of one of my clients."

Chapter 2

"Why is your client's husband lying dead on Ms. Brown's desk?" Detective Shane Klakken asked Bob as they entered David's office, along with Sabre.

"I have no idea," Bob answered.

Sabre sat down in David's chair behind the desk and Bob and Klakken sat across from her. The detective gave Sabre a disconcerting look because she had taken the big chair. It was an unconscious power play which she realized when she saw the look on Klakken's face. He hadn't missed it. "What's his name?" the detective asked Bob.

"George Foreman." Bob smirked.

"George Foreman? A skinny, little, white guy named George Foreman?" Klakken asked.

"I didn't name him. I just represent his wife."

Sabre looked at Bob, her eyebrows raised. "He's the father on the Foreman case?"

"Yes," Bob said.

"Oh, no." Sabre thought of his children and what they had already endured.

"What kind of case is it?" Klakken asked.

Sabre answered. "It's a juvenile dependency case. I represent the children—two boys."

"Please don't tell me he named them George."

"No. They're Marcus and Riley."

"Abuse case?" Klakken asked.

"Neglect, primarily. Drug use, kids not attending school, nothing that unusual."

"May I see the file?"

"Not without proper protocol," Sabre responded. "You're welcome to the reports but I would need to remove any work product first. I'm sure you know that you're not entitled to my opinions or legal theories or any notes or materials prepared with an eye towards impending litigation, such as my investigative reports or memoranda. So I would have to remove those before I could give you the file. It would probably be quicker for you to obtain the file from the Department of Social Services."

A tall, African-American woman walked into the office. "Excuse me, Klakken. You wanted an update?"

"What is it?" he asked.

"It appears that the victim was killed here, but we're still not certain. There's a large bruise across the victim's temple. It seems he had a blow to the side of his head that may or may not be the cause of death. He has a number of bruises and scrapes on his arms and a small scratch on his face, but most of them look old. There's no sign of forced entry so either the door was unlocked, he had a key, or someone let him in. His driver's license says his name is George Foreman and the address on it is La Jolla."

"La Jolla?" Klakken asked. "He sure doesn't look like a La Jolla resident."

The detective just nodded and continued. "His wallet contains a piece of paper with an address on it and two business cards—one for Marla Miller, Department of Social Services, and the other for Attorney Regina Collicott. He has what looks like an old prom photo of two teenagers. The boy looks like it could be him. The young girl is very attractive. He had no money or credit cards. He also has a vial of what looks like meth in his pocket." She handed him a manila folder. "This file was under his hand on the desk. It appears to be a juvenile dependency case. And...." she hesitated.

"What is it?" Klakken asked.

"He had a cigarette butt inside a baggie tucked into his belt."

Bob and Sabre exchanged looks. "That's odd," Bob said.

Klakken nodded to the other detective and she left the room. "We see some pretty strange things in this business, as I'm sure you do."

Klakken opened the folder and Sabre didn't object. She knew by the looks of it that it wasn't her file and even if it belonged to her, it was part of the crime scene. Although, if it was her file, she would've attempted to stop him. Sabre's conviction to her oath of office was strong. She believed wholeheartedly in the attorney-client privilege. Without it, the system failed. If a client couldn't trust his attorney and know she wouldn't betray a confidence, he would never tell her anything. It was balanced by rules of professional conduct that didn't allow an attorney to provide false information to the court. So, if a client admitted to a crime, his attorney couldn't let him testify and say he didn't because the attorney couldn't intentionally let a witness commit perjury. It made for a fair system. As a result, some attorneys didn't want to know if their clients had done the deed. Sabre didn't operate that way. She wanted to know, and then gave the best defense she could. She found it a lot easier to represent a client when there were no surprises.

The folder contained a social study from the Department of Social Services, a petition, and a detention report, nothing the police couldn't easily obtain. Sabre would've given him that much. Her only concern was her work product. She watched as he glanced through the paperwork.

Klakken turned to Bob. "How well did you know Foreman?"

"I only met him once. I had an appointment with his wife and he tagged along. He was pretty angry and I had to ask him to leave the office. Actually, it was Sabre's office."

"Your office?" Klakken said, looking at Sabre. "Here? In this building? Where he is now?"

Sabre shrugged. She hadn't realized until now who Bob had met with when he used her office.

"My office had a gas leak and so we met here," Bob said.

"I'll need to speak to your client," Klakken said. "We'll need her to identify the body. Can you have her meet us at the coroner's office? You're welcome to be present if you'd like."

"I'll get her there." Bob stood up. "I'll call the court and let them know I've been detained. Sabre, do you have court this morning?"

"Yes. When you call, let them know I'll be a little late. I'll cover what I can for you."

After Bob left the room, Klakken said, "Is there anything else you can tell me about what happened here?"

Sabre shook her head.

"Did you see anyone around when you came in this morning?"

"No one unusual. Casey, an attorney who works upstairs, drove up the same time I did. We walked up to the building together but then he went to his office."

"Did Casey come inside?"

"No, there is no entrance to his office from inside here. There's a stairwell on the outside that leads to another set of offices. I came in alone. No one else was here."

"Who else works in this law office?"

"Jack Snecker owns the building. He has the front office. He's in Hawaii on vacation." She glanced around the room. "David has this office but he seldom shows up. He has another business so this is only part time for him. Elaine is the receptionist and secretary for all of us."

"Where is Elaine?"

"She had a doctor's appointment this morning and won't be in until the afternoon."

"And they all have keys, I presume."

"Yes, of course."

"Have you given anyone a key?"

"Only Bob, the attorney who was just here." When she saw the look on Klakken's face, she suddenly wished she hadn't told him about the key.

"Who else might have one?"

"I don't know for certain. I don't think Jack changed the locks when I came here, so I suppose past tenants could have them. Jack and David are both married. Their wives may have them."

"And Jack's in Hawaii?"

"I'll get you his cell number. And Elaine might be able to help you as well." Sabre searched on her phone for Jack's cell number and gave it to Klakken. "Oh, and there's a janitorial service that comes in once a week."

"Which one?"

"I don't know, but I can look in Elaine's Rolodex."

Sabre walked out of the room and into the front lobby to Elaine's desk. She flipped through the Rolodex and wrote down the number listed under "Janitor." Bob walked in the front door carrying some folders and smelling like cigarette smoke.

Bob handed Sabre the files. "This is what I have on calendar this morning. You're on three of them and we're not protesting anything on those. The Barber case is a trial set; I wrote down some dates for you. And the Jones case will need to be continued if I'm not back. See if you can put it over until tomorrow. I don't think my client will show anyway, but I need to be there."

"I'll take care of them. Did you call your client on Foreman?"

"Yes, I just hung up."

"Did you tell her that her husband was dead?"

"Dana doesn't have a phone but the woman she's staying with does, so I called her. She's a good friend of Dana's and has been a big help to her since this case started. I told her and she was going to tell Dana. She said she would take her to the coroner's office, and I'll meet her there shortly. I'm sure Dana's pretty upset. Even though she and her husband were separated, she was very invested in their relationship. She was planning to take him back once he got his act together."

"I better call Marla, the social worker, and let her know what's going on. She'll inform the boys once the body is identified. Marla is very good at that sort of thing. Better than I would be. I'm glad she's on this case. It's going to be especially hard for Marcus. He already has so many problems."

Chapter 3

A tall, handsome man dressed in cowboy boots and a black Stetson walked in the front door accompanied by a uniformed officer.

When Sabre saw him enter she walked down the hallway to meet him. "JP, I'm glad you're here."

"Bob called and briefed me." The look on his face was a mixture of frustration and concern but, as usual, he spoke without raising his voice. "Why didn't you call me? Dang, woman, you could make a preacher cuss. I may've been able to get a few clues before they disturbed the crime scene."

Sabre put her hand on his arm. "I'm sorry."

Before she could say anything else, he said, "I'm your investigator. Didn't you think a dead man on your desk called for a little investigating?"

Sabre removed her hand. "I guess I wasn't thinking."

His tone changed slightly. "Are you okay?"

Sabre nodded her head. "Yeah, I'm fine," she said convincingly. "Surprisingly, it didn't upset me as much as I would've thought. I mean, I was shocked when I first saw him and my first reaction was to bolt, but then I took a closer look and he appeared to be dead. What was he going to do to me? So I called the police and then Bob who, by the way, got here nearly as fast as the cops."

"I'm glad he was here," JP said, as he gave her shoulder a quick squeeze. "See if you can get me in there, kid."

Sabre felt relieved. He called her "kid." That meant he wasn't upset with her, at least not too much. He never called her "kid" when he was angry. Then he called her Sabre or worse, Ms. Brown. She didn't want to upset JP. He was a great investigator and she liked him a lot. She even had the occasional romantic dream about him. But they were just dreams; nothing had ever happened between them. She couldn't let that happen, as it would surely ruin their professional relationship. Besides, she knew he wasn't interested in her. He'd had plenty of chances to show her otherwise and he never did.

They walked down the short hallway toward Sabre's office. Just before they reached the open door, Detective Klakken came out.

Sabre started to make an introduction but before she could, Klakken said, "What are you doing here, Torn?"

"My job," JP said.

"This is *my* job today. Not yours," Klakken said.

At first, Sabre thought they were friends, but she noticed some tension between them.

"I won't touch anything," JP said. "I just want to have a look."

"No, you won't touch anything because you aren't going in there. Now back off and wait in another office with Ms. Brown or you can both leave the building."

Sabre took hold of JP's arm and tried to usher him toward David's office, but JP stood his ground. Sabre tugged his arm. "Come on. Let's go."

JP hesitated for a couple of seconds. Klakken tossed him a pair of rubber gloves. "Put these on because I know it won't do any good to tell you not to touch anything."

JP caught the gloves, glared at the detective, and then turned and walked away with Sabre, sticking the gloves in his back pocket.

"What was that all about?" Sabre asked when they were in David's office and their voices out of reach.

"Nothing."

"Well, it's obviously something. You two know each other and you were so cold to one other I felt the chill. Did you work together?"

"Yes, a long time ago. We were on the force together."

"And?"

"And nothing. It doesn't matter. It won't affect this case. Klakken is a good detective. He'll figure it out. Now, tell me what you know about the dead guy."

Sabre knew it was no use trying to get information out of JP, especially something as personal as this appeared to be, so she let it go. After giving him an overview of the juvenile dependency case, she explained to JP exactly what she had told Klakken earlier and everything she had learned from the police.

"The dead man is the husband of Bob's client?" JP said.

"Yes."

"So, he didn't just randomly end up in your office. I mean...there's some connection to you."

"Perhaps, but I don't even know the guy."

"Then the real question is what was he doing here that got him killed, or why would someone dump him here if they killed him somewhere else?"

"The police think he was killed here."

"That's even worse, but there has to be some connection to the juvenile case."

"But what could that possibly be? I've been racking my brain trying to think what it might be, but it makes no sense."

"And the case is based on neglect and drug use?"

"That's right."

"Whose drug use? Mom's or Dad's?"

"Both, but the mother was trying to clean up. They were living on the streets and the only one working was Riley."

"Riley? Didn't you say he was fourteen?"

"Yes, but even after they lost their home, he continued to keep his lawn-mowing jobs with his old neighbors."

"How did he get to work?"

"He had a bicycle until his father sold it for drug money a few weeks before they were picked up."

"Real 'Father of the Year,'" JP said. "Wait, didn't you say the mother retained Bob? How did she do that if she was homeless?"

"Her stepfather paid for counsel. He apparently has plenty of money."

"He wouldn't help her when she was on the streets, but he paid for an attorney for her?"

"According to the social worker, her parents tried to help her many times, but they wanted her to leave her husband and she wouldn't leave him, at least not for long. She kept going back to him. They only retained the attorney because the children were removed and they wanted to help them."

"So, are the children with the grandparents?"

"Yes, the maternal grandmother, Celia, and her husband, Frank Davis. Celia and Frank were split up, but they went back together when this all happened. According to the grandmother, they separated because she helped her daughter one too many times."

"Do you believe her?"

"I have no reason not to. Frank Davis is loaded, but I'm sure he didn't want his money thrown down the rabbit hole. His wife enabled her daughter, basically feeding her drug habit. People talk about drug use as a victimless crime, but it isn't. Look how many people this affected—the parents, the grandparents, the children, and those are just the ones we know about."

"What can I do to help?" JP asked.

"For starters, you can investigate the Foreman case and see who might want to kill him. Try to find out why he was in my office and see if there is any connection to the juvenile dependency case. Any information you gather will also be helpful in the disposition of my case. I need to be certain we have the best placement for those boys. Come with me, and I'll make you a copy of the reports."

They left David's office and walked down the hall. Across from her door and against the wall stood eight grey file cabinets. They were covered with black dusting powder where fingerprints had been lifted. Sabre stepped toward a file cabinet and then stopped.

"I should check with Klakken," Sabre said.

JP frowned, but Sabre stuck her head inside her office where Klakken stood talking to another officer. When she caught his eye, she said, "I need to get some files out of the cabinet for court and I need to make some copies. Can I do that now?"

"Sure. Everything in there has been dusted already." Sabre thought he smiled at her as she turned around, but when she looked back he was already engaged in conversation with the coroner.

Sabre took the Foreman file out of the cabinet walked to the copy machine, and made copies of the reports she thought JP would need. She placed them in an aqua-colored file folder and handed them to JP. She then picked up the files Bob had left for her.

"I really need to get to court. Can you stay here and keep an eye on things?"

"Sure," JP said.

"And you and Klakken will be alright?"

"Of course, get out of here. I can handle Klakken." He smirked at Sabre, then put his arm around her shoulder and escorted her to the door.

Chapter 4

Sabre didn't realize until she pulled away from the office and drove off just how much the dead body had upset her. Now she could let her guard down. She no longer needed to act brave or even professional. She felt a flood of emotions hit her all at once: fear, anger, frustration, and the one she hated the most, vulnerability. She took a deep breath and tried to calm herself.

By the time Sabre arrived at San Diego Superior Court, Juvenile Division, the parking lot was full. After circling the lot several times, she finally found a parking spot in a far corner of the lot near the fence. She checked her phone for the time and when she saw how late it was, she picked up her files, Bob's files, and her calendar and hurried across the pavement. About twenty feet across the parking lot she caught the right heel of her new shoes in a crack in the pavement. She stumbled but managed to keep herself upright. When she took another step she discovered the heel was loose and her ankle hurt. She walked back to her car and retrieved a pair of running shoes from her trunk. There was not enough time to go home and change, so in spite of the fact that she felt silly in her expensive suit, her Jerry Garcia tie, and beat-up running shoes she continued on to the courthouse.

Sabre set her files on the belt of the metal detector and limped through the scanner. Her ankle hurt less if she didn't put all her weight on it. She walked directly to the attorney lounge, which was really just an old storage closet that had been converted to a work place. The room contained a small table with wire baskets where the detention reports for the day were stored. At the far end of the room against the wall was a large wooden structure divided into small cubicles, the attorneys' mailboxes. Four uncomfortable old chairs, two on each side of the room, completed the shabby décor.

Sabre took her reports and Bob's from their mail slots and sat down for a minute to get off her sore ankle and to read the reports. She glanced through them, not discovering anything too surprising. As she stood up to leave, a tall, attractive woman with a dark pageboy haircut entered.

"Good morning, Regina."

"Hi, Sabre. You're short today." She glanced down at the shoes. "Starting a new fashion trend? It looks great with the new tie. That is a new Jerry Garcia, isn't it?"

Sabre smiled. "I broke the heel of my shoe in the parking lot. And yes, it's a new tie. Thanks for noticing." Sabre received her first Jerry Garcia tie from her brother Ron when she graduated from law school. Ron was a big fan of the band, "Grateful Dead," so wearing a tie designed by the leader of the band, Jerry Garcia, brought her a little closer to her brother, who had disappeared from her life many years ago. After she received the first tie from Ron, she started a collection and wore them in his honor. She never wore any other ties—only the ones created by the "deadhead."

Sabre sat back down. "Please sit. And thanks for meeting me here."

"Sure, what's up?"

"You represent the father on the Foreman case, right?"

"Yes, for what it's worth. I've only spoken with him once and he's never shown up for court."

"Something really strange happened today. I went into my office early this morning and discovered a dead body lying across my desk."

"Oh my God! That's terrible."

"Regina, it was your client, George Foreman."

"My client? *My* client was dead in *your* office?"

"Yes."

"Why was he there? What happened?"

"I have no idea. The police are investigating right now."

"Oh, Sabre, I'm so sorry. You must be pretty shaken up."

"I'm okay now. Bob and his client, George's wife, will be meeting with the coroner soon so she can identify the body. I'm sure the police will also be talking to you. JP is investigating for me as well. Please give him any information you can."

"I will, but I don't think I'll be of much help. I really know very little about him." Regina moved her head back and forth in disbelief. "Do you or Bob need any help on your cases? My daughter has an assembly today but it's not until 12:30 so I could help with this morning's calendar."

"I'm good, but I see you have a case in Department One with Bob. It's just a review and he's submitting on the recommendations. If you want to cover that one you won't have to wait on me and it might save you some time so you can get out of here."

"Sure, I can do that. Anything else?"

"No. I can take care of the rest."

They both stood up and left the lounge. Walking past the information desk and through the crowded corridor, they parted ways when Regina went to the right and Sabre veered to the left toward Department Six. Sabre completed two of her cases and one of Bob's before she moved onto Department Four. Just after 11:30 a.m., Bob arrived.

"You're just in time," Sabre whispered to Bob, as he sat down at the defense table next to her. "This is your last case. I just submitted on the recs."

"Nice to see you, Mr. Clark," the judge said.

"Thank you, Your Honor, I apologize for being late."

"I was about to wrap this up. Is there anything you need to add, Counselor?"

"No, Your Honor. My client is submitting on the recommendations in the social study."

"Very well. The Court is following the recommendations by the Department of Social Services. All orders not in conflict remain in full force and effect," the judge ordered. "That completes today's calendar." She hit her gavel just slightly on the block, stood up, and left the room.

"Lunch?" Bob asked.

"Sure. Drive me to my car. It's clear out by the fence, almost to Children's Hospital. I'll move it now so I don't have to walk so far when I get out of court this afternoon."

Bob and Sabre left the courtroom and walked toward Bob's car.

"So what's with the tennis shoes? And are you limping?" Bob asked.

Sabre waved her hand in a dismissive gesture. "I broke the heel on my shoe and twisted my ankle a bit. It's fine. What happened downtown?"

"My client was pretty upset. I wanted to tell her she was better off without him, but I didn't."

"I'm sure he had some redeeming qualities."

"No, he was a total waste of space. I think he was abusive. Have the kids said anything?"

"No, not to me and there's nothing in the reports."

"Maybe they'll tell you now that he's gone. They may have been afraid before."

"That won't bode well for your client, if it's true. They always look first at the spouse."

"They already started questioning her but she has an alibi. She was with her friend the whole evening. I told her to talk to a criminal attorney just in case and recommended Robert Bourne. I don't know if she's retained him or not."

Bob took his keys out of his pocket. When he put them in the ignition, Sabre said, "Where's my office key?"

"What?" Bob asked.

"The key to my office building. The one with the little red ladybugs on it. It's not on your key chain."

"Oh, I don't know. This is my spare set, I guess. I only had one of your keys. One set doesn't have your key on it."

Sabre frowned at the thought of her office key being lost. "Are you sure you still have it?"

"Of course. I'm always misplacing my keys. That's why I have a second set." Bob squeezed her shoulder. "Don't worry, Sobs. They'll show up. They always do."

Chapter 5

JP sat in his home office and read every report, minute order, and motion filed on the Foreman case at least three times searching for some clue that might indicate why there was a body in Sabre's office. He didn't really expect to find the answer in the dependency file, but he hoped something in the file would provide a lead. Besides, he had a dual purpose in his investigation. He also had to help Sabre find the best placement for the children. There were so many people he needed to speak with on this case, but most were off limits for one reason or another. Foreman's wife, Dana, was too upset right now and she didn't have to answer any of his questions even if she could. He'd speak to the children, Marcus and Riley, but he didn't want to put them through any avoidable grief. His best hope was that Bob might be able to shed some light on the case. He had an appointment to meet with Dana's stepfather, Frank Davis, in about an hour and a half, followed by one with the children's grandmother, Celia. He had time to see Bob first if he left now.

JP poured a mug of coffee for the road, half decaf and half regular, put on his Stetson, and picked up the folder Sabre had given him. Louie, his beagle puppy, followed him from room to room, wagging his tail, and waited for an invitation to go for a ride.

"Come on," JP said, as he opened the door and went out into the perfect morning air. June in San Diego often meant the sky would be overcast and fog would roll in, but this was East County and warmer than the beach areas. There wasn't as much moisture in the air. JP enjoyed the beach on occasion, but he felt more comfortable in this part of town where the cowboys and the rednecks lived.

JP looked at his watch as he drove up Jamacha Road. It was nearly 7:30 a.m. on a Saturday morning. He had already been up for about two and half hours. He hadn't called Bob, but they were good enough friends that he could just drop in. Their friendship went way back—before Bob became an attorney, before the private eye business, and before JP met Sabre.

He recalled the time he first met Bob. JP was still on the force and Bob was in his first year of law school. It was the end of the first semester and everyone was celebrating. JP was on a stakeout next door to the house where a group of law students chose to party. Bob was drunk and stumbled into the yard JP had under surveillance. He could've gotten himself killed and blown JP's cover. Instead, JP handcuffed him and put him in the car. It ended the stakeout and the police arrived to check on the wild party.

Instead of handing him over to the police, JP drove him home. Bob was living with his divorced sister at the time. JP was younger and more impulsive then and although he wasn't there very long, it was long enough to meet Bob's sister. They dated for almost two years, but it ended badly. During that time, Bob and JP became good friends and remained so throughout the years.

JP drove up the steep, narrow street that led to Bob's house. He knew it was early, but this wasn't unusual. He had gone to Bob's house on Saturday mornings many times before. Louie paced back and forth from one window to the other in the back seat as JP pulled into the driveway. When JP opened the door for him, Louie bounced out of the car and ran directly for the back yard.

"Good morning, Louie," Bob said, as he reached down and scratched the dog's head. He was holding his cigarette with his left hand up and away from the dog.

JP knew Bob's habits, and it was about time for Bob to be in his back yard so he followed Louie past the side of the house and into the yard. JP stepped onto the patio that he had helped Bob build a few years earlier.

"Hi, JP. Nice to see you this morning," Bob said.

Just then Alfie, Bob's white Bichon Frise and poodle mix dog, dashed across the yard toward Bob, Louie, and JP, wagging its stub of a tail on his square body. JP reached down and patted him on the head as he nuzzled up against his leg.

"Mornin'," JP said. He didn't feel a need to explain why he stopped by, so he didn't. "Hi, Alfie." Alfie wagged his stubby tail and then shuffled off. "I swear Alfie walks like a mechanical dog. Are you sure he doesn't run on batteries?"

Bob laughed and watched Louie tackle Alfie. The two dogs rolled around, and then Alfie sped off with Louie chasing closely behind.

"Have a seat," Bob said, glancing at JP's coffee mug. "Does that need heating up?"

"No, I'm good for now. Thanks."

They sat there talking and watching the dogs play. It didn't take long before the conversation turned to what occupied both of their minds—the dead guy. This whole case left JP uneasy. Two people he cared a great deal for were somehow connected to what looked like a murder. This could only mean trouble.

"The obvious connection between you, Sabre, and George Foreman, is the juvenile dependency case. I know he was your client's husband, but he was also the father of Sabre's clients, so it may not have anything to do with you. Even if we take you out of the equation, the juvenile case is still the only common ground for Sabre and Foreman."

"True. I just somehow feel responsible. I can't help but think that if we hadn't met at Sabre's office, his body wouldn't have shown up there."

"Don't be making statements like that to the cops or you'll be their primary suspect." JP understood the reason for Bob's guilt. "Have you found Sabre's key yet?"

"No." Bob shook his head. "I found my other set of keys, but it wasn't on there. I sure can't remember taking it off my keychain. What if it was my key they used to unlock the door? What if Sabre had been there?"

"Well, she wasn't. The locks have already been changed and chances are your key is just lost. You've never been able to keep track of things."

They sat in silence for a few minutes. JP watched the concern grow on Bob's face. He knew how important Sabre was to Bob. She was his best friend and his work wife. Having worked together at juvenile court for over five years, he spent more time with her than he did with his wife, Marilee. JP was certain there wasn't anything romantic between them. In fact, Bob spent a great deal of time ineffectively playing matchmaker for JP with Sabre. His lack of success in getting them together was not because JP wasn't interested. He was. JP was confident in everything he did, except in matters of the heart. Somewhere along the line, he had lost that confidence. He didn't know if it was because past relationships had failed or if it was because he didn't think he measured up to Sabre. And he was nearly eighteen years older than her. That bothered him.

Bob's relationship with Sabre resembled what you'd see between a brother and sister who grew up actually liking one another. JP knew for a fact that Bob liked Sabre more than he did his own sister. Their relationship was based on complete trust and although JP and Bob were close friends, he knew Bob shared things with Sabre he couldn't even tell him. Perhaps it was because she was a better listener than him. After all, he had heard that many times from women in past relationships.

Bob broke their silence. "Have you checked to see if Sabre had a previous case that involved him?"

"Yeah, nothing there that I could find anyway."

"Do you have any theories as to what happened to Foreman?"

"The guy was a user. Maybe it was just a drug deal gone bad."

"But you don't really believe that, do you?"

JP shook his head. "It doesn't explain why he was killed in Sabre's office."

"Do you think someone is trying to frame her for murder?"

"It's a pretty dumb way to do it. If someone was trying to frame her, they would likely have done it somewhere else and left clues leading to her."

"That's true. And there's no reason for Sabre to want him dead."

"Maybe someone was after him for something totally unrelated to the juvenile case, and they followed him there and just took the opportunity to off him. Which brings up the question of why Foreman would be going to Sabre's office at all?" Louie ran up to JP, who reached down and scratched the dog's head. Alfie darted toward Louie and the two of them bounded off.

"Maybe Foreman thought there was something in Sabre's case file that would help him some way."

"That's possible. Another scenario is that someone lured him there, in which case they were probably making a statement."

"Like what?"

"I don't know. If we examine the juvenile case, the only one who appears to have anything to gain is his wife, your client."

"You think Dana may have killed him?" Bob walked over to a can full of sand sitting on a stone table and stuck his burning cigarette butt into it.

"No, I'm just saying no good motives have surfaced yet, unless you know something that might shed some light on it. I realize you have a confidentiality issue here that might prevent you from telling me something."

"If I had something that would help Sabre, I'd tell you. You know me better than that. I just don't see it. Dana doesn't have a strong motive. There's no financial gain, nor will she gain custody of the children with him gone."

"That's what I thought. So unless it was a crime of passion, why would she kill him? There are just too many questions. And why were they in Sabre's office?"

"Yeah, why not somewhere that he wouldn't be easily found?" Bob said.

"I just know it wasn't Sabre. But if his death is related to the juvenile case, then the killer knows Sabre and wanted to cause her trouble of some sort—either to frame her for murder or at the very least, to cause emotional pain."

Chapter 6

Just the name La Jolla sounded expensive and stuffy to JP, which is why he seldom went there. The closer he drove toward the water the more it reinforced his beliefs. The more expensive the house, the more windows it seemed to have. He zigzagged through small streets until he found the street and the house number for Frank and Celia Davis, Dana Foreman's mother and stepfather. Frank Davis' house had plenty of windows. He pulled into the long driveway and parked in front. Their house would make his look like an outhouse.

JP stepped out of the car onto the interlocking pavers that covered the circular driveway and walked up to the massive beveled-glass entry. He thought the pavers probably cost more than the flooring in his entire house. JP walked up to the front door and rang the bell, half expecting a servant to answer, but instead Mr. Davis opened the door and invited him in. They exchanged greetings and Frank led JP through the vast living room filled with green furniture and expensive paintings and into the sunroom, where they could see the waves breaking and the white foam as it dissipated when it floated back out to sea. The water lay directly below the edge of the cliff upon which the house sat. Off to either side within less than a quarter mile were gorgeous beaches with high-rise hotels.

"Have a seat," Frank said.

JP sat where he had a good view of the water. Then he realized there were so many windows, every seat in the sunroom had a good view. Frank sat across from him.

"Where are the boys this morning?" JP asked.

"Still sleeping. They would sleep until noon if I let them, but the house rule is that they need to be up by ten on Saturday. Sunday we go to church, so today is the only day they get to sleep in."

"And their grandmother? Does she get to sleep in, too?"

Frank smiled. "Not usually, but she woke up with a migraine this morning. I told her to just get some rest. Keeping up with the boys is a lot of work. Don't get me wrong, she's great with them. It's just been a whirlwind and it can be pretty stressful, but we wouldn't have it any other way," he continued, as if he thought he may have said something wrong.

"It's okay. As I told you on the phone, I work with Sabre Brown, the attorney for Marcus and Riley. Ms. Brown just wants to make sure the boys end up in the best placement for them."

"That's all we want as well. I'm very attached to those boys. They are as much my grandchildren as if they were my own." When Frank spoke about the children, his usual businesslike manner mellowed a bit. He sat forward in his chair as if he were about to stand up. "Would you like some coffee? I need a cup myself."

"Yes, thank you. Just black, please."

While Frank was gone, JP gazed out at the water. The sky was overcast and although he couldn't see very far, what he could see was spectacular. Frank returned shortly with two cups of black coffee and handed one to JP.

"Thanks." JP took a sip of some of the best coffee he had tasted in a while. "How long have you been part of the family, Frank?"

"Around twenty years. Dana was only nine when I met her mother. Such a beautiful little girl with her flaming red hair and hazel eyes. I helped raise her and helped spoil her, I suppose. I'm afraid I gave her more material things than I should have and so I take some responsibility for where she's at today."

"You mean her drug use?"

"Not her drug use, per se, but her bad choices. She grew up privileged. Her mother wanted her to have the best of everything. I don't blame her. So did I. It's just in retrospect maybe it wasn't the best thing to do."

"When did she start using drugs?"

"Looking back, we think she started drinking and using marijuana when she was around fourteen or fifteen years old. We didn't realize it at the time. We just knew she was acting out and at first we thought she was just being a typical teenager."

"What was she doing?"

"Her grades dropped from A's to B's. She skipped school once in a while. She wore too much makeup and her clothing became a little provocative. That really bothered her mother. But her behavior wasn't like some of the troubled teenagers we had heard about. We thought it would all pass."

"But then?" JP took a long drink of his coffee, enjoying it all the way down.

"Then it got worse and Dana really started rebelling. She started staying out all night and she was so nasty to her mother. She would call her awful names and refuse to do anything Celia asked. One night we received a call that she had been picked up and was being held at juvenile hall."

"For what?"

Frank stood up, walked closer to the glass, and looked out. "She and some friends were playing some kind of drinking game where they would dare each other to do things. Dana was caught in someone's backyard trying to break into a shed. The police charged her with trespass, attempted burglary, and for being under the influence."

"Did they make a true finding on the charges?" JP asked.

"No. I hired an attorney and he managed to get everything dropped. I'm not sure now that that was the best thing to do, but her mother had become so distraught at the idea of Dana spending one more night in juvenile hall. I just did what I could."

"Did she have any other bouts with the law?"

"Not really, but it was shortly after that we discovered she was pregnant. Her mother wanted her to have an abortion, but it was already too late. We considered putting her in a facility, but she begged us not to and we finally agreed to keep her at home under certain conditions."

"What conditions?"

Frank sat back down. "First, no drug or alcohol use. We had to protect that baby even if she didn't realize the importance of it. Second, we didn't want her to have any contact with George Foreman. But Dana wanted us to sign so she could marry him. She thought they could move in with us after the wedding. We were miles apart on that one because he was a bad influence on her. She finally agreed to stay without him. And while she wasn't supposed to be having any contact with him, we know she was. We just couldn't watch her every minute."

"How long did she live with you?"

"She and Riley lived with us until her eighteenth birthday. Riley was about six months old at the time. Dana moved out, married George, and for a while wouldn't even let us have any contact with the baby. It was so hard on us because his grandmother and I had both become very attached to him. Celia wanted to give her money to help her, but I was very adamant about not supporting her lifestyle. I told Celia that she'd come around when things became bad enough and then she would listen to reason."

"Did she?"

"She started asking for money for Riley, but we knew she wanted it for herself and for George. We offered to take Riley in with us until they could get on their feet, but they wouldn't do that. Don't get me wrong, they weren't living on the streets or anything. We wouldn't have let that happen, not with a baby. Dana just didn't have the luxuries she was used to. Then she became pregnant with Marcus and she started to come around a bit. We started helping more and soon we were getting to spend time with the children. I knew we were buying time with them, but it seemed to be the only way we could help the babies and it made such a big difference to Celia."

"Were Dana and George using drugs then?"

"I don't think so. When they were young, they indulged primarily in alcohol, maybe some pot. The serious drug use didn't seem to start until a few years ago. I don't know for sure, they may have been using all along, but it wasn't until a couple of years back when it became severe enough to affect their daily life."

"How bad did it get?" JP asked.

"They both lost their jobs—first Dana, then George. They were way behind on their rent and down to one car that only ran on occasion. We begged them to let us take the kids in, but they wouldn't because the kids meant income to them. Dana received welfare for them and they used the children as a bargaining chip with us. They trusted that we'd continue to give them money for the kids."

"But you stopped doing that?" JP finished his coffee and considered asking for more, but instead he set his cup on a coaster on the table next to his chair.

"We tried. At first, we would take food to them to make sure they had something to eat and clothes to keep them warm. But George wouldn't let us see them. He'd take the stuff we brought and not let us in unless we gave him money. I refused, but then Celia started giving it to them without my knowledge. When I found out, we had a big fight over it, the first of many. That went on for years. I'd find out she was giving them money and we'd fight."

"Is that why you and Celia split up?"

"Ultimately, that was the reason. We get along great most of the time. The fights over the years were mostly over Dana. We've been arguing about parenting since she was a teenager. I tried not to interfere since she wasn't my child, but sometimes I just couldn't sit back and watch Celia enable her."

JP noticed the lack of emotion in his voice. He spoke evenly as if he were in a business meeting. He wondered if it was his training in the business world or if it was just too many years of the stress that made him not show his emotion. "So, you stopped giving them money?"

"I did, and eventually Celia did too, but not before it tore us apart. I think she finally realized everything she gave them just went to drugs and not the kids. Dana and George were evicted from their apartment and living on the streets when CPS picked them up."

"That's when you decided to help again?"

"Those boys are my grandchildren and I will do whatever I can to help them. We agreed to take the children in but since we were living apart, I told Celia she could live here with the boys. We're trying to work things out between us, and it's best for Marcus and Riley that we're together right now, especially with their dad gone."

"It must be real hard on the boys." JP paused. "Do you know who may have wanted to kill him?"

"Not a clue. As I told you, we didn't see much of him the last year or so. I'm sure he made some enemies on the streets with his drug deals."

"So, George was dealing?"

"I don't know it for a fact, but once when Dana left him she told us he was. I suspected he was peddling marijuana when he and Dana first met. Who knows what he was into now. Like everything else he did, he wasn't very good at it, so I'm sure he ticked off a lot of people."

"You didn't like him much, did you?"

"No. That's no secret. I'm sorry he's dead, but he wasn't much of a father or husband. Would you want a man like George marrying your daughter?"

JP shook his head slightly. "No, I guess I wouldn't." JP absently reached for the empty cup, then realized it was empty and set it back down.

"Would you like more coffee?" Frank asked.

JP shook his head. "No, thank you. I need to run." He stood up and reached to shake Frank's hand. "Thank you for your time. Please tell Celia I'll come back another time when she's feeling better."

Frank walked JP to the front door. As JP opened the door, he turned and said, "Great coffee, by the way."

"I have it flown in from Huehuetenango, Guatemala. Since I found it, I haven't been able to enjoy anything else."

When the door closed behind him, JP paused before he started toward his car. He looked out at the beautiful blue ocean that was visible from nearly every part of the property and inhaled the salty air. As incredible as this was, he was out of his comfort zone. East County was much more his style.

Chapter 7

Sabre finished her morning run and made herself a cup of decaf coffee on her new Keurig single-cup coffee maker. She chuckled to herself about her recent purchase. She had avoided getting a "single-cup" coffee maker for some time. It made a statement that left her a little uncomfortable. It wasn't that she wanted to be married, at least not right now, but she did miss having a relationship. It had been a while now since she had met anyone who interested her.

Sabre walked out on her little veranda. From there she could look out at Tecolote Canyon. Her neighborhood was usually quiet, but it was especially so on early Sunday mornings. A song sparrow lit on the three-foot wall that separated her property from the common ground. The little bird had dark streaks on its back, a whitish underbelly, and dark streaking on its breast. His face was grey and the brown streak on the top of his head looked like a little cap. Sabre knew he was a male by his coloring. She had been watching the birds since she moved into her condo and when she'd see one she couldn't identify, she researched it online. The song sparrows were her favorites. She loved to listen to their little tunes. The songs changed over time. It seemed as though they sang one for a while and then learned another. This morning the song was so crisp and clear, it was especially melodious to her ear.

Sabre sat quietly, drinking her coffee as the little bird walked back and forth on her wall, occasionally stopping to sing. A couple of other birds joined him. She wondered if he had called them. Then for no apparent reason, other than that he could, the little sparrow flew about ten feet to the large pine tree that stood like a giant in front of her home. The other birds followed.

Sabre sat there appreciating the peaceful environment and thinking how fortunate she was to have this life. Every day she dealt with children who often had no peace; children who hated waking up in the morning for fear of what might lie ahead; children who lived in squalor; children who couldn't trust their own parents to protect them; women who were victims of domestic violence; and men and women whose lives were ruled by drugs and alcohol.

Her life wasn't perfect. She had had her share of tragedy. She missed her father who passed away when she was in college. She missed her brother, Ron, who disappeared six years ago. She and Ron had been very close. He was a couple years older than she was and although he teased her mercifully, he also protected her and she could tell him anything. Whenever she found herself in a mess, it was Ron she called. She often thought of him when she sat outside watching the birds. Ron loved the outdoors. Anything that kept him inside too long made him feel caged. He was kind of like the song sparrow flitting from branch to branch. He had a beautiful voice, too, but unlike the sparrow, his was a deep baritone.

She still had her mother who lived about an hour away, although she had never been as close to her as she was to her father. She was definitely a daddy's girl. It wasn't that she didn't love her mother, but growing up they were much more likely to butt heads. She didn't often confide in her and even now with her father and brother both gone, she wouldn't run to her mother if something went wrong. Instead she would go to Bob. He was her rock now. Guilt crept into her mind as she thought about her mother and she decided to make a greater effort to see her more often.

Sabre's phone rang and as she stood up the little sparrows flew away. She took her coffee cup, went inside locking the door behind her, and answered her phone. It was a social worker at Alvarado hospital.

"Yes, this is Sabre Brown."

"The file lists you as the attorney of record for Marcus Foreman. Is that correct?"

"Yes, I represent him in a dependency case. Is he okay?"

"He was just admitted to the psychiatric unit."

"I'll be right there," Sabre said.

Sabre felt bad for Marcus as she wondered if his fragile state of mind was due to the death of his father or if something else had happened. He had been through so much already in the few years he had spent on this earth.

She ran upstairs, took a quick shower, dressed, and drove to Alvarado. She arrived within forty minutes of the phone call. Sabre was expected to see her minor clients within four hours upon admission to a psychiatric facility. She often received these calls in the wee hours of the morning, so even though this call interrupted her peaceful Sunday morning, she was glad it was still daytime.

Sabre checked in with the receptionist who called for the social worker on the case. Shortly, a thin, young, African-American woman, who was carrying a stack of files in one arm and a coffee mug in the other, approached Sabre in the lobby.

"I'm Kim Matlock, hospital social worker. We spoke on the phone earlier." She was pleasant and cheery.

Sabre smiled back at her and was about to extend her hand, but Kim's hands were occupied so she just said, "Sabre Brown."

"Please follow me," Kim said, as she headed down a hallway at a fairly rapid pace. "I need to drop these files off." She stopped at the second door she came to. "Just one second." She opened the door, stepped in, and placed all but one of the files on a desk.

Then she came out and walked with Sabre around the corner and down the hallway toward another office. A dark-haired, dark-skinned man approached them as they walked. "Hi, Doc," Kim said.

"Good morning, Kim," the man replied.

She continued talking as she walked, greeting everyone they met in the hallway. Two women passed them and when Kim said, "Good morning," neither of them responded.

"They weren't very friendly," Sabre commented.

"Don't pay any attention to them. That's Grumpy and Bashful. We have all of the 'Seven Dwarves' here. You should see Dopey."

Sabre smiled.

"It's been a crazy morning. There must have been a full moon last night. We've admitted more than our share already today," Kim said.

"And yet, you're still smiling," Sabre observed.

"Yeah, I'm one of the Dwarves, too, 'Happy' is my moniker. If you don't make an effort to keep a good disposition in this job, you'll burn out in a week. Just look around you at the employees here; you won't see too many who are content. They're either fat because they turned to food, or drunks because they turned to alcohol, or so bitter you can't stand to be around them. I like my work and I want to continue to like my work so I decided to keep a good attitude, and when I can't, I'll move on."

Kim continued down the hallway. Sabre wondered if she was in a hurry this morning or if this was her normal speed. Perhaps the pace was part of her whole plan to stay positive. She appreciated a person who moved from task to task without wasting time. Sabre did it herself. Bob and other colleagues often complained to her for "running" when she could have been walking. For a while Sabre tried slowing down for Bob but decided it wasn't worth it. She had too much to get done before she stopped each night.

Kim stopped at a tiny office that held only a desk with a small file cabinet and two chairs. She nodded toward a chair and seated herself behind the desk before Sabre sat down. She picked up a file on the desk and said, "Marcus came in a little over an hour ago. You'll be able to see him in a few minutes."

"How did he get here?"

"The police brought him in."

"Do you know what happened?"

"According to his grandfather, Frank something...." She looked at the paper in her folder and continued "Frank Davis is his name." She continued partly reading, partly speaking from memory. "He said Marcus was upset because he had to get up this morning, and by the time they made it to the breakfast table he was grumbling and complaining. He got angry and threw his plate across the room, and when his grandmother reached out to him and tried to calm him he swung his arm around and hit her in the head. She lost her balance and fell backward. The grandfather said he had never seen him so enraged, so he grabbed him and threw him down. He held him on the ground, but even with all his weight on him, it was a struggle, so he had Riley call the police. He held him there until they arrived, which apparently was within just a few minutes."

"An officer must have been close to the scene," Sabre said.

"Or maybe when you have that kind of money they respond a little quicker," she said. She sounded a little sarcastic, but not bitter.

Sabre didn't respond to her comment. "Did the grandparents come in?"

"They did, but I sent them home. There was no need for them to hang around. I told them Marcus would likely remain here on a seventy-two-hour hold and if not, we would call them."

"Has the doctor seen Marcus yet?"

"Yes. Marcus had to be sedated, but he was given something pretty mild. It was just enough to calm him down. I haven't spoken to the CPS social worker yet so all I have is an intake sheet and the little information I obtained from the grandparents. Can you give me some history of the case?"

"For starters, his father just died; he was possibly murdered. Marcus' life has been in turmoil pretty much from birth. His parents chose drugs and alcohol over parenting their children. They moved from place to place, disrupting his schooling and a chance to make solid friends, until they finally ended up homeless. An anonymous report was made about Marcus running the streets at night. That's when social services removed the children."

"But his grandparents appear to be pretty well off. Didn't they help?"

"They tried, but in many ways their help only made the situation worse. When Marcus' parents would get money they'd spend it on their habits. And it was difficult for the boys because they knew life could be so much better than what they had. They'd spend some time at this beautiful mansion with a swimming pool and a maid and then go back to squalor. It was like that all their lives. There would be periods of overindulgence alternated with chaos."

"Does Marcus have any delinquency history?"

"A few weeks ago Marcus tried to steal a bottle of liquor from an undercover cop. It caused quite a stir, though, because it almost blew their investigation. We're in the process of dealing with that right now. We're hoping to get it dismissed because it appears that he did it because his father told him to, but Marcus isn't ready to give his dad up yet."

"Does Marcus have any history of violence?"

"According to the reports, he has always been more difficult to handle than Riley, but I'm not aware of anything out of the ordinary. Riley lived his first few years in a somewhat stable environment with the grandparents. Marcus didn't get that opportunity. The mother freely says, 'Riley is my good boy,' with the obvious implication that Marcus is the 'bad boy.'"

"It's likely Marcus has tried to live up to his title. Children often do," Kim said.

"May I see Marcus now?" Sabre asked.

"Let me see if they have him ready for you." Kim picked up the phone and spoke to someone in the hospital. She stood up. "I'll take you to him."

They walked down a hallway to the door of another room. Sabre asked, "Is he restrained?"

"Not now. We had to restrain him when he first came in. He kept banging his head against whatever he could, including the attendants, and screaming. 'I know. I know.'"

"What do you suppose he meant by that?"

"The doctor thought it was just his way of trying to get us to stop whatever we were doing...you know, agreeing with us. We'd tell him to stop fighting and he'd say, 'I know, I know.' But to me the tone of his voice didn't fit. It seemed like he was trying to tell us something else." She patted the air with her hand in a gesture of dismissal. "It was probably nothing. Just my lame attempt at amateur sleuth."

Chapter 8

Marcus appeared almost angelic with his tussled, dark, curly hair, his round face, and droopy eyes. He sat very still on a bench with his back against the wall. Sabre pulled a chair up close to him and touched his hand lightly.

"Hello, Marcus."

"Hi."

"Do you know who I am?"'

"Uh huh."

"Who am I?"

"My attorney." He spoke slower than normal but coherently.

Sabre had seen him enough times before to know he had been sedated even if the social worker hadn't told her. Sabre didn't like the use of mind-altering drugs on children. She saw them used too often and she had fought many a battle in court over the excess use of prescription drugs. She wondered if it was necessary this time. From the account she was given, it likely was but she would look into it later.

"And my name?"

"Sabre Brown."

"That's right. How are you feeling, Marcus?"

"Alright," he shrugged.

"Do you remember what happened this morning?"

"Grandpa made me get up and I didn't want to."

"Why not?"

"I was tired."

"Were you up late last night?"

"Sort of."

Sabre tipped her head to the side and gave him a questioning look. "What were you doing?"

"When everyone fell asleep I snuck into the office and used the computer."

"Were you playing games?"

"No. I was just reading stuff on there."

"What kind of stuff?"

"Just stuff." He rubbed his eye with the back of his hand.

"What kind of stuff?"

"Just different stuff." He looked guiltily at Sabre.

"Marcus, were you looking at porn?"

"Naw," he said, shaking his head. "I'm not into that. I was reading about astronauts. Did you know that the word astronaut means 'space sailor'? It's Greek, I think."

"No, I didn't know that. Would you like to be an astronaut?"

"Yeah, but I probably won't."

"Why is that?"

"Because you have to go to school a really long time and I don't do so well in school, but someday I'm going to be a pilot. My friend's dad was a pilot. He sprayed crops."

"Why did you stay up? Were you having trouble getting to sleep?"

"I was asleep at first, but I had a bad dream and it woke me up."

"What did you dream about?"

"My dad. These guys were beating him up and then they saw me and they said they'd kill me if I told."

Sabre laid her hand gently on his. "Were the guys someone you knew?"

Marcus shook his head.

"Did you ever see anyone beat your dad up for real?"

"One time we were sleeping in the alley behind the pizza place. I woke up and saw two guys punching him. When they saw I was awake, one guy kicked me and then they left."

"Were these the same guys in your dream?"

"I don't know. I couldn't see their faces. In my dream my dad kept dying over and over again."

"I'm so sorry," Sabre said.

Marcus' sad face cut into her heart. Sabre moved over to the bench and put her arm around him. He leaned into her. They sat there for a couple of minutes, neither of them talking.

Finally, Sabre said, "Tell me what happened after you woke up this morning."

"I went down to breakfast and I got mad and threw my plate. I didn't mean to hit my grandma."

"What made you so mad?"

"I don't know. Sometimes I just can't help it."

"You said something when you came in like, 'I know. I know.' What did you mean by that?"

He shrugged, "I dunno."

Sabre put her hand under his chin and raised his face slightly so she could see his face. "Marcus, do you know who killed your dad?"

He moved his head away and looked down at his feet, shaking his head from side to side. "It was just a dream," he said.

Sabre tried to get him to explain what he meant, but he wouldn't or couldn't, and when Sabre rose to leave, Marcus said, "Please don't tell my grandparents I used the computer. They'll kick me out."

Sabre turned back to him. "Why would you think that?"

"Because."

"Because why? Did someone say something?"

"They get mad when I do bad things."

Sabre put her hand on his shoulder. "Honey, parents and grandparents get angry sometimes. They have to correct children, teach them, and keep them safe. That's why they have rules, but it doesn't mean they're going to make you leave because you did one little thing that you were told not to. Adults get afraid sometimes, too, and when you lashed out at your grandmother and she fell, it scared everyone. But they love you very much and they want you to come back home."

"But I do a lot of bad things. I try to be good like Riley, but I'm just bad."

"You are not bad," Sabre said emphatically. She sat back down and hugged him, her heart aching for this little boy. She just wanted to keep him from hurting and take away the eleven years of pain he had already suffered...but all she could do was hold him and maybe give him a moment of comfort.

Chapter 9

Juvenile Court was more crowded than normal, even for a Monday morning. Sabre entered the attorney lounge and picked up the detention calendar. She checked the schedule and saw Regina Collicott's and Richard Wagner's names on the list with her. She sighed when she saw Wagner's name. It's not that she didn't like him. He was actually a decent attorney, but doing cases with him always meant you were at the end of the calendar. He never seemed to be where he was supposed to be, and as a result the court clerks just put him at the bottom of the stack and called his cases last.

When Regina walked into the lounge, Sabre said, "We're on detentions together. There are three of them, a tox baby, a six-year-old boy whose stepmother put red-hot chili peppers on his genitals so he wouldn't touch himself, and a two-year-old with gonorrhea."

"Geez," Regina said, shaking her head.

"We also have Wagner on with us, so it might be awhile," Sabre said.

"We can go ahead and divide up the cases. I just spoke with Wags in the hallway. I told him to come in so we could sort out who we'll be representing. He said, and I quote, 'Just give me the fathers on the cases. I don't have time to make any home visits this week to see kids and I'm sick of dealing with crazy women.'"

"Well, he's in rare form this morning." Sabre picked up the reports and started to peruse them.

Regina pointed to one of the detentions. "I already represent the mother on that one, the State case. I represent Tammy State and Bob has the dad, Bill State. This is their seventh drug baby. They've lost them all to adoption."

Just then Bob walked into the lounge and said to Regina, "I just saw Billy State in the hallway. Did they have another drug baby?"

"Yup, number seven."

"Just the name they gave him alone is reason enough to go straight to a .26 hearing and terminate their parental rights," Sabre said. She handed the petition to Bob. "Who names a child California Is a Police?"

"State," Bob added the last name. He smirked. "You have to give them credit for creativity."

"It's as bad as the last two names they gave their kids," Regina said. "They named them after universities."

"Actually, it was their favorite football teams, Michigan State and Iowa State," Bob said.

Sabre asked, "But California Is a Police State? Really. Do they blame everything on the system?"

"Pretty much," Regina said.

Bob was still smiling about the name. "They can call him Cal for short. Hey, did you notice? His initials are CPS, as in Child Protective Services. I'll bet they didn't mean to do that. I can't wait to point it out to Billy. He'll be furious." Bob took his report and petition and started toward the door. "I'm going to see Billy and listen to him rant. He always spices up my morning."

Sabre read through the report on the chili pepper case. "I thought I recognized these names. This was my first drug baby case when I started here. He was adopted by a nice young couple."

"What happened?" Regina asked.

Sabre read further. "It says the adoptive mother was killed in a car accident two years ago. The father remarried six months ago. Stepmom apparently isn't doing too well with little Dylan."

"Okay," Regina said. "You get little Dylan. Wags gets the father and I'll take the stepmom if they appoint for her. I have the mom on the State case so you get baby Cal." She took a quarter out of her purse and flipped it in the air. "Heads or tails?"

"Heads."

"Heads it is," Regina said, as she looked at the coin on the back of her hand. "Your call."

"I'll take the child on the gonorrhea case. You get the mom; Wags gets the dad."

Regina gathered up the petitions and reports. "I'll take Wagner his paperwork. Are you ready on Foreman?"

"Yes, I'll meet you in Department Four."

Bob had been running from one courtroom to another in an attempt to complete his calendar when Sabre met up with him in front of Department One.

"They're ready on the Foreman case. I'll be in Four," Sabre said.

"I'll be right there." Bob turned to speak to a gaunt, fidgety, African-American man. "You have to test clean if you want any chance of seeing your kids," Sabre heard him say as she walked away.

She thought about how many times she had said the same thing to her clients. Get in a program. Stay in a program. Test clean. Sometimes she thought if drugs and alcohol weren't involved, her caseload would drop by about ninety percent. As she walked down the hallway she looked at the rows of dejected people sitting on the benches waiting for their hearings. Most of them didn't stand a chance of getting their lives in order, and the children were the ones who would suffer the most. They were hauled into court, a Band-Aid was put on the wound, and once in a while one of them made it out healed. But even those clients carried the scars for life and the children had the biggest scars of all.

The crowd thickened and the noise level increased as Sabre entered the lobby area. Most of the people were waiting to speak with their attorneys or be called into court. Sabre squeezed through an extended Mexican-American family gathered outside of Department Three; passed the information desk and the metal detector; left the lobby; and entered the hallway leading to Department Four. Bob arrived within a minute or two and they went inside to hear the Foreman case.

The court clerk called the case. The County Counsel then announced his presence, "David Casey on behalf of the Department of Social Services."

"Robert Clark, attorney for the mother, Dana Foreman, who is present in court."

"Regina Collicott, attorney for the father, George Foreman. Since my client is deceased, Your Honor, I would respectfully ask to be removed from this case."

"So ordered," Judge Hekman said.

"May I be excused, Your Honor?"

"Yes, counselor."

Regina left the table, but remained in the back of the courtroom. Sabre stood up. "Sabre Brown, on behalf of the minors who are not present in court."

"Are we prepared to go forward this morning?" Judge Hekman asked.

County Counsel said, "We are, Your Honor."

Bob stood up. "We're requesting a continuance, Your Honor. As you know, the father passed away on Friday. There are a lot of unknown circumstances surrounding his death, and as you may well expect my client is pretty distraught. In the alternative we would ask for a trial date."

Sabre responded, "We have no objection to continuing this matter. My client, Marcus, is on a seventy-two-hour hold at Alvarado Hospital and I'd like him to have a psychological evaluation."

"No objection, as long as it's not used for jurisdictional purposes," Bob said.

"No objection," County Counsel said.

The judge said, "Do you expect Marcus to be released in seventy-two hours, Ms. Brown?"

"I do, Your Honor. I've already set a hearing."

"And do you want him returned to his grandparents, assuming they want him back?"

"They do want him back, Your Honor," County Counsel said.

"Are you sure that's a good idea, since he hit the grandmother?" Judge Hekman asked.

County Counsel responded, "It appears to have been an accident. We don't believe he intentionally struck his grandmother. We do realize something needs to be done about his rage if he is to remain in any home placement."

The judge looked at Sabre. "Ms. Brown?"

"Yes, Your Honor, I think the grandparents offer the best solution at this time. Right now he seems to need family more than ever. He's pretty upset about his father's passing."

Dana whispered something to Bob. He raised his hand and said, "One moment, Your Honor." He spoke with his client and although Sabre couldn't hear what they were saying, it was evident Bob didn't agree with what she wanted. Bob stood up. "The mother is not certain that returning to the grandparents' home is the best alternative for Marcus."

"Why is that, Mr. Clark?" the judge asked.

"She wants to make sure Marcus receives the treatment he needs and she thinks that his needs might be better served elsewhere."

"Anything else, Mr. Clark?"

"No, Your Honor."

The judge turned to her clerk and said something the attorneys couldn't hear, then turned back. "The case is set over for one week from today. Hopefully, we'll have more information on the death of the father by then. Psychological evaluations are ordered for both Marcus and Riley, neither to be used for jurisdictional purposes. When Marcus is released, he will return to the home of the grandparents. All other orders remain in full force and effect."

Dana started to complain about the ruling, but Bob cut her off and shuffled her out of the courtroom.

When Bob returned for the next case, Sabre said, "What was that? The mom doesn't want Marcus to go back to his grandparents' home?"

"Nope. I told her it was her best shot at getting him back to her, but she doesn't want him there."

"Why? Is there something I should know?"

"Not that I know of. She doesn't get along with her mother. My guess is that they're fighting again."

"I hope that's all it is. I don't want Marcus going back there if it isn't safe."

CHAPTER 10

JP felt a tingle when Sabre's name appeared on his phone. He wondered what it was about that woman that always made him feel like a long-tailed cat in a room full of rockers. He tried not to show it when he was around her and she never let on if he did. So either she didn't notice or she was kind enough to not embarrass him.

"Hi, kid," he said.

"Good morning...or is it afternoon?" Sabre said.

"Nope, it's still morning. What can I do for you?"

"Are you working on Foreman today?"

"Yes, I'm on my way to see the grandmother right now. I'm just about to pull into the driveway. Why?"

"See if you can find out what's going on between the mom and the grandparents. Dana doesn't want Marcus to return to that home when he's released from the hospital."

"Will do." He stopped in front of the house, still overwhelmed by the view and the size of the residence. "These folks sure don't ride to town two on a mule," JP said.

"What?" Sabre asked.

"This family has a lot of money. It just goes to show you that even money can't solve everything." JP shut off the car. "Anything else?"

"Yeah, join us for lunch if you can around noon."

"Pho's?"

"Yup."

JP stepped out of the car and walked up to the door. Frank Davis answered the door and led JP into the sunroom where they had met the last time. The view was even better today. There was no cloud cover and JP could see miles of ocean.

"You're here to see Celia, correct?" Frank said.

"Yes. We have an appointment."

"I'll go get her. She's been resting. Would you like some coffee?"

"That would be great."

Frank left the room. JP took out a little notepad and set it on the table. It was at least five minutes before Frank returned with Celia, a thin woman in her early sixties. Frank carried a silver tray holding two white china mugs with a fancy, cursive H scrawled across the side of each one, a little dish with sugar cubes, and a vase-shaped dish full of cream with the same design on the side. Frank presented the tray to JP and as he reached for the mug closest to him he breathed in the delicious smell of rich gourmet coffee along with a hint of brandy. When he took his first sip he knew the liquor was in the other mug, not his. Frank set the second one down on an end table next to an antique, straight-backed chair near the wall of windows.

Celia wore a light blue, silk dress with a darker blue cardigan sweater. Her hair was in place and her makeup perfectly applied, not exactly what JP expected of someone who was resting.

"Thank you, ma'am, for joining me."

"No problem. Please have a seat."

JP noticed a slight quiver in her voice as he sat down in the nearest chair. He wondered if she was nervous or if she always sounded that way. He would ask Sabre what she had observed. Celia seated herself in the chair next to her coffee mug. Frank sat down on the love seat closest to her.

"Frank filled me in on a lot of things, but I have a few questions for you, ma'am," JP said.

"Go ahead," Celia said and reached for her coffee cup, wrapping both hands around it.

"What was Dana like when she was young?"

Celia's face lit up just a little when she spoke of Dana's childhood. "She was such a happy little girl and so well behaved. We'd sit for hours playing games and talking. We lived in El Cajon back then. We were close to downtown and we'd walk to the stores and look in the old thrift shops. Together we'd make up stories about old pieces of furniture or little trinkets, about the lives of the people who owned them."

"When did things change for Dana?"

Frank answered, "When she was about fifteen she really rebelled."

"She changed before that, Frank," Celia said, and although she was speaking to Frank, she didn't look at him. "You didn't know her before my divorce. It crushed her. She was never quite the same after the split. Life was harder. We had to move to a small apartment and I had to go to work, so we didn't have as much time together. She was still a very good girl, but kind of sullen." Celia lifted her mug to her lips, both hands still attached, and took a long, slow drink of her coffee.

"How old was she when you divorced?" JP asked.

"She was eight years old when her father left. It was a nasty divorce and I know that didn't help. Things were a little better after I met Frank. She loved Frank and the lifestyle he gave us. She made new friends and was involved in lots of activities at school. Everything was good again. And then she met George." She took another drink and continued to do so after each question JP asked her.

"What was it like in the beginning with George?" JP asked, as he jotted down the different ages he had just been given.

"We didn't even know about him at first. Dana didn't bring him home for a long time. I'm sure she knew we wouldn't approve. She dropped her cheerleading and her debate team and her grades fell. She started dressing like a floozy and wearing a lot of makeup. I tried talking to her, but she would just sass me. Frank tried, too, but it didn't do any good."

"So, how did you finally find out about George?"

"I went through her room and found his name scribbled on a lot of her papers and on her notebook. When I confronted her, she said she loved him. We told her to bring him to dinner. We thought maybe he wouldn't be so bad. But we were wrong. He came to dinner and he didn't even attempt to make a good impression. He was rude and obnoxious. He kept leaning over and sticking his tongue in Dana's ear. He bragged about how tough he was and how he had already dropped out of school. It was disgusting. *He* was disgusting. And he never got any better."

JP sipped his coffee and listened as Celia continued to tell her story, periodically writing notes on his notepad.

"When she turned up pregnant I was devastated. I was so angry at them both but I kept it to myself in order to keep my daughter home with us. But as soon as she turned eighteen she left. I kept hoping she'd come to her senses and leave him, but she never did. I tried to help her financially at first, mostly for the sake of the children. Eventually I realized she and George were just wasting the money. Frank continued to help Dana. He could never say 'no' to her."

Frank looked at Celia and wrinkled his brow. Celia didn't seem to notice. JP wrote a note on the pad indicating that there was a discrepancy in what Frank and Celia said about helping Dana. Each blamed the other. "But they ended up homeless. How did that happen?"

"Their priorities had become so skewed. Everything they had was all going to drugs and alcohol at the end. We begged them to let us have the boys, but that was George's meal ticket. He wasn't about to let go of them. In retrospect, I realize I should've reported them to CPS years ago, but I didn't."

"So, how are you and Dana getting along now?"

"On and off. The plan was for her to stop using drugs and then come live with us and the boys. For the first time, she was finally talking about leaving George."

"You say 'was.' Has she changed her mind about coming home?"

"No. I guess not. Some days she is reasonable and others she's like the old Dana."

"You mean like when she was drinking or using drugs?"

"Yes. She gets so angry at me. She just screams."

Celia finished her coffee and Frank reached over and took her empty cup from her. "Excuse me," Frank said, looking at JP. "Would you like more coffee?"

"No, I'm good. Thank you." Frank walked out of the room.

"Do you think she's still using?" JP asked.

"She says she's not. Her attitude has been worse since George died. Maybe she's grieving. And the worst part about George dying is that now he's like a hero to her and I think she lashes out at me because she can't berate him."

"Let's hope that's what it is. If you see any signs that she might be using or drinking again, please let us know. Ms. Brown needs to keep those children safe."

"Of course. Those children have been through enough."

JP recalled the smell of brandy in her coffee and hoped he was wrong. Perhaps it was one of those fancy flavorings, he thought, but he knew better. Just then Frank returned with a full mug of coffee and handed it to Celia. She wrapped her hands around the mug as if she were cold, just as she had done earlier. The sun was shining in the room, making it comfortably warm. Too warm, JP thought, to warrant her behavior. Perhaps it was habit.

JP looked from Celia to Frank. "Do either of you know anyone who would want to kill George?"

"Anyone he ever met," Frank said.

"Now, Frank," Celia said. "The man is dead."

"And the world is a better place for it. I'm not suddenly going to pretend I liked the man."

"It's true. He wasn't very well liked." Celia said. "But we didn't see much of him last year. He came by here about a week ago, even though there were court orders for him not to come to our house. His visitation is supervised at another location."

"So, he came here to see the boys?"

"I don't think so. At least he never asked to see them. His eyes were dilated and they looked glassy. He wasn't alone, either. Another man drove him here."

"What did he want?"

"He never said. He asked if he could come in and I told him it wasn't a good time. The other guy didn't take it too well. He started spouting off about how I wasn't very hospitable and he called me a 'rich bitch.' That's about the time Frank came to the door and asked them to leave. The guy put his face right next to Frank's and said, 'Who's going to make me, old man?' I was scared, but it didn't sit well with Frank. He moved closer to him and said, 'I am, you little punk.' And he told him to get off our property. I thought the man was going to hit Frank but before he could, George took the guy's arm and pulled him away."

"What did he look like?"

"He was tall with short, reddish hair," Celia said.

Frank added, "He stood about six-foot. He had strawberry blond hair—short, but in need of a haircut—and a thin, gaunt, red, freckly face. His nose wasn't remarkable. A poor attempt at growing a beard left peach fuzz on his chin. His blue eyes were deeply set; they were possibly more exaggerated because his face was so thin. And he had a scar about an inch long that ran across his left eyebrow."

"Your eyes are keener than a rat's in a trash pile after the carnival left town," JP said. "Had you ever seen him before?"

"No. I just make it my business to study a man before I annihilate him."

Frank's voice conveyed neither anger nor humor. It was just businesslike. JP wondered if that's how he became so rich or if that was at least how he maintained his wealth. He couldn't remember reading anything in the reports about how he accumulated his money. He would see what he could find out.

"Did they leave then?"

"Yes, but the guy yanked away from George and grumbled something like, 'I told you this wouldn't work. I want my money, man.' And then he turned around and jabbed his finger in the air at us and yelled at Frank, 'This ain't over, old man.'"

Chapter 11

Bob and Sabre were already seated at a corner table with the usual pink polyester tablecloth and single, fake flower vase when JP walked into Pho's. Sabre spotted him as he passed through the archway into the room. Her eyes followed him as he sauntered to the table, admiring his 'cowboy' demeanor. He never hurried when he walked unless there was a real crisis. His plain, black Stetson hat and his basic boots spoke to his simple nature. But he wasn't simple, Sabre thought. In fact, he was very complicated. He just didn't like a lot of conflict or drama, at least not outside his profession. He didn't talk much about himself, which made it difficult to get to know him. JP remained a mystery to Sabre. For a second she wondered about his love life. She imagined he was slow and methodical about everything he did.

"Hi, kid," JP said to Sabre as he approached the table. He nodded his head at Bob, "Bob."

Sabre found herself blush a little, embarrassed about her recent reflections about JP's personal life. "Have a seat," she said, as she moved into the chair nearer the wall and freed up the chair next to her. JP sat down. Sabre felt uncomfortable by his closeness. She searched for the reason and blamed it on her earlier thoughts.

The waitress approached just as JP sat down.

"I know what I want," Bob said.

"Of course you do," Sabre said. "You never get anything but the 124."

"Can you get the124 with chicken instead of pork?" JP asked.

Bob shook his head. "Not for me. I like the pork."

"Number 124 come with chicken and pork," the waitress said in a heavy Vietnamese accent.

"Could you please bring us two orders of rice paper rolls while we decide?" Sabre said. She sat her menu down and asked JP, "How did Celia's interview go?"

He gave a detailed account of the visit, including his suspicions about the brandy in the coffee and the visit from George and his friend. "I'm going to try to track down the man with George and see if it helps find the killer. Frank gave me a good description of him, but I don't have a name." He looked at Bob. "I was hoping I could speak to your client and see if she knows who he might be." He turned to Sabre. "The boys as well," he said.

"Sure," Bob said. "In fact, Dana is coming to my office this afternoon. I'm meeting her right after lunch. You can talk to her then, if that'll work for you."

"And I'll make arrangements for you to see Marcus and Riley when you leave there," Sabre said. "You should have time to get to the school before Riley leaves. He stays late several days a week in a special study hall so he can catch up from all the school he's missed. He wants to play football in the fall, but he has to bring his grades up now or he won't be able to participate in the summer program."

"That'll be better than talking to him at his house," JP said. "And Marcus?"

The waitress came back with the rice paper rolls. She set them down in the middle of the table and placed three small plates with dishes of sauce in front of each of them. "You ready for order now?" she asked.

"I'll have the #124," JP said.

"I'll have what he's having," Bob said.

"Me too," Sabre handed her menu to the waitress and turned back to JP. "I'll call when we leave here and set up the time for Marcus. Maybe around 6:00?"

"Sure."

The conversation turned to sports, then local politics. There was a judge up for re-election, whom Bob and Sabre thought to be one of the best on the bench. However, it was recently discovered that he and his wife were involved in sex-sharing, where several couples would meet and exchange partners. The adults were all willing participants and weren't violating any laws, but it was sure to affect the outcome of the election.

The waitress returned with their dishes and walked away.

"This doesn't look right," Bob said. "They've changed the way they fix the pork." He took a bite of the meat. "And it's really dry."

"Yeah, it's not very good," Sabre said. "So, do you think Judge Harris will get re-elected?"

"Probably not. The public will be more concerned about his private life than what kind of judge he is," Bob said and then took another bite. "This is awful. It's about as dry as my sister-in-law's Thanksgiving turkey."

"I agree," JP said. "They won't re-elect Harris. There's a very active religious group campaigning against him. They don't even mention his work, just his immorality."

"Why would they change the pork?" Bob said. "It's all I've ever eaten here. Now I need to find another dish or we'll have to go somewhere else for lunch."

Sabre took another bite of her meat and removed a small, thin bone from her mouth. The meat was not very tasty, so she set it aside and finished the rest of her dish. "This really is awful pork."

They continued to chat as they finished their meals. The waitress returned with the check. Bob said, "I have to ask. Why did they change the pork in the #124?"

"You no order pork. You order chicken...#124A."

"No, I ordered #124."

The waitress looked at JP. "You ask for chicken." She turned to Bob. "You say, want same as him."

Bob raised his right hand slightly and waved it back and forth, smiling as he spoke. "It's okay. I'm just glad you still have the pork."

By the time the waitress left the table, all three were laughing. "I can't believe we ate the whole thing and didn't know it was chicken. I should've realized it when I compared it to the Thanksgiving turkey," Bob said.

"Or when I found the tiny bone. Pigs don't have tiny bones."

"We were just so set on eating pork," JP said, still laughing. His phone rang. JP looked at the name on the screen and said, "Excuse me." He stood up and walked out of the restaurant to take his call.

When JP returned, Bob and Sabre were still chuckling about their keen observation skills. JP looked somber.

"What's wrong?" Sabre asked.

JP wrinkled his forehead. "That was my friend Greg Nelson. He's a detective with the San Diego PD."

"I remember him," Sabre said. "He was on the Murdock case. Nice guy."

"Yeah, that's him. Well, Klakken won't give me any information on the Foreman investigation so I asked Nelson to keep me updated." JP looked straight at Bob and hesitated.

"What's the problem, JP?" Bob asked.

"Remember they found a cigarette butt in a baggie tucked in Foreman's waistband?"

"Yeah, why?" Bob asked.

"It has your fingerprints on it."

Chapter 12

JP sat with Bob in Bob's office as they waited for Dana to arrive for her appointment.

"I hope she gets here soon or I'll miss Riley at school," JP said. Bob didn't respond. He stared at his desk as if he were studying a scratch on the edge of it. "Bob," JP said a little louder.

Bob looked up. "What reason can you think of for one of my cigarette butts to be in Foreman's possession?"

"He lived on the streets. Maybe he just picked up your butts to smoke later."

"And put it inside a baggie and concealed it in his waistband?"

"Okay, not likely."

"So, what do you really think?"

"Perhaps he was trying to frame you or prove something. There is no indication that the guy was crazy. Conniving, stupid, and maybe even mean, but not crazy, so I think it was a calculated move. The question is whether or not it had something to do with his murder."

"Yeah, it's not every day they find a dead guy with my fingerprints in his pants."

"Not even the time you went to the Brass Rail Bar?"

Bob gave JP a sideways glance. "You're a funny guy."

"Seriously, you know Klakken will be calling you soon to ask more questions. Maybe we should try to figure this out first."

"What do you mean?" Bob asked.

"They're going to want to know how many times you saw Foreman, when, where, etc. So, why don't you tell me first." JP took his notebook from his pocket and reached for a pen on Bob's desk.

Bob thought for a moment. "If I were advising a client in this situation, I'd tell him not to say anything to the police."

"Why? Does your hypothetical client sound guilty to you?"

"Not necessarily, but first of all, I wouldn't know for sure if he was involved in the murder, and second, even if he were innocent he might say something else that could implicate him."

"So, is that the way you want to play it?" JP asked.

"I don't know. I know I didn't kill him, but because my fingerprints were on him I could be implicated some way." Bob cocked his head to the side. "Do you think I have reason to be concerned?"

JP sighed and chose his words carefully. "Klakken is good at what he does, but when he gets his claws into something, getting him to let go is tougher than trying to put a dress on a worm."

Bob chuckled. "I'll answer your questions first and let's see how it sounds."

"Okay. Let's start with the first time you saw anyone on the Foreman case."

"Dana came into my office with her stepfather, Frank Davis, to retain me on the dependency case."

"How did they happen to pick you?"

"Sabre referred him to me at the detention hearing. Frank didn't like the attorney who was appointed by the court so he asked Sabre for a referral."

"Why would he ask her?"

"Because she was representing the minors. That's not unusual. It happens all the time. Anyway, she gave him three names—Richard Wagner, Roberto Arroyo, and mine. I was at the top of the list. They came to me first and retained me."

"Okay, when did you see them next?"

"We had a jurisdiction hearing about a week later. Dana, her mother, and stepfather were there, but not George. The boys were detained with the grandparents. Dana and George were both given supervised visits with the children as long as one or both of the grandparents served as the supervisor, but George's visits were more limited than Dana's."

"How so?"

Bob reached inside his pocket and took out a full pack of cheap cigarettes. "Dana could go to their house three times a week. George had his visits elsewhere and only once a week. That's all the grandparents were willing to supervise for him, and since he didn't appear in court that's all his attorney could negotiate for him. Dana had already enrolled in drug treatment and the plan was for her to leave George, clean up, and then move in with her mom. We continued the jurisdiction hearing in hopes the social worker would go along with that plan, which she was amenable to, but only if Dana did everything she was supposed to."

"Was Dana doing what was expected of her?"

"I thought so, but then George came with her to an appointment we had at Sabre's office." Bob opened the cigarette pack and removed a cigarette. He put it in his mouth, then took it back out, held it upright between his finger and thumb, and tapped it on the desk as if he were packing it down.

"Why were you meeting at Sabre's office?"

"Because there was a gas leak in our building and we were shut down for a couple of days, so I made arrangements with Sabre to use her office."

JP made a note on his pad. "Was she there? Sabre, I mean?"

"No, it was late Friday afternoon and everyone had left already. I would've put the meeting off except that Dana's hearing was scheduled for Monday morning."

"And that was the first time you saw George?"

"Correct. I talked to them both for a bit, but he was flying high. When I asked him to step out so I could talk to my client privately, he flipped out. He started cussing at me and saying I just wanted to break them up like everyone else. I told him to get out so I could help his wife or they could both leave and she could hire someone else. To tell you the truth, I felt a little uncomfortable. I was alone in the building and I had no idea what this guy was capable of."

"Did he leave?"

"Dana convinced him to go. She had to practically push him out the door. On his way out, he raised his fist to me cussing and grumbling something I didn't quite catch because Dana was yelling, 'That's ridiculous. That's just stupid.' By then I hoped she would leave, too, but she didn't. She closed the door behind him and sat down. Then she made all the excuses for him— how rough life has been, now he was losing her and the kids, and blah, blah, blah. I took the information I needed from her, advised her as to what she needed to do for and at the hearing on Monday, and I left there as quickly as I could." Bob tapped the cigarette again.

"Do you need to smoke that thing or are you just going to beat it to death?" JP asked, pointing to the cigarette.

"I'm thinking about quitting again." Bob laid the cigarette on his desk. "It's not easy. I've been smoking since I was twelve."

"That's when I started too."

"Those wise decisions we make when we're young are those foolish ones we have to live with when we're old."

"Yeah, but unlike you, I was smart enough to quit many years ago," JP said. "So, did George show up for the hearing?"

"No. And the next time I saw him he was dead and sprawled across Sabre's desk."

JP heard the front door jingle as it opened into the reception area. He looked at his watch. Dana was twenty-three minutes late. He wondered if she would apologize. Bob's office door stood open and he saw her from his desk. Bob motioned her to come in.

This was JP's first meeting with Dana and he was surprised to see she hadn't lost all her natural beauty to the streets. He had seen photos of her at her mother's house and she was a gorgeous young woman. She wore no makeup now, her unstyled red hair was pulled back in a clip, and she was far too thin. In spite of all that, she was still physically attractive by most standards. Personally, he liked a woman with a little more meat on her bones.

"Dana, this is JP. He's the investigator for the children's attorney. He'd like to ask you a few questions, if you don't mind. He's in a bit of a hurry, so I thought he could go first and then we can talk," Bob said, as he motioned her to a chair.

"Okay," she said, and sat down next to JP.

"I'm sure you've answered a lot of the same questions for the police, and I know you're mourning the death of your husband, but we need to try to figure out how he died in order to do what is best for your children. Is that alright?" JP said.

She nodded.

"Do you have any idea who may have wanted him dead?"

"You mean besides my mother and stepfather?"

"Why do you say that?"

"They've always hated him. They decided the day they met him that he wasn't good enough for me and they've hated him ever since."

"Did either of them ever threaten to kill him?"

She looked at JP like she couldn't believe he was asking the question. "All the time."

"Did you take them seriously?"

"Sometimes."

"Any time recently?"

"Last time I talked to my mother, she said she was glad he was dead."

"Those were her exact words?"

"No. She said it would be better now with him gone. Same thing. I know that's what she meant."

"And is that why you don't want the children at her house?"

"I don't want the children there because they aren't safe," she snapped. Dana's attitude made JP question whether or not she had remained clean and sober.

Bob raised his eyebrows at JP and JP realized he had ventured beyond the subject matter he was allowed to explore. "I understand, Dana. Is there anyone else who might have wanted to see your husband dead? Did he have any fights with anyone recently?"

"He was a scrapper. I think he liked to fight. He'd come home with bruises and cuts all the time, but he didn't usually explain them. The day they took our kids away from us, he had a big gash on his lip and a black eye. He seemed to be more worried than usual about that fight. George told me he owed money but didn't have it to pay. He said they'd kill him if he didn't pay it soon. He wanted me to try to get the money from my folks."

"Did he say who *they* were? Or how much he owed?"

"No. He said it was his business and he would take care of it. He just needed me to get a little money for him."

"Did you get him the money?"

"No. I was going to try, but then CPS took our kids and everything got all crazy." She brought her clasped hands up to her chin and looked over them. "I should've gotten him the money. Do you think that's who killed him?"

"I have no idea, Dana. I'm sure the police are looking into it. You did tell them about that, right?"

"I'm not sure. Maybe not."

JP was going to explain to her that she should make sure the police knew everything there was to know about possible suspects, but then he decided to leave that to Bob. Instead, he asked her about the man who went with George to her mother's house. When JP described the man, she seemed uneasy. "Do you know who that man was?"

"It sounds like Sammy."

"Does Sammy have a last name?"

"All I ever heard was Sammy."

"When they were at your mom's house, Sammy said he wanted his money. Could that be the same guy who beat him up the day before the kids were removed?"

She shook her head. "Naw. He and Sammy were friends. He only got mad at Sammy when he flirted with me. George had a temper, especially when it came to me. He got in fights all the time when guys would come on to me."

"He was a pretty jealous guy, huh?"

"He just loved me so much," Dana said. She sniffled as she fought back tears.

"I'm sorry for your loss," JP said. He paused for a moment. "I just have a few more questions."

She nodded.

"Did you ever hear anyone threaten him?"

She shook her head. "Not really, just the normal stuff that happens in the streets. Nothing I took seriously."

"Was there anyone who showed extra interest in you? Someone who may have wanted to protect you from him?"

"My mother said that all the time. She just wanted to 'protect me.'" She looked up at Bob. "And you. You said you could protect me from him. He was very jealous of you. That's why he acted so badly that day in that other office. He saw us together once and it set him off." She smiled at Bob.

JP stood up. There was something about this woman's behavior that left him uneasy. "I need to go. Thank you for your time, Mrs. Foreman." He motioned with his head toward the door. "Bob, could you come out to my car with me? I have something I want to leave with you."

"Sure," Bob said, and stood up. "I'll be right back."

When they were outside the building, JP said, "Is there something going on between you two?"

Bob placed his hand on JP's shoulder. "No, of course not," Bob said indignantly.

"Just watch your back. That woman's as dangerous as a hungry bear at a nudist colony."

Chapter 13

Riley's school was nearly deserted by the time JP arrived. Eight cars remained in the parking lot and he didn't see any students in front of the school. Inside the office, a young man sat at a round table about ten feet from the reception desk. He was hunched over some papers with his straight, dark hair hanging over his eyes and face. He held a pencil but spent more time tapping it on the table than actually writing anything.

JP checked in and the receptionist directed him where to go, explaining that she couldn't leave the student alone.

JP walked toward the back of the school and out toward the rear parking lot where there was a row of four portable classrooms. He looked at the numbers and found #104 was the first room on the end. He walked up the metal steps that were attached to the temporary building and opened the door. An auburn-haired boy was sitting at a table and a girl was walking toward the front of the class. Her light brown hair hung at least three feet long. She couldn't have been much over five feet tall and her hair covered at least two-thirds of her body.

"Excuse me, miss," JP said. When the girl turned around he discovered she was a grown woman, not a student as he initially thought, and an attractive one at that. He surmised her age to be about thirty-five. "I'm JP Torn. I'm here to see Riley Foreman."

She walked toward him. "Hi, JP. I'm Cheryl Cox, Riley's teacher. I've been expecting you." After shaking his hand, she motioned her head in the direction of the auburn-haired boy. "That's him over there. I'll give you two some privacy. I need to go make some copies anyway."

"How's he doing in school?" JP asked.

"He's quite a ways behind, but he works really hard and he's smart enough that if he keeps this up he'll make it. He's a good kid, worth saving." Her face reddened. "I didn't mean to sound like some kids aren't worth it. It's just that by the time I get them, no matter how hard I try I can't get through to some of them. They're so entrenched in their drug and gang worlds that school is their last priority."

JP smiled his half smile and said, "I knew what you meant. It's a tough job you have. Seems to me, teaching kids these days would be like being pecked to death by a chicken. Slow and painful."

She smiled. "I couldn't have said it better myself." She looked over at Riley. "Have you seen him before?"

"No, this is our first meeting."

They walked over to Riley. He looked up from his math paper. "Riley, this is JP Torn. He's a private investigator for your attorney, Ms. Brown, which basically means he works for you." She turned to JP. "Right?"

"That's right."

JP reached out his hand to Riley. "Pleased to meet you."

Riley shook his hand and nodded, and then after a slight hesitation said, "Sir."

"Please, call me JP. I'm much more comfortable with that." JP sat down on a chair across from Riley. He heard the door open and close as Cheryl left the room.

"What are you working on?" JP asked.

"Algebra word problems."

"My favorite. Maybe I can help. I was never much for schoolin' but math always came pretty easy to me." JP looked at the problem Riley was working on. "It's like solving a puzzle or a mystery. Read it to me."

Riley read the problem. JP asked him a couple of questions which led him down the right path and Riley came up with the answer.

"Wow. How do you do that?"

"You just need to know what questions to ask. It's the same with trying to figure out other things in life—for example, who killed your father. If I can ask the right questions it'll lead me to the evidence and to the people who have the answer. Do you think you could help me?"

"But I don't know who killed him."

"But you may know something you don't even know you know and that could lead me to the killer."

"Sure. I'll help."

JP wanted to tread lightly. After all, this child had just lost his father, and as bad as Foreman was, he was still his dad. Riley wasn't showing a lot of emotion, other than being a little fidgety, tapping his pencil. He was fourteen, too big to cry in front of other men. JP watched his demeanor. He appeared almost stoic. Perhaps he hadn't really accepted the death yet.

"Do you know anyone who would harm your father?" JP asked.

"Lots of people, I suppose."

"Why do you say that?"

"He didn't get along well with some people."

"Did he have physical fights?"

"He got in a lot of arguments and even some fights when we were living on the streets."

"Do you know of anything recent?" JP asked.

"He looked like he had been in a fight the day CPS picked us up."

JP wished he would elaborate a little. Riley was either not very talkative or just guarded, so JP continued to break it down for him. "Do you know who he fought with?"

"Nope."

"But he had been beaten up?"

"He had just returned from somewhere and he was bleeding."

JP decided to take another tack and ask a question that might elicit a narrative. "So, what happened then?"

"Nothing."

That didn't work. "Did you talk to him?"

"No, but Mom did."

"Did she say what happened?"

"She started to explain to us that dad was okay, but then the social worker showed up with the police and Dad ran off."

"He left when they were taking you in?"

"No. He spotted the cops before they got very close to us. He probably figured he was going to be taken in for something. He didn't like cops much."

"Riley, do you know a man named Sammy?"

Riley looked directly at JP and then his eyes shifted off to the side.

"Yeah, why?"

"Did your dad ever fight with him?"

"He yelled at him a couple of times, but they were good friends. He got along better with him than anyone."

"Did you get along with Sammy?" JP wondered about Riley's reaction when he mentioned his name.

"He was alright," Riley said, not showing any emotion.

"Do you know Sammy's last name?"

"No."

"Did he live on the streets?"

"Mostly he stayed in his car."

"What kind of car was it?"

"I don't know."

"Did you ever see it?"

"Yeah, a couple of times. It was an old, white junker. That's about all I know."

JP asked a few more questions and was about to wrap it up when the teacher returned to the room. "Thank you, Riley. You've been a big help."

He shrugged. "I don't really know anything."

"Every piece is important," JP said, as he stood up.

"Do you think Sammy did it?" Riley asked.

"I don't know."

"I don't think it was him," Riley said.

"Thanks, Riley. I'll keep that in mind as I investigate."

Chapter 14

Sabre waited in the reception room at Alvarado Hospital until JP arrived. When he walked in, Sabre said, "Right on time. Marcus was just put in an interview room."

"Good. I hope he's more talkative than Riley. That kid doesn't volunteer any information without a direct question, and even then he doesn't say much."

"Riley is kind of shy and very guarded, but Marcus is quite the opposite. He loves to talk once you get him started."

A tall, heavy-set woman led them down the hallway and into a small room where Marcus sat talking to an orderly. The young man stood up and said, "Just push the buzzer on the wall when you're finished and I'll come get him. See you later, Marcus."

Sabre introduced JP to Marcus and explained he would be asking most of the questions and that the confidentiality rule was still in effect. She observed that Marcus' behavior was quite different from the last visit. He didn't appear to be over medicated, but he was calmer than the first few times she met with him. She assumed it was from a balanced dose of medication. She listened as JP questioned him.

"Did your father have any enemies?"

"Yeah. Like everybody he met. Nobody liked my dad. He could be a real jerk most of the time. He'd steal people's things when they weren't looking and he'd get in their face when anyone would call him on it. He didn't mind punching them out, either, if they messed with him." He spoke as if he were proud of the way his father behaved. Sabre hoped that was more about the mourning process than his true feelings.

"You saw him get into fights?" JP asked.

"All the time. If he wasn't fighting with someone, he'd pick a fight with my mom. He'd scream at her for everything. It was always her fault. He blamed her for losing our home, for not having work, for not having enough alcohol or drugs. He was always yelling at her to move back with my grandma 'cuz Mom could get money to help support them. When she said she couldn't get any more money, he told her to steal stuff from Frank's house and he'd sell it. But she said she wasn't ever going back there."

"Did you see who your dad fought with the day you were picked up by CPS?"

"Not exactly, but we had been working the streets the night before trying to get some money for food and this really big guy got mad and came after us. We ran off but he chased us. Dad always told me to split up when that happens. That way at least one of us would get away. The guy followed Dad. A couple of hours later, Dad came back to where we were sleeping. It was dark and I didn't see his face, but later Riley asked me what had happened to him because his face was pretty messed up. He said he looked like he'd been in a fight. I told him about the guy chasing us but that's all I knew."

"So you didn't see your father at all that morning?"

"No. I was asleep when the social worker and the cops came. Riley said Dad took off the minute he saw the cops. I would've, too, if I'd been awake."

"You said you were working the streets. What did you mean by that?"

"Dad took me with him to help him get money. He always said we were going to 'work,' and he was teaching me the ropes. He taught me a lot of things. He said I needed to learn how to survive in 'the concrete jungle.'"

"What kinds of things did he teach you?" JP asked.

"Like how to spot an easy mark on the streets, especially the ones who would give money to kids. He showed me where the best dumpsters were for food. Some restaurants threw better stuff away at the end of the day. And I had to learn my way around—which alleys didn't dead end, or what fences or walls I could climb so when we split up I wouldn't get lost or caught if someone was chasing me with a car," he said with pride in his voice.

"Did that happen often?"

"We got chased a lot but only a few times with cars. That was actually easier 'cuz I knew where to hide. When they were on foot, I had to just outrun them. I'm pretty fast, though. Dad said I was almost as good as him at getting away."

"What kind of work were you doing that night?"

Marcus hesitated. He shifted in his seat and started rubbing his finger and thumb together in a circular motion, a gesture Sabre had noticed before when he was uncomfortable about something. "Just the usual stuff...getting money where we could."

JP looked at Sabre, raising his eyebrows as if he were asking if he should continue. She shook her head slightly from side to side and he changed his line of questioning.

"Marcus, do you know a man named Sammy?"

"Yeah. He's my dad's friend. He'd go out with us sometimes. It was easier then because he had a car. He was cool, except he lied a lot. He was always telling stories about all these things he had done. Like one time he said he was an ultimate fighter and he told me all about beating some guy up in the ring. He said one time he robbed a bank. I didn't believe him most of the time, but I liked to hear his stories anyway. And he always had marijuana. One night after we came back from work, we sat in his car and we shared a joint."

"You and Sammy?"

"And my dad."

Sabre asked, "Did your mom know?"

"No, she would've been mad so we didn't tell her."

"What about Riley? Did he ever use any drugs or alcohol?"

"No. Riley's too square for that."

Sabre was tempted to lecture Marcus on the dangers of drugs, but then she thought about the fact that she hadn't objected to his medication and it all seemed so hypocritical. And she knew if she said anything right now, it would probably just keep him from speaking freely about what happened.

"Do you know what kind of car Sammy has?" JP asked.

"It's a white 1989 Acura. Sammy said he had his license plate made special with his name on it, but that didn't make much sense to me because it didn't really have his name on it. I think it was just another one of his lies."

"What was on the plate?"

"SMS8925. He said it meant Sam's '89. When I asked him what the twenty-five was for, he said he needed two more numbers so he used his age.'"

"Thank you, Marcus. You've been a really big help," JP said. "Oh, one more thing. Do you know Sammy's last name?"

Marcus thought for a second and then shook his head. "No. All I ever heard was Sammy."

Sabre put her hand on JP's shoulder. "If you don't mind, I'd like to speak with Marcus alone for a moment."

JP stood up. "Sure. If you don't need me here, I'm going to take off. I have to check out a few things."

Sabre nodded. She knew he was going to try to find Sammy's car.

After JP left, Sabre took Marcus by the hand. "Are you doing okay in here?"

"Yeah. It's not so bad, but do I get to go home soon?"

"I don't think it will be more than a few days. The doctor says you're doing well. We have a hearing set for Wednesday. If the doctors aren't willing to release you at that point, then they'll have to show good reason to keep you here."

"Do you know when my dad's funeral is?"

"Nothing has been set yet. The medical examiner has to release the body first and that takes a little while…sometimes." Sabre said cautiously.

"You mean because he was murdered?"

"Yes, they have to gather all the evidence they can first."

"Will I go to his funeral?"

Sabre found his question curious. He didn't ask if he could go, but rather if he was going. Then she thought about her own father's funeral. She hadn't wanted to go because she knew it would make his death real, but her brother, Ron, encouraged her. Later she was glad she went because it also gave her a chance to say goodbye and start healing.

"I'll do everything within my power to get you there."

"Okay."

After a few minutes of talking about his routine at the hospital, Sabre decided to pursue the earlier line of questioning. "Marcus, what happened that was different the last night you 'worked' with your dad?"

He shook his head. "Nothing."

"Why was the big guy chasing you?"

"Dad took his money, but the guy didn't get what he paid for."

"What had he paid for?"

Marcus looked down at his feet and his voice dropped so low it was barely audible. "Me," he said.

Chapter 15

Three hours of sleep was all Sabre managed after her conversation with Marcus. She was so angry at George she thought she would have killed him herself if he weren't already dead. He had tried to run a scam with his son as the bait. She couldn't even think about what would have happened if Marcus hadn't gotten away. She could only pray that it was a con and that he wasn't pimping him out. Marcus said nothing had ever happened, but Sabre wasn't sure she could believe him. What if he didn't always get away? What had that poor boy had to endure at the hands of his father?

When Marcus had told her about that evening, Sabre's face had reddened with anger and though she tried to hide it, she was sure Marcus had seen the horror on her face because he stopped talking.

Sabre showered, fixed her hair, applied her eyeliner and mascara, and dressed, but it was still too early to go to court. When dawn broke she called JP. She was certain he was up by now. He seldom let the sun rise before he did. He answered on the first ring.

"Good morning, kid," he said in a chipper afternoon voice.

"I take it I didn't wake you?"

"I've been up for almost an hour."

"It was still dark an hour ago." Sabre often wondered if JP just liked the morning hours, or if it was a habit carried over from the military or police department. So she asked, "Why do you get up so early?"

"Someone has to get up to wake the roosters."

Sabre smiled aloud. It felt good after her somber night.

"This is mighty early for you. What do you need?"

"I couldn't sleep last night. I would've called Bob but I'm sure he isn't awake yet. You're the only one I know on this coast who gets up this early." After she said it, she thought how bad it sounded, as if he were her last choice. He wasn't, really. Besides Bob, there wasn't anyone else she'd rather talk to. She was about to apologize when she heard JP's voice.

"Would you like to get a cup of 'joe'? I have a few things I'd like to discuss with you anyway."

"I'd like that. Coffee Bean?"

"See you there in about fifteen minutes."

Sabre opened the door to her shoe closet. It was a custom closet made when she rebuilt her condo after a fire had burned it to the ground. This closet housed only shoes, all forty-eight pairs, which was considerably less than she had before the fire. She put on a pair of navy blue Louis Vitton pumps that matched her suit perfectly and drove to the coffee shop. She was glad she had called JP. She felt a little better already.

Sabre pulled into the parking lot and parked next to JP's pickup. He looked like a real cowboy as he stood leaning against his tailgate. But then he is a real cowboy, she thought. About as real as they come. He may not have the ranch, but he walked, talked, and lived like a cowboy. She thought for a moment that he was born about a hundred years late. She could picture him riding a horse and stopping at the local saloon, holster on his hip, everyone looking up with respect as he passed through the swinging doors.

Sabre was so engrossed in her time travel that she was startled when JP opened her car door.

"You're as jumpy as spit on a skillet," JP said.

"Sorry, I didn't see you walk up."

They went inside The Coffee Bean, ordered their drinks, and sat down at a small round table across from one another. When Sabre told him about the rest of the conversation with Marcus, she could see the anger move across his face. The muscles tightened and his jaw clenched. Then he took a deep breath and reached across the table, wrapping his hand around Sabre's.

"Don't worry. I'm going to find Foreman's killer, if for no other reason than to shake his hand and thank him for removing that skunk from God's green earth."

For just a second Sabre felt herself a little unnerved by his touch and she wasn't sure why. It wasn't a creepy feeling, but rather an unexpected warmth. "You may have to get in line. Other than perhaps Sammy, his kids may be the only people on this earth who didn't want him dead." She relaxed a little and just as she began to feel comforted by his hand on hers, he pulled it away.

"Yeah, and I wouldn't count Sammy out, either. Don't forget the visit they made to Frank Davis' house. George apparently owed him money, too. Who knows what that was about. It may have been a scam they ran where he didn't get his cut or payment for the marijuana Sammy seemed to be supplying. Whatever it was, money is a huge motive for murder. Speaking of which, I drove around downtown San Diego last night looking for Sammy's car but I didn't see it. I asked around a little bit. A few people knew who he was but no one admitted to having seen him recently. The consensus on the streets is that Sammy is all hat and no horse. No one takes him too seriously."

Sabre took a sip of her decaf mocha. She sat silently for a moment, then looked at JP.

"What are you thinking?" JP asked.

"Why do you think Foreman was in my office? And how did he get in?"

JP shook his head. "I don't know. I've been tossing that over and over in my mind but that has me as confused as a goat on Astroturf."

Sabre laughed aloud. She thought about her anger with Foreman, herself, and her self-consciousness when JP put his hand on hers. Everything seemed to come together and release itself in a burst of laughter when she visualized the poor goat on Astroturf.

JP smiled and winked at her. "That's better," he said.

Sabre did feel better. She decided the next time a visual of young Marcus running from some creepy pedophile popped into her head she would try to conjure up the goat on Astroturf instead. "I'm good. Thanks. But I think I'll stop on my way to court and see how Marcus is doing this morning. Are you working on the Foreman case today?"

He glanced at his watch. "I'm going to call one of my friends at the department, Ernie or Greg, and have him run Sammy's plate as soon as they're in. I can try Greg shortly. He's usually in early."

"Have you heard anything from Klakken?"

"No," JP said. His response sounded blunt.

"What is it with you and Klakken?"

JP shook his head. "It's old history." JP stood up. "I should get going. You should, too, if you want to see Marcus."

Chapter 16

Bob waited for Sabre outside the front door of juvenile court while she finished her morning calendar. When she walked out carrying her usual armful of thick manila folders, she spotted him smoking a cigarette near the California buckeye tree in the concrete planter. She so wished he would quit again; she really hated the smell of cigarette smoke. Bob never smoked in the car when they were together and he was the most courteous smoker she had ever met. He was especially careful to hold his lit cigarettes in a position so the smoke best avoided whomever he was near. But she worried about his health. He had been smoking since he was twelve and he went through a couple of packs a day.

"You were late getting here this morning," he said. "Did you sleep in?"

Sabre smiled. "Hardly. Before court I had already had coffee with JP and made a visit to Alvarado Hospital to see Marcus."

"How's he doing?"

"Marcus or JP?" she asked, even though she knew who he meant.

"Marcus. I know how JP is." Bob spoke softly and slowly using a Texas drawl. "He's 'happy as a teenage boy in a whorehouse'...or some other 'JPism.'"

Sabre laughed when he misquoted his friend. "I've never heard him say that one."

"I ad libbed a little."

"JP would be proud. And to answer your question: Marcus is doing okay; it looks like they'll release him tomorrow. Is your client still objecting to his going back to his grandma's?"

"I don't know. I told her it has to be better than putting him at Polinsky or a temporary foster home."

"I don't get it. Unless there's a problem at his grandma's that we don't know about, why wouldn't she want him there?"

"She hasn't said. I think she's just mad at her mother and Frank for not liking George when he was alive."

"Nobody liked George when he was alive. How can she defend him? He was such a creep!"

Cocking his head to one side, Bob looked at Sabre. "Did you learn something new about him?"

Sabre nodded. "But for now it's attorney client privilege. Just know he wasn't a very nice man." Sabre took a step in the direction of the parking lot. "It's only ten thirty, a little early for lunch."

Bob snuffed out his cigarette and followed her. "I need to pick up some things from my office for my trial this afternoon. Come with me and then we'll go to lunch from there."

"Why not? If we get back here early, I'll spend the time on prep for my trial."

When Bob and Sabre walked into Bob's office building, they were greeted by Detective Klakken.

"Mr. Clark, may I ask you a few questions?"

"Certainly." Bob led him into his office and took a seat behind his desk. "Please have a seat." He motioned to a chair in front of his desk. Sabre followed them in and sat next to the detective. Klakken looked at Sabre as she sat down. Bob said, "She's with me. Now, what can I do for you?"

"How well did you know George Foreman?"

"I only saw him one time."

"And that was in Ms. Brown's office?"

"Yes. I had an appointment with Dana and he came along."

"You said he was angry. What about?"

"He came in with a chip on his shoulder. I spoke with the two of them together first, but I wanted to talk with my client alone and he became irate when I asked him to leave."

"Do you know why Foreman would be carrying a cigarette butt with your fingerprints on it?"

Bob shook his head. "I have no idea."

"How would he get it?"

"I don't know. I don't smoke inside my office, but I do put my cigarettes out in the large stone ashtray in the outside hallway. I suppose he could've taken one from there."

"Are you having an affair with Foreman's wife?"

"What!" Bob and Sabre both said at the same time. Then Bob said, "Of course not."

Sabre said, "Why would you even ask that?"

Klakken looked straight at Bob when he answered Sabre's question. "Because his wife said George was jealous of you, Mr. Clark. I'm just trying to determine if there was any basis for that jealousy."

"The guy was a druggie," Bob said. "He didn't need a reason for his jealousy."

"Where were you on the night when Foreman was murdered?"

Bob tilted his head and spoke slowly. "I was home. I went straight from home to Sabre's office and you were already there."

"Do you have someone who can corroborate that?"

"Am I a suspect?" Bob said a little louder.

"Just asking," Klakken said.

Bob stood up. "This is over. If you have any other questions, you'll have to take me in."

Klakken stood up and started for the door. "That won't be necessary, Mr. Clark." And he walked out. The door closed behind him.

"What the heck was that?" Sabre asked.

Bob snickered. "I think I'm a suspect."

"That's not funny."

"Sure it is. Klakken is chasing his ass."

"But this could turn into a nightmare."

Bob waved his hand in dismissal. "I didn't do anything. How could he possibly find enough evidence to arrest me, much less convict me?"

"Yeah, because that never happens. Innocent people are never arrested or convicted," Sabre said, rolling her eyes. "Heck, even an investigation could ruin your reputation. You better take this seriously."

"I am taking this seriously. I seriously think the guy is an idiot."

"Bob," she pleaded. "You need to talk to an attorney."

"I am talking to an attorney," he said, smiling.

"You know what I mean." Sabre paced back and forth in front of his desk. "Someone who can advise you and represent you if you need it. You know *I* can't do that. I have a conflict."

"Why? Just because you represent the dead guy's kids, you can't represent the guy who's accused of killing him? Well, how silly is that."

Sabre stopped and looked Bob directly in the eyes for about three seconds before she spoke. "I mean it. I'm worried. This could get out of hand."

Bob continued to act cavalier, but his smile seemed a little forced and his eyes showed concern. He finally walked around the desk and put his arm around Sabre's shoulder. "Okay, Sobs. I'll talk to Leahy. He's the best around...besides you, of course."

"Of course." She smiled a half smile but the thought of Bob going to jail made her ache inside. She loved Bob like a brother, almost as much as her biological brother, Ron, and she had already lost Ron. She couldn't stand the thought of losing Bob.

Chapter 17

JP thought about Bob's predicament as he drove to Bob's office. He knew his friend hadn't committed a murder, but he worried about Klakken. By now Klakken would know that a close friendship existed between him and Bob, and he feared the anger the detective felt for him would cloud his judgment. JP knew him to be an honest man, but an angry one. JP hoped Klakken had let his resentment of JP go after twenty years, but when he thought about what had happened between the two of them, he wasn't sure he would be very forgiving, either.

When he walked into Bob's inner office, he saw a dark-haired man who was approximately fifty years old standing near Bob's desk. The man reached out his hand, "Jerry Leahy. I'm not sure we've met."

JP reciprocated, shaking his hand. "JP Torn. I've seen you around the courthouse but I don't believe we've been formally introduced. However, your reputation precedes you. Nice to meet you."

"My reputation? Professional or social?"

Just then Bob walked in.

JP paused. "I was speaking professionally, but you are definitely loved by the women."

Leahy smiled a devilish smile. "Please tell me. Is it good or bad? My reputation, that is. Is it good or bad?"

"Good, I'd say," JP said.

"Ah, Mr. Leahy's reputation," Bob said. "Let me tell you what that is. Have a seat." JP and Jerry sat down. Bob walked behind his desk and sat down as he continued his description. "You are known as the 'Columbo' of juvenile court....Very clever, but you don't flaunt it and as a result your abilities are deceptive, especially to those who don't know you, and consequently you are often underestimated. You can go into a courtroom on a case with very few facts or little information and still know exactly what to do. You've been practicing over twenty years, which means you're seasoned, but unlike many attorneys in your position who have seen just about every scenario and have long since become stale in their defense tactics, you approach each case like it's your first." Bob paused. "How am I doing so far?"

"Great," Leahy said. "Keep it coming."

"You're good natured, helpful, and a charmer with the ladies. I can't see the attraction myself, but JP is right, the women love you. It must be that Irish charm."

JP said. "Yup, I've heard you're smoother than a sun possum's belly, both in the courtroom and out."

Leahy laughed. "I don't think I've ever been described quite like that before, but I think it was a compliment." Still looking at Bob, Leahy moved his head to the side gesturing towards JP. "Your friend here just called me 'smooth' while he compared me to the underside of a rodent and yet he left me feeling flattered. Now that's what I call 'smooth.'"

"You were just hit with a 'JPism,'" Bob said.

When they stopped laughing, JP said, "Well I'm just glad to see you're helping Bob. Sabre speaks highly of you and that's enough for me."

"Now there's a woman," Leahy said, looking directly at JP.

JP's face turned a little red.

"Is she...are you...?"

Bob interrupted Leahy. "Yeah, he's smitten with her. But he won't admit it to himself or her. I keep telling him he's an idiot. He needs to make his move before he's too old to hear her response without a hearing aid."

"My friend, you've got tongue enough for ten rows of teeth." JP said, his face reddening. "How about if we talk about Foreman now?"

Bob explained his situation to Leahy. He told him about his meetings with Dana, his client, and the mishap with George in Sabre's office when George became angry when he was asked to leave. He explained George's obsession with his wife and his jealousy, how Sabre found the body in her office, and Klakken's questioning which left him feeling vulnerable and a little ticked off.

JP filled in details about Sammy and other possible suspects. And he added, "I don't trust Dana Foreman. My take on her is that she's been using her looks for many years to manipulate people."

Jerry listened without interruption. Then he asked Bob two questions. "Do you know who killed him?"

"I have no idea."

"Was there any basis for Foreman's jealousy of you?"

"None."

"Okay, then. You now have an attorney. Here's what you do. You can talk to the police, but only when I'm with you. Go about your business as if nothing were wrong. Continue to represent Dana Foreman. If you become an official suspect or if you are arrested, then you'll obviously have to conflict off. But do not have any private meetings with her. It will only give them fodder for their jealousy theory."

Bob nodded.

Jerry stood up and took a few steps toward the door, then turned back—not unlike Columbo—and said, "And, Bob, take this seriously. It's potentially a nightmare."

"I will," Bob said with conviction.

"Now, I have to leave. I have a hot date with a pretty, young, Spanish interpreter." He walked out the door.

JP and Bob looked at one another and smiled, neither of them sure if he was yanking their chain.

"Does Klakken really think you may have something to do with this?" JP asked

"Between you and me, he has me worried," Bob said.

"What does he have, really?" JP asked and then answered his own question. "He has your fingerprint on a cigarette butt in the victim's waistband. Which by itself doesn't mean anything. You had a key to the building where he was killed, which you didn't actually have because you lost it so it could be in anyone's possession. You have an alleged affair with a married woman whose husband was obsessed with his wife and jealous of every man who came around her. You wouldn't cross that line anyway. There's no real motive, no real means, and it happened in the early morning hours. You and I both know you wouldn't be up that early." JP smiled. "So, you have an alibi. You were home with your wife and kid."

"That's just it. I wasn't home with my wife," Bob said.

"What are you talking about?"

"Marilee and I had a fight and she took Corey and went to her sister's house. I was alone that night."

Chapter 18

Sabre stepped up to the information desk at Alvarado Hospital and asked for Kim Matlock. The receptionist said, "She had a family emergency and left early."

"I'm sorry to hear that," Sabre said. "I'm Sabre Brown, attorney for Marcus Foreman. We have a hearing here in about five minutes. Could you please direct me to the room or to someone who can help me?"

The receptionist typed something on her keyboard and looked at her computer screen. "It looks like that hearing was canceled."

"Canceled? They wouldn't cancel the hearing because the social worker left. Where is Marcus?"

"It says here he was 'released to the grandmother.' I remember them now. The grandmother had to wait for Marcus to change out of the hospital issue garments. Sweet kid, Marcus. I'm sorry that you weren't notified of his release."

Sabre shook her head. "It's fine. I'm sure Kim would've called me if she hadn't had an emergency. Please let her know that I hope everything is alright."

Sabre drove to La Jolla to check on Marcus in the home. She decided she wouldn't call but instead make a surprise visit. She took Highway 56 across to the I-5 exit, only to get stuck in a long line of other vehicles waiting to enter I-5 North. There weren't many things that annoyed Sabre more than sitting in traffic, and she was still irritated that she had driven to the hospital instead of the shorter drive to Marcus' home. Exiting the freeway, she drove through a coffee kiosk that she had spotted a few days earlier. She ordered a decaf mocha, set it in the cup holder, and edged her way back onto the freeway.

Sabre was frustrated because no one called her to let her know that the meeting had been canceled, but she also knew they were leaning toward releasing him and she should've known to call and check before she'd driven there. She continued to drive, sipping her coffee, starting and stopping in the traffic, thinking she should just go home, but decided she had gone this far and she really wanted to see Marcus.

It was nearly six o'clock by the time she reached the grandparent's home. She took a deep breath of clean ocean air as she stepped out of the car. The sun had just started to set, creating a spectacular view from the driveway and Sabre suspected from inside the home as well. She felt rejuvenated. This was her first visit to the home and it was as impressive as JP had described. She was anxious to see inside.

Frank answered the door. "Hello, Sabre. Come on in. Were we expecting you?"

Sabre stepped inside. "No. I went by the hospital and they said Marcus had been released so I came to see him and Riley. I hope I'm not interrupting your dinner or anything."

"No. We generally eat around 6:30. I'll get Marcus. He's in his room."

"Actually, I'd like to see him in his room if that's alright."

Celia walked into the room carrying a glass of wine. "Celia, Sabre is here to see Marcus," Frank said.

Sabre and Celia exchanged greetings, and Frank continued toward the sunroom. "Riley," he called. "Will you please take Ms. Brown upstairs to Marcus' room?"

Riley stepped out of the sunroom wearing khaki shorts and a surfer t-shirt. He looked like he belonged in this house, but she had a hard time picturing Marcus in this atmosphere.

"Hi, Riley."

"Hello, Ms. Brown. Follow me." He started up the stairs.

"I'd like to speak to you as well, Riley. Can we do that after I finish with Marcus?"

"Sure. My room is right here. Come when you're finished." He pointed to a door as they passed it. A few steps further down the hallway, he stopped. "This is his room." He knocked, but no one answered. He knocked again.

"Do you think he might be asleep?"

"No. I was just in his room, like two minutes ago. We were playing a Nintendo game and talking, but he was acting like a goober so I quit and went downstairs." He knocked again. Nothing.

Sabre tried the door. It was unlocked. She opened it and stuck her head in. "Marcus," she said. "It's Sabre Brown, your attorney." She didn't hear anything and she couldn't see him. She and Riley stepped inside. The room was simply but tastefully done. The bed was made and everything was in its place except for a few video games scattered around. The Nintendo Wii game still flashed on the television screen on the table in the corner. "Maybe he's in the bathroom. Could you check?"

Riley left and Sabre walked around the room. The closet door was partway open. She pulled the door the rest of the way and gasped. Then she screamed. Marcus was hanging from a bar in the closet, his feet not touching the floor. The crude yellow noose around his neck was made of a twisted polypropylene rope. He was a strange shade of blue—a frightening, gut-wrenching blue.

"Marcus," Sabre shouted. He was unresponsive.

Riley ran in and Sabre stepped forward trying to shield him from this sight, but it was too late.

"Oh my God!" Riley shouted. He stepped in closer to Marcus. "I'm sorry. I'm sorry."

"Get Frank," Sabre commanded. "And then call 9-1-1."

Sabre quickly shook off her feeling of helplessness and reached for Marcus, attempting to lift him and release the pressure on his neck. Frank must have heard her scream because he was there in about two seconds. He lifted Marcus up while Sabre slipped the rope over his head. Frank laid him on the floor and began CPR. Sabre felt Marcus' pulse. It was weak but rapid. She wasn't sure what that meant except that he was still alive.

Celia ran into the room. "What's going...Oh, no!" she screamed and Sabre saw her white coffee cup hit the carpeted floor and bounce, black liquid flying through the air and then settling on the cream-colored surface like the first splash of a paint brush on canvas. "No! No!" she screamed again and again.

Riley stood beside his grandmother in silence like a statue with his hands over his mouth.

"Riley, did you call 9-1-1?" Sabre yelled.

He just stared at Marcus, not responding. Sabre stepped over to him, looked at him directly, put her hands on his shoulders, and said, "Riley?"

He moved his head from side to side in quick, short movements. Sabre pulled her phone out of her pocket, moved closer to Marcus and Frank, and dialed 9-1-1.

"Tell them it's Frank Davis' house," Frank said between breaths.

Celia continued to shriek until the sirens grew louder than her screams.

"I'll get the door," Sabre said. She bolted downstairs and opened the door before the police knocked.

"Where...?" One of the policemen started to ask.

"Upstairs. Last door on the right," Sabre said, pointing to the staircase before the policeman could finish. He ran upstairs.

Someone asked her a question that she didn't quite comprehend. Then she saw a tall, dark man—another uniformed officer—standing next to her in the doorway. "Ma'am," he said.

Sabre shook her head. She heard more sirens blare. "Yes." she said.

"Can you tell me what happened?"

"Marcus tried to hang himself."

"Marcus?"

"He's only eleven." Sabre saw more red lights flashing outside. A fire truck. And then more men in uniform, six of them, moving quickly up the walkway and into the house. They blurred past her. Another siren and more lights. Two paramedics emptied out of the white van, grabbing a stretcher and following directly behind the firemen.

The policeman put a hand on Sabre's shoulder and moved her out of their pathway. He directed them upstairs, then turned back to Sabre. "Tell me exactly what you saw."

Sabre watched them dash up the stairs. She felt like she was in a fog and couldn't see clearly. She had to gain control. She took a deep breath.

"His brother, Riley, took me to his room. I knocked on his door but he didn't answer. I went inside and found him hanging in the closet." She took another deep breath but it caught in her chest as she breathed and her body shuddered. She felt like crying, but there were no tears, just confusion.

Two of the firemen came down the steps and walked outside.

"Are you okay?" the officer asked.

She breathed in again, this time inhaling deeply. "I'm sorry...I've never...I'm sorry. I'm fine." She breathed a little easier now. The two firemen came back in carrying a second stretcher. She wondered if there was something wrong with the first one. Watching them climb the steps, Sabre continued to explain what she had seen earlier. "I screamed. When I saw him hanging there, I screamed. I tried to take him down, but I couldn't. I was too little."

"Little?"

She wondered herself why she used that word. It was such a strange choice of words. "I wasn't strong enough, but Frank ran in, picked him up, and laid him on the floor."

A paramedic on each end of the stretcher and a fireman on each side carried Marcus down the steps. Sabre breathed deeply again. She had to be strong for Riley and Celia. "Will you take him to Children's Hospital?" Sabre asked, as they passed her.

"No, Scripps on Genesee is closer," one of the paramedics said. They carried the stretcher out and into the white medical van.

The second stretcher descended the stairs with the help of the other four firemen. This one carried Celia.

"Is she going to be okay?" Sabre asked.

One of them, a short man with a reddish face, responded. "I believe so."

Sabre was frustrated at herself for not being more calm. She prided herself in being rational in most situations, but the sight of Marcus had thrown her into a state of disorder. She could see more clearly now. All the figures passing by her had faces again.

She felt her pocket for her keys. "May I leave? I want to go to the hospital."

"First I'd like you to go upstairs with me and show me what you saw," the officer said.

"Okay." Sabre quickly ascended the stairs, the policeman close behind.

When they walked into the room, Frank was talking to a policeman. Riley stood alone by the desk. Sabre walked over to Riley, put her arm around his shoulders, and squeezed tenderly. He leaned in for just a second and then straightened up. She let go.

"I'm sorry," Riley whispered. "I should've been with him."

"It's not your fault," Sabre said.

"I called him a 'goober,'" he said a little louder and left the room.

The policeman who had come upstairs with her said, "Please show me what you saw."

Sabre walked over to the closet and pointed to the yellow rope still hanging from the bar. Clothes were pushed back on their hangers on either side. A new pair of bright orange tennis shoes lay in the corner. One of the shoes was on end against the wall, partly on top of the other, as if both had been thrown in. A one-step footstool was turned over on its side on the floor almost directly under the rope, the spot where Marcus hung just minutes before. Sabre shuddered at the thought.

Frank approached with Riley at his side and said, "We need to go see my wife and grandson now, if you don't mind." He sounded so calm and professional, the way Sabre wanted to be right now. She wondered how he really felt. She had found herself in many situations where she kept calm in the storm and people asked her how she did it. Not this time. This time was different. He was just a child and she couldn't help thinking that if she hadn't stopped for coffee, she might have prevented the hanging.

"I need to go as well," Sabre said. She walked out of the room without waiting for a response. She had to see how Marcus was. She prayed that he was alive and hadn't hurt himself too badly. She picked up her pace as she left the room, dashed down the steps, and went out the front door. She took her phone out of her pocket and called Bob before she was out of the house. He needed to contact his client. She felt sorry for Dana. Her husband was dead and now her son was in danger of losing his life. The phone rang three times.

Sabre sprinted down the front steps and saw her car was blocked by the fire truck. The men were loading their equipment onto the truck. Bob's voice mail picked up. She said hastily into the phone, "Call me," and hung up. She yelled to the firemen, "I need to get to the hospital." She sounded rude even to herself. She lowered her voice and pleaded, "Please."

Chapter 19

Sabre was sitting in the waiting room of Scripps Hospital when Bob arrived with Dana. As soon as Dana spotted Sabre she yelled, "Where's Marcus?"

Sabre stood up and walked toward them. She could hear the fear in Dana's voice.

"I want to see Marcus," Dana yelled, as she and Bob approached.

Sabre said, "We'll let them know you're here, but you can't get in to see him just yet."

Dana pushed herself into Sabre's space, their faces about six inches apart. Sabre smelled the alcohol on her breath. "I need to see Marcus." Hostility emanated this time.

Bob touched Dana on the shoulder. "I'll check on him. Wait here."

Dana shook her head, flopped down in a chair, and started to cry. The cry soon turned to a wail. All eyes in the waiting room were on her. Sabre sat down next to her and put her hand on Dana's, trying to calm her. "Dana, if it helps at all, your mother is doing better. Would you like to go see her?"

Dana flung Sabre's hand away and screamed, "She can go to hell!"

Bob returned and sat next to Dana. He put his hand on her shoulder. Sabre caught his eye and he removed his hand. Bob was used to touching people in distress. He often made physical contact with his clients when he spoke to them. He always hugged Sabre when he comforted her, but this client was different. He was in dangerous territory.

"You'll be able to get in soon," Bob said.

"How is he?" Dana asked, a little calmer.

"All I know is that he's still alive."

Sabre was glad Dana had stopped wailing. She felt bad for her and she knew she had been through a lot, but she couldn't help but think the alcohol added to the drama. Sabre felt a little guilty for her thoughts; after all, she didn't have any children so she didn't really know how Dana felt. Perhaps she would have reacted the same way. Sabre thought about her initial reaction earlier in the evening when she'd found Marcus. She couldn't even imagine how she would've reacted had it been her own child.

"Where is Riley?" Dana asked.

"He's in the room with your mother," Sabre said. "Frank's in there, too."

"Is he okay? Riley? Is he okay?"

"He's pretty shaken up."

"I need to go see him." Dana stood up. "Where do I go?"

Bob stood. "Come on," he said. He asked someone at the desk for directions to Celia's room, and then led her to the door.

"I can go from here," she said and walked off.

Bob returned with an unlit cigarette between his fingers to where Sabre sat.

"What the heck are you doing?" Sabre said.

"I'm not smoking it. I'm just holding it."

"Not that. Why were you alone with Dana?"

"I'm not alone. You're here." He made a sweeping motion with his hand around the room. "And all these lovely people are here."

"Don't make light of it. Did you drive her here?" Before he could answer she asked, "Didn't you tell me Leahy said not to be alone with her?"

"I called to tell her about Marcus and her mom. She doesn't have a car, her friend wasn't home, and she didn't have money for a cab. What was I supposed to do?" Bob tapped the cigarette on the back of his hand.

"Why didn't you call me? I would've picked her up. Or you could've paid for the cab when she got here. Or called JP."

"Sabre, her son may be dead. It was on my way. It just seemed like the decent thing to do."

She shook her head. "You know she's been drinking?"

"Yes. I noticed that, but I don't know if she started drinking before or after I called her. And I didn't know she was drinking until she was already in the car."

"Would that have made a difference?"

"Probably not." He put the cigarette in his mouth and let it hang there.

"I just don't like this whole mess." Sabre sighed. "And why are you playing with that cigarette? Go outside and smoke it if you need to."

"I'm quitting. This is my last pack and I'm just making them last as long as I can. Do you know that cigarettes cost over five dollars a pack? And that's in California. In Alaska and Hawaii they're almost ten dollars a pack."

"Are you planning a move I don't know about?"

"No, but if I did I wouldn't be able to smoke there. I can't even afford them at five dollars a pack."

"So, damaging nearly every organ of your body, increasing your risk of a heart attack or stroke, depleting your bones of calcium and Vitamin D, or dying an agonizing death from any number of types of cancer or some horribly painful pulmonary disease aren't enough reasons to quit, but the cost is?"

"That pretty much sums it up."

"Well, I'm glad you're quitting for whatever reason." She slumped down in her chair. "I'm tired of meeting at hospitals."

"At least we're at a different one this time." Bob looked around. "This is a nice facility. The last time...."

"Please, don't mention the last time. I remember it all too well." Sabre shifted in her chair. "I wish I knew how Marcus was. Bob, you should've seen him. No, you shouldn't have. It was awful. He just hung there, lifeless. I thought he was already dead at first, but I think Frank's CPR was effective." She hit her hand on the side of the chair. "He's just a kid."

"I don't know what to say, but they're still working on him, so he's still alive and as long as he's alive, there's a chance."

His words weren't very reassuring, but at least he didn't just say "He's going to be fine." She could count on Bob to not lie to her or even placate her. And it helped just having him there.

"I stopped for coffee on the way there."

"Sabre, don't even go there. Don't beat yourself up for things over which you have no control."

"But...."

"But nothing. If you hadn't stopped you may have arrived there before it happened, and then he probably would've done it after you left and no one would've found him until morning. So, you may have saved his life."

"I know. You're right."

"Of course I'm right, Sobs. I'm always right." He smiled.

She smiled back, but it was forced.

They waited. They talked. Sabre paced and Bob played with his cigarette. Finally, Bob stood up and said, "Let's go outside."

"I better wait here in case someone comes out."

"You could go in and find out what's happening."

"I'd just be in the way," Sabre said. "Do you think Dana went looking for Marcus?"

"Wouldn't you if he were your kid?"

"Yeah. I just hope she hasn't had too much to drink to not know where to draw the line."

"Who cares? If they throw her out, they throw her out." He walked out the door with his cigarette in his mouth and his lighter in his hand.

Sabre wished she could share Bob's attitude about his clients. She always felt disappointed when her adult clients didn't follow court orders, partly because it made her work harder, but primarily because she didn't want them to fail the children. Bob, on the other hand, had little faith in most of his clients. He expected them to mess up, and when they did, he just saw it as a new challenge.

Sabre wondered if anyone had reached the social worker, and just then Marla walked into the waiting room. Sabre wasn't surprised to see her. In Sabre's estimation, she was the best social worker in the business.

"Marla, how is he?" Sabre asked.

"Better. He's in the intensive care unit now," she said. "I'll try to explain it the best I can. I don't know all the medical terms."

"Let me get Bob so you only have to say it once. Besides, he understands the medical jargon better than I do."

Sabre returned with Bob, who said, "Hi, Marla."

"Hi, Bob." She looked from Sabre to Bob as she explained. "They had to do an endo tube something...."

"An endotracheal intubation. It's used to ventilate the lungs and to prevent airway obstruction," Bob said.

"That's it. He must have gained consciousness on the way to the hospital because they had apparently inserted it at the house, but he pulled it out in the ambulance and they had to put it back in."

Sabre remembered their carrying him out and she recalled he had something black sticking out of his mouth.

Marla continued. "There doesn't appear to be any cervical spine or spinal cord injury, which according to the doctor often happens in these situations, especially if it's a long fall. Fortunately for Marcus, it wasn't. And the CT scan on his head appears normal. He does have what they're calling aspiration pneumonia and I think that's one of their biggest concerns right now."

"So he's going to be here a while," Bob said.

"Yes, for a few days anyway, maybe longer. I guess there can be delayed airway and pulmonary complications they'll watch for, and right now he's still on the ventilator. He's still unconscious."

"And Celia?" Sabre asked.

"It appears it was just anxiety. Her EKG came back normal, so she didn't have a heart attack at least. She also has some pains in her stomach. They're keeping her overnight for observation."

"How's Riley doing?" Sabre asked.

"As well as can be expected. He doesn't show much and acts pretty tough, but he has to be hurting inside. He's been Marcus' protector for a while now."

"He blamed himself for not being with Marcus when it happened. He said they were playing games and it sounds like they had a little disagreement. Riley called him a name and left. That poor kid."

"I'll get him some professional help tomorrow. I'm going back to the hospital room. Do either of you want to come with me?"

"No," they both said.

"I'm just going to go home," Sabre said.

Marla turned to Bob. "Thanks for bringing Dana here. I'll see to it she gets home if you want to leave."

"That would be great," Bob said.

Marla left and Bob put his arm around Sabre's shoulder as they walked outside. "Are you going to be okay, Sobs?"

She put her arm around his waist. "Sure." They walked together to the car.

Chapter 20

Sabre opened the door and walked inside of a little yellow house. She yelled, "Dinner time." Dark shadows filled the walls. She felt sick to her stomach and very afraid, but she walked further inside. She gasped and tried to scream but nothing came out of her mouth. Two dead bodies hung from the rafters. She couldn't see their faces but it looked like a man and a young boy. Then more hanging bodies appeared. She turned to run but she was so tall, about eight feet, and every time she turned dangling body parts hit her head. More bodies emerged until there were dozens of them with no facial features; all were a sickening shade of blue. She tried to reach the door to escape but she was caught in the maze. Then all of a sudden she was very small, just a child looking up at a blue sea of bodies with no features, just blue faces.

A man appeared in the doorway. He didn't look like the others. He was bright and glowing, like an angel. She moved toward him, but her steps were so small she couldn't get there quickly and the bodies started dropping. She reached deep down to muster up a scream. This time she heard the sound, "Daddy! Daddy!"

Sabre bolted upright in her bed. She felt sick inside and afraid. Trembling, she lay back down and tried to relax as she told herself it was only a dream, but she couldn't forget the images from her dream...or the image of Marcus. She tossed and turned for several minutes before she gave up and stepped out of bed.

After turning on the light on her night table, she picked up her iPhone and pushed the button to see the time. It was only 2:23. Sticking her phone in her pajama pocket, she walked downstairs to her kitchen and took a mug out of her cupboard. She cut a lemon in half, squeezed it into the mug, set it on her Keurig coffee maker, and drew a cup of hot water. Carrying the lemon water, she went into the living room and sat down on the sofa.

It was only a dream, she thought, a dream triggered by the day's events. But it had been frighteningly realistic and left her very uncomfortable. She wondered if Marcus was still alive. She thought she would've heard if something happened, but she knew better. No one would've called in the middle of the night. They'd just wait until morning. She took out her phone and called the hospital. A night nurse reported there had been no significant changes. Marcus was still on the ventilator and they were treating the pneumonia with intravenous antibiotics.

Sabre turned her television on and flipped the channels until she found an old black and white movie with Katherine Hepburn and Cary Grant. She lay her head down on the sofa pillow and pulled the sage green blanket from the back of the sofa over her and joined Katherine and Cary in a simpler time.

She watched for nearly an hour before she drifted off to sleep. She didn't remember seeing the last few scenes of the movie, but she knew how it ended anyway. Boy gets girl and they lived happily ever after.

Marcus lay in his bed in the critical care unit at Scripps Hospital, the ventilator still attached. His face was slightly mottled and marks from the rope around his neck made last night's events a tragic reality. Sabre was sitting by Marcus' bedside and holding his hand when Bob entered.

"Your client just left," Sabre said.

"Yeah, I passed her in the hallway. Is she going home?"

"Yes. The doctor encouraged her to get some sleep, but I think she's just going home to freshen up. Celia was released and Frank took her home. Frank offered his house to Dana, but she's so...." She stopped as she realized Marcus may be able to hear. "Let's go into the waiting room. There's free coffee there."

With a Styrofoam cup of coffee in her hand, Sabre said, "Dana's so angry at her mother."

"I know. I thought her attitude might change, given her mother's stay in the hospital, but it hasn't." Bob opened the door from the ICU and held it for Sabre.

"Does she blame her mother for George's death?" Sabre asked.

"I don't know. She hasn't said that exactly."

"Well, I know she blames her for not liking him when he was alive," Sabre said. "She has made that abundantly clear."

"What was there to like about him? The guy was a scumbag."

At first Sabre didn't respond, although she felt the same way about him. She just didn't say the words out loud. Although the man was dead, she could find very few redeeming qualities about George Foreman.

Bob continued his rant as they entered an empty waiting room. "He was a lousy husband, a lousy father, and no one liked him. He was a drug-dealing thief and doper who cared far more about himself than his family...basically a useless human being who left damage in his wake."

"Damage in his wake? Well, aren't you poetic this afternoon."

"I'm just saying. I didn't like the guy alive. I'm not going to like him any better now that he's dead. I never understand why people do that, why they feel the need to canonize dead people."

Sabre poured more decaf coffee into her cup. Bob filled his from the other coffee pot. They sat down on cushy chairs, far more comfortable than those in most waiting rooms.

"I suppose it's because they can't defend themselves," Sabre said. "But I know you're right. The man wouldn't qualify for any humanity awards."

"How's Marcus?" Bob asked.

"He's still in critical condition, but he's doing better, I think. I spoke with the doctor this morning and she was cautious but encouraging in her prognosis. The tests aren't showing a lot of damage but she said she can't be sure how much, if any, long-term impairment there will be until he is fully conscious. She said, 'if any.' That means he could be okay, right?"

"The tests are a real good indicator," Bob reassured her.

"The doctor seemed pretty concerned about the pneumonia, and when she checked his eyes, they were dark red."

"Subconjunctive hemorrhaging. It's like bruising of the eyeball. It looks different because you're not seeing the bruising through skin, but it's the same principle."

Sabre looked at Bob, her eyebrows furrowed, a look of amazement and confusion. "I'm always amazed at how much you know about the medical field."

"My father was a doctor."

"He was an urologist," Sabre said mockingly. "What did he know about the eyes?"

"It's amazing how one thing is connected to another, and he spoke 'doctor-speak' all the time. It's like another language, you know. You just learn it."

"That's kind of cool, having a father for a doctor."

"It was no picnic. He was a much better doctor than he was a father. It was all about his work," Bob said. He didn't sound bitter, just straightforward. "Speaking of work, the mother didn't show on your case this morning, so her attorney submitted on the recs."

"I'm not surprised. I heard the mom had dropped out of rehab so I didn't really expect her to show." Sabre shook her head. "Another baby with a druggie mother who cares more about her habit than her child. That's really getting old. Oh, thanks for covering that for me, by the way." Sabre yawned.

"Are you okay?" Bob asked. "You look awfully tired."

"Yeah, I just didn't get a lot of sleep last night."

"Less than usual?"

"I kept dreaming of dead people."

Bob smiled. "I love those dreams."

"You're sick."

"These were people hanging from rafters. I felt so creepy when I woke up. It was so vivid and it seemed so…real."

Bob changed his tone. "I'm sorry, Sobs. I know finding Marcus was awful for you." He put is hand on her shoulder. "Do you have a trial this afternoon?"

"No. My calendar is clear. I just need to do some prep for tomorrow and make some phone calls."

"You really should go home and get some rest."

"I'm going to check on Marcus and then go back to the office for a bit. I'll leave early."

Bob stood up. "I need to go meet JP. He called on the way over and wanted to see me. I wanted to check on you first, but I better get going."

When Bob left, Sabre tossed her coffee cup in the waste basket and went back to sit by Marcus' bedside.

Chapter 21

JP had just reached the park bench when Bob arrived. Setting his folder down and shaking Bob's hand, JP asked, "Hey, partner, how are you doing?"

"Confused. Why are we meeting here?" Bob asked.

JP's eyes scanned the park. "I didn't want to go to any of your usual haunts. So just sit down and humor me. I need to ask you some serious questions and I want you to be straight with me."

"Okay. Shoot." Bob remained standing across from JP, but raised one foot and put it on the bench to support himself.

"Are you having an affair with Dana?"

Bob wrinkled his face. "No. Of course not." Then he jokingly added, "I mean she's 'do-able' and I might under the right circumstances."

"Please, I need you to be serious," JP raised his voice, which he seldom ever did. "You may be in a lot of trouble. Have you ever had sex with that woman?"

"No." Bob responded in kind to the tone in JP's voice.

"Have you kissed her or done anything that could be construed as having an interest in her?"

"No. I told you that before."

"Have you ever had an affair or inappropriate physical contact with any client?"

Bob took his time as if he were thinking. "Just that druggie guy with no teeth and...."

"Bob, please." JP pleaded, as he stepped closer.

Bob stepped down from the bench and looked directly at JP. "Look, you know me well enough to know how much I love my wife. Marilee and I have our problems like everyone else, but I would never cheat on her, and certainly not with a client. I'm not that stupid. So, what's with all the questions?"

"I talked to my friend, Greg Nelson, at the department. He said Klakken is really out to get you. He's hanging his hat on your relationship with Dana."

"So he's an idiot. He's got nothing. My relationship is totally professional." Bob removed a cigarette from a half-empty pack he had retrieved from his pocket and lit it up.

"He has a witness," JP said in his usual, quiet tone.

"That's ludicrous. Who?"

"Dana."

"Dana?" Bob said, disbelievingly.

"Yes, apparently she told Klakken you two were an item."

Bob's face turned red with anger. He threw his hands up in the air. "This is unbelievable!" He took a few steps to the right and then back again. "That lying bitch. What's her game? What can she possibly gain from saying we're having an affair?"

"I don't know. Maybe she's hoping you'll be arrested for Foreman's murder."

"Why?" Bob's face appeared to know the answer to his own question before JP answered.

"Maybe she's working a blackmail scheme, or setting you up for a lawsuit. Or maybe she killed him."

Bob took a long drag off of his cigarette. He just stood there in silence for a few seconds.

"So, what do you want to do now?" JP asked.

"I guess I better start by calling Leahy. And I'll need to conflict off the dependency case."

"Can you do it without using this information? Because we don't officially know this and I would just as soon Klakken didn't know there was a leak."

"I'll talk to Leahy. We'll come up with something." Bob paused.

"I understand if you have to use it, but if you don't it may benefit us in the future. Either way, you have to get off the case before that woman gets you alone again."

"Oh, damn," Bob said.

"What?" JP said a little sharper than he intended.

"I picked her up at her house last night and took her to the hospital to see Marcus."

"Geez, Bob." He shook his head. "For a smart guy, sometimes you're about as sharp as a mashed potato."

"I haven't done anything wrong. I didn't seriously think I'd be a suspect."

"Well, you are."

"Do you really think they may arrest me?"

"I still don't think they have enough for an arrest, but they may have enough for a search warrant." JP tipped his hat back. "I know you haven't done anything. I believe what you're telling me, so bear that in mind when I ask you: Is there anything that might appear incriminating in your house or office?"

"In my house?" Bob's face suddenly displayed a look of awareness of what was really happening. "They could search my house," he said dejectedly.

"Most likely, they'll do both. That is, if they can even get a warrant. I'm not sure they can."

Bob shrugged. "I don't know what they could possibly find. I haven't done anything."

They stood there in silence for a few minutes, Bob blowing smoke rings in the air, JP deep in thought, trying to figure out how to protect his friend.

Bob broke the silence. He sounded like a lawyer again. "Now I see why you wanted to meet me in the park. But Greg did say they weren't going to arrest me, right?"

"No, not yet. They're trying to get a warrant as we speak. If they do, they'll be out soon."

"I haven't done much criminal law so I'm not certain what it takes to get a warrant, but I do remember a few of the basics from law school...like they can't just be on a fishing expedition. They have to have probable cause. How could they possibly establish probable cause?"

"A lot of it comes down to the judge issuing the warrant and what his relationship is with the DA or the detective making the request."

"You mean, if the judge likes the guy, they get their warrant?"

"No, not if he likes him, if he respects him. Some cops are too lazy to do their investigations themselves and get what they need. They go right into search warrant mode. Others do their due diligence and so when they ask, the DA is more likely to fight for them and the judges are more likely to trust their assessment. I'm not saying judges don't weigh the facts and make the correct legal judgments. I'm just saying there's a human factor and if it's questionable then personalities come into play."

"And Klakken? Where does he fall on this 'respect' continuum?"

JP sighed. "Right at the top."

Bob finished his cigarette and then took out another, counting the eight cigarettes left in the pack. He put it in his mouth, lit the tip, and breathed in a long deep drag. "I guess I picked a lousy time to quit smoking."

Chapter 22

JP knocked on the door of a small house in North Park. It was an older neighborhood where many of the houses stayed occupied by the same families for fifty or sixty years. The front lawn was small but well manicured. Flowers lined the walkway to the house, and an enormous bird of paradise, perfectly groomed, stood near the entrance. JP could hear someone moving about inside. He waited while he watched to make sure no one left from another exit. After several minutes an old man answered the knock on the front door.

"Are you Ludwik Bernard Sampulski?" JP asked.

"Yes," the old man said.

JP extended his hand. "I'm JP Torn. Do you have a minute?"

"Sure, I was just about to have some tea. Would you like to come in and join me?" Ludwik said in a heavy Polish accent.

JP entered cautiously, surprised at the open invitation to a stranger. The furnishings inside the house were simple but tasteful. The house smelled old, and although it was cluttered with items accumulated over many years of daily living, it was clean and tidy.

"Please," Ludwik said, pointing to a chair at the small maple table which sat in an extension off the undersized kitchen. JP sat down and the man shuffled the few steps to the kitchen. He removed two teacups from a wooden mug rack that sat on a mint green tile counter and slipped his left index finger through the handles. The room obviously hadn't been remodeled since it was built in the early fifties. The quaint style and the smells conjured up fond memories from JP's childhood visits to Aunt Norma's home.

"Have you lived here long?" JP asked.

"Just over fifty years. I bought this house shortly after I came to America with my wife Tekla." He picked up the teapot, walked back to the table, and looked around with pride. "A poor boy from Poland never could have had such a lovely home. Ah, but in America, hard work can buy you many belongings. I was good with my hands back then. I made beautiful things." The old man poured two cups of tea, shaking a little as he poured. "Now, I'm not so steady."

Ludwik went back to the kitchen and obtained two spoons and a container of cream before he seated himself in a chair adjacent to JP.

"It's a very nice home," JP said.

"After my dear Tekla was killed, I thought about returning to Poland. At times I wished I had never come here because then maybe she would still be alive."

"Do you mind my asking what happened to her?"

"She was killed by a drunk driver as she walked to the market."

"I'm so sorry," JP said.

Ludwik poured a good dose of cream into his tea. "It happened many, many years ago. And she was very happy for two years in her new home. America was her dream. By then I had had a taste of freedom and couldn't return to the Communist oppression that ruled the country."

JP strained to make out the words through the thick guttural sounds, but Ludwik seemed lonely and appreciative of the company and JP found him fascinating. Though he would rather sit there and listen to Ludwik's stories, he decided he better broach the subject he came there to discuss.

"Mr. Sampulski, you are listed as the registered owner of a 1989 white Acura, license plate SMS9925. Is that your car?"

"Yes, that's my car, but I don't have it anymore. My son Ludwik has it." He took a deep breath. "That boy has gotten himself in trouble again, hasn't he?"

"I'm not sure, but I need to talk to him. You called him Ludwik. Does he ever go by the name Sammy?"

"Yes. He never liked his name...my name...my father's name. I was proud to have my father's name. I thought my son would be, too, but from his first day of school he wanted to change his name. He said the kids teased him. I told him stories about his grandfather, hoping to instill some pride in him. I told him how his grandfather was a member of the Polish Underground State and fought for educational and social reforms. He also fought against Nazi Germany and the Soviet Union. Ludwik Bernard Sampulski," the old man said with great pride in his voice, "was not a Jew himself, but he fought against the oppression of the Jews. He fought for freedom. He loved his country but he dreamed of bringing his family to America where they could live in freedom. He was shot and killed before he had the chance to come here."

JP was caught up in the old man's stories, even though it took great effort to understand much of what he said. He enjoyed listening to history through the eyes of people who had experienced it because he heard the emotion as well as the facts. This gentle, kind man who sat before him exuded pride and pain in his narration.

"But *you* did. You completed your father's dream."

"Yes. I kissed the earth when I landed in America and then I gathered up a handful of dirt for Tatus." JP must have looked confused because the old man quickly said,

"For Papa. I saved the dirt." He stood up and walked to a shelf in the living room and took down a small mason jar with a faded, flowery cloth fastened over the lid and tied off with a red ribbon. "Here's the dirt I picked up. I always intended to return to Poland one day and lay it on my father's grave, but I never made it back there. I carried it in a match box for many years, but Sammy's mother, Clarice, made this new home for the dirt when the match box started to fall apart."

"So, you remarried after Tekla passed on?"

"About ten years later I met Clarice. She was a lovely lady but very different from my Tekla. She was a good wife and a good mother to our two children. It was Clarice who gave Ludwik the name Sammy after many fights at school over his name. I fought her at first, but I finally let it go."

JP looked at the clock on the wall. The time had slipped by and he was running late. "Does Sammy live here with you?"

"He lived here until about six months ago. Even then, he would come and go. He never held a job for very long and he has been in trouble since he was a kid. He had a hard time even when he was very young, and when he was six years old his mother was diagnosed with cancer. Two years later she died and it got a lot worse for Sammy. I tried to be a mother and a father to him, but I'm afraid I wasn't very good at it. I never really understood why he did the things he did. He was always stealing something, mostly from other kids and from stores. The last few years he stole things from our house and sold them. When he took my car, my daughter put her foot down. Her husband came over and changed the locks on my doors. Sammy came back once but left when he couldn't get in."

"Did you report your car stolen?"

"No, his sister wanted me to, but I didn't. I can't drive anymore anyway. It's my last gift to Sammy."

"Do you think your daughter may know where he is?"

"I doubt it. They've never been close." Ludwik looked up from his teacup with a concerned look on his face. "What has Sammy done?"

"He hasn't done anything that we know of, but a friend of his died and we're trying to gather information about the friend." JP didn't think it would do any good to tell him that George had been murdered. It would only worry the poor man. So, JP asked a few more questions and left.

Chapter 23

Marcus had been on the ventilator for just over thirty-six hours when Sabre received a call from the hospital on Saturday evening that the ventilator had been removed. He regained full consciousness shortly after extubation, but remained in critical care. Sabre waited until morning and then drove to the hospital to see him. He was asleep when she arrived so she sat by Marcus' bed. When he opened his eyes, she could see the deep redness had already lightened a little; the bruising on his neck was starting to take on a slightly yellowish color.

"Good morning," Sabre said.

"Morning," Marcus said with a weak, raspy voice.

"Does it hurt to talk?"

The slight movement of his head and the closing of his eyes indicated to Sabre that he was trying to say "yes."

"You don't need to say anything. I just wanted to stop by and see how you're doing. I spoke to the doctor this morning. She says you're much better."

He looked so innocent and vulnerable as he lay in the hospital bed. He was just a little boy who had already suffered so much pain, enough that he didn't want to go on living in this world.

"It was stupid," Marcus muttered.

Sabre took his hand. "It's over now. You're going to get better. I know life sucks sometimes, but it's going to get better."

Sabre thought how unfair it was that this little boy was born to parents who cared more about themselves than their children—a mother who couldn't satisfy the needs of her children until her own were met, and a father who used him as a pawn in his schemes. Sabre knew some of their behavior was drug and alcohol driven, but that was a choice, too. They were the adults. This child should not have to pay for their weaknesses. Sabre decided right then to not let Marcus suffer one more day.

Sabre was reluctantly driving to the Starbucks on the corner of Balboa and Genesee for a blind date. Her friend, Jennifer, had been encouraging her to meet some new men and arranged this meeting with a friend of a friend. Jennifer herself hadn't met this man but her friend had told her how wonderful he was. He was new in town, a transplant from Wisconsin, and he wanted to make some new friends. After much discussion and Jennifer calling in some favors, Sabre agreed to meet for coffee. He wanted an evening date, but Sabre refused to go that far.

The closer Sabre got to Starbucks, the more she dreaded her decision to go. The only positive thing was that it might distract her from dwelling on another restless night filled with more nightmares.

She arrived about fifteen minutes early, bought her own decaf misto to avoid the awkwardness of who was going to pay, and took a seat at a small table on the southeast corner of the small café. With her back against the wall she could see who entered. She looked around to confirm he wasn't already in the room, but didn't see any man over twenty who was alone.

Sabre relaxed and sipped her coffee. She thought about Marcus. Although he remained in the critical care unit and had already made great strides toward recovery, how was she going to help him survive everything else in life?

A man entered the café alone. He stood about five-foot-nine, had a slightly round but attractive face, and his hairline had just begun to recede. That wasn't exactly how he had been described to her, but she watched him anyway. He walked directly to the counter, ordered his coffee, and left without looking around.

Jennifer's friend, whom Sabre had met once while she was dating Luke—the last of a string of bad relationships—assured Jennifer that the man from Wisconsin was Sabre's type. Sabre smiled to herself at that comment. Did it mean he was dark and handsome like Luke? She didn't know she had a "type" and if she did, what the heck was it. Though she had dated a lot, she had only had a few serious relationships. She thought all the way back to high school about the men she had dated, but she couldn't conjure up a "type." She wasn't so shallow that physical attributes would make or break a relationship for her because once she grew to know someone all that changed. But she was no different than anyone else in that when she first met a man there was something in her brain that said "attractive" or "unattractive."

While she waited for her mystery man she watched everyone who entered the coffee shop and gave them the litmus test. Most of them she didn't find attractive. She did notice one thing: She definitely wasn't attracted to the suits.

This little game kept her mind occupied for a while, but it didn't take long before the visions from last night's dream entered her head. She remembered the hanging, dead bodies; sometimes they had faces, sometimes they didn't. The numbers of bodies had accelerated from one to dozens. The ages of the men or boys changed, but they were always male and always at the little yellow house.

She wondered why the scene wasn't at the mansion in La Jolla and why her father always came to her rescue. But she was grateful for his presence because for a few minutes each night she saw her father again even though she was filled with fear.

Sabre watched more people come and go—families with small children dressed in church clothes, couples holding hands, girlfriends sharing time together, and students with laptops who were studying. A few single men came and went, none giving her even a first glance. The arrangement was for the mystery man to approach her. He had seen photos on Facebook and he assured her he would recognize her.

Sabre was about to get up when a man walked in and held the door open while looking around the room. His eyes stopped on Sabre for just a second, then he continued to span the room. Apparently satisfied that he hadn't found who he was looking for, he stepped back out and let the door swing closed behind him.

Forty-five minutes had passed which made him thirty minutes late, enough time to account for traffic or getting lost. Besides, he had her cell number and could have called. Sabre finished the last bit of her coffee and opened the door to the parking lot. Outside, she saw a man exit a dark, pearl-blue F-150 Ford pickup. He looked about forty-five, handsome, and rugged. He wore jeans, a t-shirt, and a belt with a big shiny buckle. Something about him made her feel comfortable. Maybe he was her mystery man. He headed in the direction of the café. Sabre stopped outside the door and waited. He walked up the sidewalk and continued around the corner past Starbucks.

Late or not, he would have been worth going back in for, Sabre thought. I guess that's my type.

Chapter 24

It was Sunday evening and JP had spent most of the weekend driving the streets of downtown San Diego in search of the 1989 white Acura. So far, he hadn't had any luck. He had talked to several people who recognized Sammy from the photo his father had been kind enough to give him, but everyone he asked said Sammy hadn't been around for over a week.

JP drove up and down the streets from Seaport Village to Little Italy and back through the Gaslamp Quarter, zigzagging across town in what he thought would be the most likely spots for Sammy to hang out. As he drove east on Market he saw a white Acura parked on Eleventh Street. The car was facing the wrong direction on a one-way street. He drove to Twelfth, made a right, then another right, and drove slowly past the car. He could make out enough of the license plate to know it was the correct vehicle, but he didn't see anyone near it and as far as he could tell there was no one inside. He circled the block and parked in a small lot on the opposite side of the street from Sammy's car. He sat there for a bit, assessing the situation. Street lamps illuminated the area on each street corner but provided very little light in between. Most of the buildings were dark; some businesses were closed and some had been abandoned. JP couldn't see any building on this street where someone might be visiting or conducting business. A woman staggered past him down the sidewalk and into the darkness.

From where he sat, he would be able to see if anyone approached the car. Except for the occasional pedestrian and the infrequent vehicle, the street was deserted. He wondered if Sammy's car had been deserted as well, but JP was confident the car wasn't there last night when he canvassed these streets.

After nearly an hour of surveillance without any action, a tall, thin man fitting Sammy's description and two males, who appeared to be no more than eighteen years old, approached the Acura. Sammy removed something from his trunk and handed it to one of the boys. JP couldn't see well enough to know what it was or if they gave him anything in return, but it appeared as if Sammy slipped something into his back pocket. The two boys walked off with an extra bounce in their step, seemingly excited about their transaction.

JP wanted to bust the guy, but he was no longer a cop and that wasn't his mission. Right now he had to learn more about him. He wondered if Sammy was going to drive away, in which case JP intended to follow him. Instead, the man retrieved an item from the trunk, stepped toward the building, and leaned against it where he lit up a cigarette or a joint—JP couldn't tell which—but the way he handled it, his guess was a joint. Sammy slipped into a nearby alcove to finish his smoke, returned to his car and re-opened its trunk, removed a small bag and shoved it into his pocket, and started walking towards Market Street.

JP exited his car, leaving his cowboy hat behind so as not to draw attention, and began trailing him to Fifth Street and into the Gaslamp Quarter. He dressed differently when he went on a stakeout. He wore a baseball cap instead of his usual Stetson; no shiny belt buckle glistened from his waist; and tennis shoes covered his feet where leather or snake-skinned boots generally lived.

JP hung back behind Sammy for the first few blocks as there were very few people on the street, but the closer they got to Fifth, the more people there were. Sammy was apparently oblivious to JP's presence, as he never once looked back. He stopped every once in a while and talked to people in an obvious attempt to sell his wares. Most of them were teenagers, which made JP like this guy less and less.

On Sammy's sixth attempt, he exchanged a joint for cash. The two boys didn't appear to be virgins in this endeavor. Next, he approached a young couple. JP wasn't close enough to tell just how young they were, but they and Sammy turned around and began walking towards JP. Standing near the entrance to a café as if he were in line to go inside, JP kept his back turned away from them until they passed and he then followed them to Market, where they turned left. JP crossed the street and walked in the same direction on the opposite side of the street. Confident they were headed to Sammy's car, JP picked up his pace in order to arrive there before Sammy did with his latest customers.

When he reached the car he positioned himself in the modest alcove where he could watch unseen as they approached. He wondered if Sammy was bringing them to the car to purchase something besides the marijuana or if he only took one joint at a time to sell. That would be the smart thing to do when he was dealing. If he were caught, it could appear to be his own personal stash and he could possibly avoid felony charges. From JP's experience he knew most criminals weren't that smart and Sammy didn't appear to be any exception Only a few minutes had passed before Sammy and his customers approached the car and Sammy opened the trunk.

"This is some really good stuff, man. Worth every penny," Sammy said.

The young girl said, "I don't know, Darrin. Maybe we shouldn't do this." JP shifted a little to see if he could see them better, but they both had their backs to him.

"Hey, man," Sammy said. "You're gonna love it."

"We'll take it," the young man said.

The girl tugged at Darrin's arm, pulling him around. JP could see their faces and estimated their age to be somewhere between twelve and fourteen. It really angered him that Sammy preyed on such young kids.

The girl protested again, but between Sammy and Darrin they convinced her. When the couple was once again facing away from him and Sammy turned to take the goods out of the trunk, JP stepped out and with two quick, quiet steps he was standing next to them and almost directly behind Sammy. As Sammy stood up, JP reached his arm around Sammy's head and grasped him into a choke hold.

"Oh," the girl squeaked.

Darrin started to pull the girl away, but she froze in place.

"Stay still," JP ordered. Darrin stopped. He looked so scared JP was afraid he might bolt. "What's your name?" he asked the girl. When she didn't answer, he turned to the boy. "What's her name, Darrin?"

"How do you know my name?"

"I know a lot of stuff. Now, what's her name?" Sammy squirmed and tried to complain. JP squeezed his arm tighter, jamming two fingers into his back emulating a gun.

"Halle," Darrin said.

"Last name?" JP asked.

Darrin looked at the girl, reluctant to give any more information. "Thomas," she said in almost a whisper.

"How old are you?" JP asked, looking directly at Halle.

Sammy said, "Don't say…." JP squeezed tighter and jammed him harder in the back. When he stopped trying to talk, JP let up a little. He didn't want to choke the guy, just hold on to him.

"Thirteen," she said.

"What are you two doing downtown?"

"We went to a movie," Halle said, still quietly.

"We were just going to get something to eat and then go back to the mall," Darrin added. "Halle's mom is picking us up there in about an hour."

"And you thought you would stop and get some drugs along the way?"

"No, it wasn't like that," Darrin protested. "We didn't plan to get anything. We don't use drugs."

JP surmised by their tasteful, age-appropriate clothes, their trim haircuts, and their demeanor that he was likely telling the truth. If they were users, they weren't very experienced at it. "And let me guess, when this fool offered you drugs, you thought you would be 'cool' and impress your girlfriend?"

Darrin didn't respond, but the look of consternation said it all.

JP turned to Halle, "Are you impressed?"

"No," she said, shaking her head and fighting back tears.

"See that, kid? She's not impressed. It looks to me like she's just plain scared. I think you best take another tack. What kind of grades do you get in school?"

"All A's," Darrin said, with more shame in his voice than pride.

"For a smart kid, you sure are dumb. A two-eyed dirt clod would have more sense. Don't you know how dangerous this is? You have no idea what's in this crap he's selling. And do you really want to go to jail over something this stupid?"

Darrin shook his head.

"Listen to me, son, and you too," he said, turning to Halle who had tears running down her face. "I'm going to let you go but I'll be watching you both. If I ever see or hear of you using drugs again I'll hunt you down and beat some sense into you myself. You understand?"

They both nodded their heads.

"Now, get out of here!"

They turned and started off and JP thought he heard a "thank you."

"And go straight to where you're meeting your ride," he called after them. He watched as they picked up speed and started to run toward Market Street.

He turned his attention to Sammy. "What the hell are you doing selling drugs to babies? What kind of low life are you?"

"Times are tough, man. I need to make a living."

JP did all he could to keep from slamming him against the car. Instead he said, "How would you like to spend the night in jail?"

"You're not a cop," Sammy said, with a cocky air.

"You're right. I'm not, but I have plenty of connections. Right now all I want from you are some answers. First, close the trunk and give me your keys." Sammy followed the directions. JP dropped the keys in his pocket. He released the chokehold on Sammy and turned him around where he could see his face, keeping a good grip on his skinny arm. "If you answer my questions truthfully, I won't call my buddies."

"What do you want to know?"

"Do you know a guy named George Foreman?"

"Yeah, he's a friend of mine. So?" Sammy shuffled his feet.

"So, he's dead." JP watched his face for surprise or concern. He saw neither.

"Yeah, I heard that on the street." Though his face didn't say much, his body language did. Sammy continued to move around nervously shifting his head from side to side, making every effort to not look at JP.

"When did you last see him?"

"It's been a week or so. He wasn't around so much after they picked up his kids."

"What can you tell me about how he died?" JP asked.

"I just heard someone killed him. That's all I know."

"You knew him better than anyone. Who would want him dead?"

Sammy turned his head to the side. "Lots of people, I suppose. His in-laws for starters. They hated him. And his wife, Dana."

"Why do you say that?"

"She was tired of the way he treated her."

"She didn't like you much, did she?"

Sammy's head riveted back toward JP and he looked him in the eye. "Are you kidding me? She wanted me. I told her no way, I wouldn't do that to my friend. But she kept flirting with me anyway. George didn't like it. He was pretty jealous but he knew I wouldn't ever do that to him."

"Yeah, you're a real stand-up guy," JP said sarcastically. "Who else might want to kill George?"

"He made a lot of enemies. He was always pulling scams and sometimes he got caught in them. Some big guy beat him up about two weeks ago. He almost killed George then."

"Did you see the guy?"

"Yeah. He was about six-foot-four or so, dark hair, probably weighed about 250. He didn't look real muscular, but he was solid, not flabby looking. He was wearing a suit when I saw him."

"Facial hair? Tattoos? Scars or anything distinguishing?" JP shook his arm slightly when he didn't respond right away.

"No. He was clean-shaven and I didn't see any tattoos. Nothing unusual except he wore a suit."

"How old would you estimate he was?"

"About forty, maybe."

"Did you see his car?"

"He drove a new, black Mercedes."

"Do you know what year? License plate? Anything?"

"It was brand new. There were no license plates. It still had the registration thingy in the window."

JP continued to question him but he wasn't forthcoming with the rest of his answers. Before JP let go of his arm he admonished him once again about selling drugs to kids and walked away, clicking the button on Sammy's key chain to make sure all the doors were locked.

"Hey, I need my keys," Sammy yelled after him.

"Then you should've been straight with me."

JP walked back to his car and stepped inside, but before he drove off, he called his friend in vice.

Chapter 25

Juvenile court was relatively quiet even for a Monday morning. The busiest days were generally Tuesday and Wednesday since that's when the detention hearings were heard for the weekend roundup of dependency and delinquency cases. On the weekends, more kids caused trouble and more abuse occurred, and since the department had a seventy-two-hour window in which to file the petitions, mid-week received the majority of action.

Sabre sat with Bob outside of Department Four waiting for their cases to be heard.

"How was your blind date yesterday?" Bob asked.

"I give up. I'm going to join a convent."

"He was that bad, huh?"

"Worse than that. He never even showed, or he came in, took one look at me, and left."

Bob reached his arm around her shoulder and gave it a little squeeze. "I'm sorry, snookums. What a fool! He doesn't know what he missed."

"Oh well. I was leery of the whole thing anyway."

At the far end of the hallway Sabre spotted Dana huddled with her mother, Frank Davis, and a man in a suit who she recognized as Dave Carr, a well-respected defense attorney. She assumed he was Dana's new attorney. She changed the subject. "How did Dana take it when you told her you had to conflict off?"

"Leahy called her for me. He thought it was best if I didn't have any contact with her. He said she seemed a little upset, primarily because she had to explain everything again. And that doesn't make a lot of sense because...."

Sabre interrupted him. "None of what she has done makes sense. She's up to something, or else why would she lie about your having an affair with her?"

"But do you think she killed him and is trying to set me up? Or is she just running a scam so she can sue me?"

"I don't know, but either way she's dangerous."

Bob looked down the hallway toward his client. "Who's the new guy? Do you know him?"

"That's Dave Carr. I had a case with him once before. He did a good job. He does a lot of criminal work and has a good reputation downtown. Besides, he once told me I had the best looking legs in the courtroom."

Bob cocked his head to one side. "You gotta love a guy who'll come on to you during a case."

"No. It was a joke. I was the only female in the room under two hundred pounds. The case was filed because the family was obese. The youngest girl was only six and already weighed over two hundred and fifty pounds. The older girls were even heavier. Mom came into court in a scooter and the dad was too heavy to even get out of bed."

"I remember that case. That woman was huge. It was right around Thanksgiving, right?"

"Right. The kids hated foster care and were afraid they wouldn't be home for Christmas. And at home they weren't teased about their weight."

"So, how did it resolve?"

"We settled it with a 'dirty-home' charge." Sabre wrinkled her nose. "The house was really nasty. It smelled horrible and was so cluttered you couldn't walk safely through any room. Mr. Carr made sure the family had the resources they needed to clean it up. He obtained in-home counseling for them and the medical attention they needed. And the social worker agreed to make regular visits and to monitor them until they were able to function on their own. Three days before Christmas, Carr had everything in place and the kids were returned with a voluntary agreement."

Sabre was so engrossed in her story she didn't see the attorney approach.

"Counselor, may I have a word with you?"

"Oh, hi, Dave. Sure." She stood up. "By the way, this is Bob Clark," she said, looking at Bob. "Bob, Dave Carr." They shook hands.

"Pleased to meet you," Dave said.

"Are you taking over the Foreman case?" Bob asked.

"Yes. I'll be substituting in this morning."

"Good. Let me know if you need anything."

"Thanks. I think I'm good. My client gave me all the reports that have been filed so far. There weren't that many, actually." He turned to Sabre. "Can we go talk somewhere?" Dave said.

Bob stood up. "You can stay here. I'm leaving." He looked at Sabre, smirked, and said, "Later, Legs."

"I see I'm not the only one who thinks you have great legs," Dave said.

"No, it's not like that. I just told him the story about our case with the obese family."

He gave her a crooked, flirtatious smile. "So, you were talking about me."

Sabre's face reddened. "Not about you. About the case."

"And my interest in your great legs."

"I told him the joke you made. It was funny."

"And, by the way, I waited for you to call me after our case ended. What happened? You never called, you never wrote," Dave said with an exaggerated, sad face.

"I was supposed to call you?"

"Yes, remember? I asked you to call me when the case closed."

"And your phone doesn't make outgoing calls?"

"I didn't want to impose myself on you if you weren't interested, but since you insist, I'll call you when we're done with this case."

Sabre shook her head. "I didn't insist on anything." But she had wondered why he hadn't called the last time. She was seldom attracted to men in suits and really wasn't interested in having a relationship with another attorney, but she found him quite charming. He was attractive, but not drop-dead gorgeous, and about five-foot-ten. He had dark hair and eyes that twinkled when he smiled, but mostly she was impressed with his intelligence and his incredible wit. "Let's talk about Foreman. What can I do for you?"

"I was very impressed with the way you handled the last case we were on, so I trust you'll do the same with this one."

"This case is very different from that one, but I can assure you I will do what I think is best for the children."

"I wouldn't expect anything less. As you know, my client would like to get her kids back. What is your position on that?"

"I don't think she's ready, but I'm sure you'll see that she gets into the programs she needs."

"What does she need to do to get ready?" he said in his all-business tone.

"Stop drinking for starters."

"I'll get her in a 'ninety meetings for ninety days' AA program."

"She needs to have a stable place to live."

"She can do that."

"Parenting classes."

"Check," Dave said.

"There are other things that need to be sorted out as well—like who murdered George, and Marcus' mental and physical health. By the way, is she still objecting to the boys staying with the grandparents?"

"She's okay for now with a temporary placement, but she wants them back with her."

"Is she willing to live with them at Grandma's?"

"No," he said, almost too quickly.

The bailiff came out of Department Four and called out, "Parties on the Bantam case."

Sabre picked up her files and stood up. "That's my case. I have to go."

"Wait." Sabre turned back, almost bumping into him as he took to his feet. "Is that your Foreman file?"

She looked at her stack. "Yes, the one on top."

Dave retrieved a pen from inside his jacket and leaned in toward her. He was so close she could smell him. It was a clean smell with just a hint of woodsy cologne. He wrote his name and a phone number across the top of her folder.

"Just in case you need me…or want me…or whatever," he said with a sheepish smile.

Sabre took a deep breath and looked at Dave with concern. "Bob did not have an affair with your client."

"You know that for a fact?"

"I'm certain of it. He's like a brother to me and the one person I know I can trust, which means your client lied to the police over something pretty serious." She paused. "Just watch your back."

Chapter 26

It was mid-morning and Sabre dozed off while sitting in an uncomfortable chair next to Marcus' bed at Children's Hospital. He'd been asleep when she'd come in, so she was waiting for him to awaken. The nightmares continued to haunt her every night and her lack of sleep was starting to catch up with her.

She woke to the raspy hello coming from Marcus. Sabre smiled. "You sound better today."

"Yeah, it doesn't hurt as much to talk, either."

The redness in Marcus' eyes was fading rapidly and the marks around his neck weren't nearly as bold. A tube led from his arm to the bag on the metal stand which held intravenous antibiotics for his aspiration pneumonia.

"How are you feeling?"

"Good, but I sleep a lot."

"Are you up for a few questions?"

"Yeah."

"You told me about a really big guy that chased you and your father. Can you tell me what he looked like?" Sabre could see the fear ripple over Marcus' face and he began to make that circular motion with his thumb and forefinger. She wished she didn't have to question him, but she knew from what Marcus had said earlier that this guy was bad news. She waited for an answer.

"He was real big." Marcus squirmed. "My face hit him just below his chest."

Sabre's heart sank as she realized he had been close enough to make that observation.

"Do you remember the color of his hair?"

"Brown. Dark brown."

"What was he wearing?"

"A dark blue suit. Oh, and he had shiny fingernails."

"Shiny?"

"Yeah, like they were polished, only with no color."

"Marcus, did you see his car?"

"Yes, it was black."

"A Mercedes?" Sabre asked.

"Yeah. How did you know?"

"Sammy told us. We were trying to figure out if it was the same man he saw. Did you happen to see the license plate?"

"Yeah. Dad taught me to get the license plate number on the marks. He said it would help when we got to Stage Two in our work." Marcus coughed.

"What was Stage Two?"

"I don't know exactly. We never got there, but it was a way to get more money from the marks. Dad said once we had pictures, that part would be easy."

"Did you get the license number?"

"No because he didn't have one."

That fit with what Sammy had said about it being a new car with the temporary permit in the window. "Was there a sticker in the back window?"

"Yeah."

She knew it was a long shot but she asked anyway. "Did you or your father happen to get that number?"

"No, but it said C250 on the back of the car and the frame for the license plate said Mercedes-Benz, Fallbrook, CA."

"Very observant."

"My dad taught me a lot of stuff," he said proudly. Then he added, "Other kids hit the marks, too, but most of them worked for Tuffy. But dad said we didn't need

Tuffy 'cause we could do this ourselves and why should we share the money with him."

Sabre cringed at the thought of the things Foreman had taught his son. "Who's Tuffy?"

"I never met him. Nobody knew who he was. He did everything 'anomonusly.'"

Sabre didn't correct his pronunciation. She knew what he meant. "Is there anything else you can tell me about the man in the Mercedes?"

"I think he's an Alabamacan." Marcus coughed. "He got real mad when I asked him if he was one."

"What's an Alabamacan?"

"They talk funny, like my friend Jermaine. He talks funny, too. When the other kids teased him, Jermaine would say he talks like that because he's from Alabama and they couldn't do it because they're not Alabamacans."

"Jermaine sounds like a very smart and brave young man." Sabre hesitated before she asked the question that burned on her tongue. "Marcus, did the big man hurt you?"

Lowering his eyes toward the floor, he said, "Not that time."

"Had you seen him before?"

"Just once, a week or so before. I tried to get away but I couldn't. He was too strong." The tears welled up in his eyes.

Sabre swallowed. "What did he do to you?"

"Awful stuff." Marcus coughed. "I don't want to talk about it." All of a sudden he was coughing more and struggling to get his breath. "Please don't tell anyone."

"It's okay, Marcus." Sabre pushed the button on his bed to call the nurse. She took his hand in hers. "Try to calm down. Someone will be in shortly to help you."

She had no sooner spoken the words when a nurse came in the room. Sabre stepped out and let her treat him. When the nurse came out of Marcus' room, Sabre said, "I'm afraid I upset him. Is he okay?"

"It wasn't your fault. This happens a lot. It's the pneumonia and the infection is pretty bad. I'm afraid he's not out of the woods yet."

When Sabre returned to the hospital room, Marcus was lying quietly. He had stopped coughing, but he looked drained. The color had faded from his face and he seemed to be having trouble keeping his eyes open.

Sabre stood by his bedside and leaned over. "I'm going to go now, but I'll be back in a day or so. Thanks for your help today. I know it's difficult."

Marcus reached up with his hand and touched her lightly on the arm. "Can you let my mom come see me? Please, please."

"She hasn't been here?" Sabre was sorry she showed such surprise when she saw the look of disappointment on his face.

"I haven't seen her. Just my grandparents have been here."

Sabre didn't know why Dana hadn't been to see her son and she didn't want Marcus to think his mother didn't care about him. "She stayed with you around the clock when you were first brought in. I'm sure she wants to be here." Marcus' face didn't show any relief so Sabre continued. "You know, your mother loves you very much. She's trying very hard to get you back with her. She has a lot of programs to attend every day and she doesn't have a car so it's difficult for her to get places. I'll see if the social worker can help her come here."

As soon as Sabre left the hospital she called Marla Miller, the social worker on the Foreman case.

"How's my favorite attorney?" Marla asked, as she always did when Sabre or Bob called.

"I've been better. I'm at the hospital with Marcus. He says his mother hasn't been to see him since he regained consciousness. Does she need bus tokens or someone to supervise or something?" Sabre spoke, as she walked to her car.

"I gave her extra bus tokens and I told her the hospital staff was supervision enough. She doesn't need to have anyone else with her in his hospital room. Dana told me she had been going. Are you sure she hasn't been there?"

"I know she was there on Wednesday night when Marcus was admitted and on Thursday because I saw her, but I haven't seen her since and I've been here several times. Marcus says he hasn't seen her and I spoke briefly with the day nurse and I inquired at the desk. No one has seen her."

"That's crazy. Why wouldn't she go visit him? By the way, how is Marcus today?"

"He was talking a little better, but he was coughing pretty hard. The pneumonia is still a risk and he's very lonesome for his mom."

"I'll follow up with Dana and get back to you." Before Sabre could respond, Marla added, "Did you hear they set Foreman's funeral for Saturday morning at ten o'clock?"

"No, I hadn't heard. Thanks. Do you think Marcus will be released from the hospital by then?"

"I don't know, but he told me he didn't want to go to the funeral."

"Really?" Sabre said. "The last time we talked about it he sounded as if he wanted to go. Come to think of it, he asked if he was going, not if he could go."

"I just worry that he'll regret it later if he doesn't go."

"Me, too, but we have a few days yet. He may change his mind and if he does, we'll do our best to get him there. If he doesn't want to go, maybe being in the hospital will be a good excuse for him. Then he won't have to feel guilty about not going."

Sabre had reached her car just as she hung up her phone. She took the Foreman case file out of her trunk, saw Dave Carr's phone number, and dialed it.

"Well, hello, Ms. Brown," Dave Carr said in a pleasing voice. "I hoped you would call but I didn't expect to hear from you quite so soon. Does this mean you couldn't resist my charm?"

"This isn't a social call," Sabre said dryly, caught off guard that he answered his phone. She expected his secretary at his office. When she heard street traffic, she realized he had given her his cell number. Of course he did.

"What a shame," he chided. "So, counselor, what 'unsocial' thing can I do for you?"

She was a little irritated that he turned her words around, but at the same time impressed that he could, and she would ordinarily find it funny, but she was too concerned for Marcus right now to appreciate the humor. "Do you know why your client hasn't visited her son in the hospital since last Thursday?"

"No, but I'll check with her to see what's going on."

"Thanks," Sabre said, her voice softer. "Marcus really needs to see his mother. We don't need a repeat of the act that landed him in the hospital."

"You're right. I'll talk to her. And thanks for not objecting to my request for a continuance yesterday."

"I understand you need to get familiar with the case. Besides, my clients are in the best placement for them right now and maybe some of this will sort itself out with a little time."

"Maybe we should meet for coffee and discuss the case," Dave said.

"You're relentless."

"I'm intoxicated by your beauty. And I've been waiting—what's it been, six months or more—for you to call. Now that you've called, I don't want to miss my chance."

"I'm sure. Besides, if I remember correctly, you were in a relationship when we met."

"No. My relationship had just ended. You wanted to give me 'healing' time. For the record, I'm completely healed."

Sabre smiled and then wondered if it showed in her voice. "I'll see you in court," she said.

Chapter 27

"Thanks for coming by," Sabre said from behind her desk, as JP walked into her office.

He peered around the room. "Does it creep you out that there was a dead body in here not long ago?"

"A little, especially when I first come in. I feel a little apprehensive, like I don't know what I might find in here. But once I'm here I settle in and it doesn't bother me anymore, and each day gets a little easier. I think it would be a whole lot worse if I had witnessed the murder, or if there was a pool of blood left behind." Sabre looked at the spot where the token of her brother sat for so long. "And I miss seeing the hourglass every day."

JP took a seat across the desk from Sabre. "I'm sorry about your hourglass. I know how important it was to you."

"Of all the things they had to take, it had to be something of Ron's. I have so few things of his left after the fire." Though she knew the answer, she asked anyway, "I take it the police haven't found it."

"No. And they're convinced it was the murder weapon so even if they do find it, it'll stay in the evidence lock-up until this murder is solved."

"I'm sure it has been destroyed or dumped by now, anyway."

"You said you had some info on the black Mercedes?" JP asked.

"Yes, and before I forget, Marcus said the big guy had a funny accent. He compared it to his friend from

Alabama, but it could be from some other southern state." Sabre relayed the story about Jermaine. "About the car, Marcus said there was a frame with no license plate that read, 'Mercedes-Benz, Fallbrook, CA.' Could you check that out? How many people have bought a new black C250 Mercedes in a small town like that in the last month? There can't be that many."

"The trick will be getting the info without a warrant."

"Please see what you can do, because if we can find him I think your buddies at the police department will be happy to go after him. He's out there trolling for kids and from what Marcus says he's doing more than talking to them."

"Did he tell you that?"

"He said the man 'hurt' him. That he tried to get away but he couldn't. He didn't elaborate, but the pain on his face said it all."

"Wait until I get my hands on that son of a...."

"Don't go getting yourself in trouble. The problem is Marcus doesn't want me to say anything, and I can't violate his confidence. Nor can you."

"So we just let him go?" JP's face turned red and he flung his arm in the air.

"No. What we need to do is find the guy, watch him, and get something else on him that we can hand over to the police."

JP stood up. "Oh, I'll find him alright, and I'll get something on him."

"In the meantime, I'll keep working with Marcus. He isn't stable enough to deal with much right now, but I think he's beginning to trust me more and more. And keep in mind, this might be the guy who killed Foreman."

"One way or the other I'll see that he pays for what he did to Marcus."

Sabre arose from her chair and walked around next to JP. She put her hand on his. "Are you alright? I don't want to have to worry about your going all 'cowboy' on me."

"Don't fret. I'm on the right horse and I ain't sittin' backwards."

"See, that's what I mean." Her eyes pleaded with him.

He squeezed her hand. "Hey, kid. I'm not going to do anything stupid." He looked Sabre in the eye and one side of his mouth rose, forming a tiny smirk. His Texas accent rose to the occasion. "But we both know that man's going to hell. I'm just gonna pave the road for him."

"Oh, and while you're at it, see what you can find out about someone who's known in the streets as Tuffy."

"Tuffy? What a lame name. It doesn't even sound tough."

"That's what I thought. It sounds like something you'd name a little kitten."

"Got anything else on him?" JP asked.

"Just that he's either running a sex-trafficking ring with homeless kids, or at the very least using them in a scam like Foreman did with Marcus."

"If that's the case, maybe Tuffy didn't like Foreman working on his own and taught him a lesson."

"That's what I'm thinking."

Following a little research on the car dealers in Fallbrook, JP still had plenty of time to make the hour drive. He pulled off I-15 and wound his way through the small mountain road to the town. He passed several ranches, four nurseries that had plants ranging from huge palm trees to small succulents, and a sign of a giant triple ice cream cone on his way into town. He liked this area and often thought it might be a place he could call home someday. The town felt secluded from the rest of the world and had a "country" feel to it.

His new GPS took him directly to the Mercedes dealership. He parked his pickup and was immediately approached by a tall saleswoman who was about forty years old. Her blonde hair laid in soft curls over a layer of brown that lit on her shoulders. She looked like she belonged in her dark blue suit and red silk blouse.

"Good afternoon," she said, smiling broadly. "Welcome to Mercedes-Benz Fallbrook." She reached her hand out to shake his. "I'm Shannon Shafer."

"JP Torn," he said, extending his hand.

"Are you looking for a new or a previously owned car today?"

"New, ma'am, if you don't mind."

"Is there something specific you're looking for?"

She walked with him past a lot full of used cars toward the showroom. "A C250 in black."

"Good choice. It's a very comfortable car, has high but efficient performance, and offers all the safety features. Plus it has sporty handling at a reasonable cost."

JP opened the door for her and let her pass in first. He wondered what she considered a "reasonable cost" as they passed an S600 Sedan with a sticker that read $159,500. Holy cow, JP thought. Even if I were rich, I wouldn't pay that for a truck, much less some fan-dangled luxury car.

"Mercedes is known for its performance and handling. This car's four-cylinder engine has the new 1.8 liter turbo-direct injection, which delivers more torque than the previous V-6. It reduces fuel emissions and consumption as well as noise."

JP noticed the lack of color in the showroom. Most of the cars were black, gray, or silver. He couldn't remember if he had ever seen a brightly colored Mercedes sedan, although he assumed they existed.

Shannon stopped at a black C250. "Here it is. It's not only a beauty; it offers the highest safety features in the business as well as the industry's first seven-speed automatic transmission, which as you probably know results in better highway fuel efficiency. With these skyrocketing gas prices we need all the help we can get."

The sticker on the C250 read $35,220 leading JP to think the pedophile wasn't rich or he would've bought a more expensive Mercedes. This was the "wannabe" car, the low-end luxury car.

"Do you sell a lot of these?" JP asked.

"It's a very popular choice among Mercedes owners," she said.

JP walked around the car as if he were interested. "How many would you say this location sells in a month?"

"I don't know that exactly, but I can assure you our customers are very satisfied when they buy this car. It has agility control suspension and an advanced breaking system which includes Predictive Brake Priming and Automatic Brake Drying."

JP listened as she continued her sales pitch. He knew that she was trying to figure out where he was going with his questions so she could give the correct responses. "How many of these did you personally sell in the last month?"

"Only one, but if you're concerned about my ability to help you, please don't be. I can assure you I will give you a good deal and you won't be disappointed with my service. Besides, we have a whole team to take care of you."

"I can see you're very good at your job." JP opened the door and looked inside. "What color was the one you sold?"

"Silver. You said you were interested in black, right? Because we also have it in the Palladium Silver on the floor if you'd like to see that."

"You just carry the black and silver?"

"Other colors can be ordered as well, but the black or silver suits you," she said.

"How many other salesmen or women are here?"

"Eight." This time she didn't even try to continue her pitch. Instead she said, "Go ahead, sit in the car. See if it fits."

"I bet you sell more cars than anyone here. You sure seem to know what you're talking about. Tell me, did the other sales people all sell at least one of these particular cars in the last month?"

"A few of them did. We stand by our products and this car in particular is exceptional. One of the salesmen even bought one himself," she offered.

"Oh, really? What color did he get?"

"Black."

"Do you own one?"

"I drive a Mercedes, but not this model. I've had mine for several years. They're very durable and also remain classic in their design."

"Could I talk to the salesman who bought the C250?" Her expression gave way to concern. JP added quickly, "Don't worry, you're my go-to person. I just want to ask him a few questions about how he likes it and such. What's his name?"

"It's Warren Smithe and I'm afraid he's not here today, but we can take the car for a drive if you'd like to see how it handles."

JP squinted his eyes and wrinkled his brow as if he were deep in thought. "Warren Smithe? That name sounds familiar. Is he a big, tall guy?"

"Yes, do you know him?"

"Not really. I came in here a while back with a friend of mine who was looking at cars and I think that's the gentleman who helped him. Does he have a southern accent?"

She nodded. "Yes, but he has tried real hard to get rid of it. It mostly comes out when he's excited or nervous about something. We joke about how he becomes more southern the closer he gets to closing a deal."

JP lowered his voice, "To tell you the truth, I wasn't nearly as impressed with him as I am you. He seemed a little odd."

"That's Warren, but he's a nice enough guy, just hard to get to know. He keeps to himself for the most part."

"Are you working tomorrow?" JP asked.

"Yes, but I can make you a good offer on the car right now."

"I'm afraid I'm out of time right now." He turned to leave and then turned back. "Do you know if Warren is working tomorrow? I'd still like to ask him a few questions before we seal the deal."

"I believe he comes in at one."

"I'll see you tomorrow then."

Chapter 28

Sabre dozed off as she sat in the back of the courtroom waiting for her case to be heard. Bob nudged her. She shook her head to help wake up, stood up, and walked out with Bob close behind her.

"Are you okay?" Bob asked, as soon as they were in the hallway.

"I'm just tired."

"Do you have some wild affair going on that you haven't shared with me?"

"I should be so lucky. Believe me, if I were having wild sex I'd be yelling it from the rooftops. No, I'm just not sleeping. These horrible nightmares of hanging dead bodies are haunting me. They seem so real, especially when they first start out—almost like a memory instead of a dream."

"Your memory of Marcus isn't a dream. It is real. And I know it was hard for you to see."

"Yeah, but there's the man with a blue face, too. He also seems real. And last night I was just a little girl and was just tall enough to reach up and touch his foot. I tugged on it and then my dad ran in and grabbed me."

"Are you only seeing Marcus and the man with the blue face?"

"Sometimes it's just the two of them. Other times there are lots of faceless bodies. It's just plain creepy. Whenever the dream goes on for any length of time, my dad always comes to rescue me. And it's always in that same little yellow house. Sometimes I think I actually remember that house, but then I realize it's probably just from the dream."

"Maybe you should see your doctor. You know, the good-looking one with the pretty eyes you always talk about. He can give you something to help you sleep."

"I don't want something to help me sleep because when I sleep I dream. That's the problem. I'm afraid to go to sleep."

"This isn't healthy. You look terrible. Your eyes are all puffy and red and you have dark circles, like something out of a horror movie."

Sabre reached up and touched her face around her eye. "Do I look that bad?"

"Okay, maybe not that bad, but I'm worried about you, Sobs. You need to go and at least talk to the doctor. Maybe if you sleep deeply enough you won't have the nightmares."

"You think?"

"I don't know, but it's worth checking into."

"Okay. I'll call the doctor as soon as I finish my calendar."

They started back toward the courtroom. "And if he gives you any good psychotropic drugs or pain pills, save them for me," Bob said.

She smacked him lightly on the arm. "You nut."

"I just know your aversion to taking pills and I wouldn't want you to waste some perfectly good mind-altering drugs."

After completing her calendar, and before leaving the parking lot at juvenile court, she sat in her car while she called her doctor and made an appointment. Bob was right. She did enjoy seeing her doctor. He was easy on the eyes and had a great sense of humor. And although she was pretty certain he was married and was never flirtatious, it was still embarrassing when she had to see him about something personal. Fortunately, she wasn't sick much.

She was able to get an appointment for the next day at 4:00 p.m. She marked it in her phone calendar and checked the time. It was too late to stop and see Marcus at the hospital as she had planned, so she drove directly to Riley's school for her scheduled appointment with him. She had given a lot of attention to Marcus and she didn't want Riley to feel neglected. He attended school regularly, his grades were improving, and socially he seemed to be fitting in well. He certainly wasn't as needy as Marcus, but he had suffered the loss of his father as well and she wanted to make sure he was okay.

Riley was waiting for her in study hall when she arrived at the school. He didn't hug her when she walked up like Marcus always did, but Sabre didn't expect that from him. He smiled and said, "Hello."

"Hi, Riley, how are you doing?"

"Good."

"Is everything okay at school?"

"Yes."

Sabre noticed a sketchpad on his desk, but Riley closed it before she could see what he was drawing. She said, "I understand your study hall teacher has been giving you extra help."

"A lot of students are here as a punishment and they won't do anything, so the few of us that want her help get it."

"That's great. I also hear that you'll likely be able to play football in the fall."

"They're going to let me take tests for math and English. If I pass them, I'll get credit for the classes and I'll be a sophomore when school starts. Then I'll be able to play." He tapped the pencil he held in his hand on the desk absentmindedly.

Sabre glanced at the pencil and he stopped. "And you started your counseling?"

"Yes, I've gone twice."

"How is that?"

"It's okay." He shrugged.

"Riley, did you see the man who beat up your father the day before the social worker came?"

He shook his head back and forth. "Nope."

"We know that your dad took Marcus out on the streets with him sometimes. Did you ever go out with him?"

He started tapping his pencil again. "Just once."

Sabre ignored it. "What did you do with him?"

"He just showed me places to get better food, and he wanted to run some scams on people but I wouldn't help him."

"Did he get upset with you?"

"Yes. He got mad and told me to leave. He said I was too old anyway for what he wanted to do and Marcus could do a better job." More tapping.

Sabre looked at his pencil again. This time he laid it down. She asked, "Do you know what he meant by that?"

"No. I just wanted to go home."

"Home to where you were staying on the streets?"

"Yes."

"And what about Marcus?"

"He wanted to go with Dad, especially at first. The last few times, though, he didn't want to go, but Dad made him. Marcus was too afraid to say no to him."

"Do you know why Marcus didn't want to go?"

Riley lowered his eyes and said, "No."

"Riley?"

"He never said. I don't know." He responded in the same tone of voice.

Sabre could tell she wasn't going to get any more information from him on this matter and moved on.

"How are things at home? Are you getting along okay with your grandma?"

"Yes. She's good to me. I like it there."

"And Frank?"

"He's fine. He even helps me with my homework sometimes."

Sabre watched Riley's behavior as they visited. He seemed much more relaxed than when she first met him. He was more talkative but not overly so and seemed proud of the changes he had made in his life. The casual observer would probably think this was an average fourteen-year-old with a typical home life. She thought about how different he was from Marcus and hoped he had been spared some of the things she knew Marcus had experienced. Sometimes the children in these situations can move on from them and grow up to be functional adults. With the court's intervention, she thought Riley had a shot at that. At least she could hope. And then there was Marcus. Poor Marcus.

Chapter 29

Several people wandered around the Mercedes-Benz Fallbrook lot. They were either being followed or led by hungry salesmen trying to close a deal. Consequently, JP wasn't greeted in the parking lot. He walked into the showroom and saw a man fitting the description of Warren Smithe talking with the receptionist at the service counter. Before JP could make it across the floor to speak with him, he heard Shannon's voice."

"Welcome back, Mr. Torn."

"Thank you."

"I know how interested you are in that C250. I took the liberty of talking to my boss and wait until you see the deal I was able to get for you. It's a deal you won't be able to refuse."

"I appreciate that." He started to walk toward the car, which put him closer to the reception desk. "Do you mind if I have another look?"

"Why, of course not."

JP walked around the car, then stood back as if he were sizing it up.

"When we spoke yesterday I don't think I mentioned all of the safety features this car has, such as the advanced brake system, a blind-spot assist, and the eleven-way air bag protection. It also has an Electronic Stability Program that can detect plowing or fishtailing and compensate for it."

JP raised his hand to stop her pitch. "Excuse me, ma'am. You're doing a fine job of explaining all the features, but if you don't mind I'd like to ask Mr. Smithe a few questions before I sign on the dotted line." He looked toward the service desk. "Is that him over there? That looks a lot like the man we spoke to last month."

"Yes, that's him. I'll go see if he can give you a few minutes."

When she left, JP positioned himself behind the car with his digital camera so he could get a photo when they walked up. He wanted it to look like he was taking a picture of the car.

Shannon stood there talking to Smithe for several minutes. JP saw them look in his direction. He guessed the stall was part of the tactic to make him want to sign. Little did they know that if he were really interested in buying a car he would've left after the first hard sales pitch. He hated to be sold on anything. He usually did his research before he ever went to make a purchase and if the salesperson was polite and not pushy, he would buy and leave.

When they finally started to walk toward him he held his camera up and took a couple of pictures of the car. When they were almost to the car he took a couple more shots, making sure they were in them.

JP looked directly at Shannon. "I wanted to get a couple of pictures of this fine car. Perhaps after I make the purchase, I can get one of you as well—with me and the car, of course."

She smiled. "Of course." She turned toward the other salesman. "And this is Warren Smithe. Warren, JP Torn."

Warren and JP shook hands. JP thought how weak and unmanly his handshake was and his shiny fingernails coupled with the touch of Smithe's skin against his made his stomach feel queasy. He couldn't even imagine what poor Marcus had to endure. "It's a pleasure, Mr. Smithe, but I believe we've already met. You've worked here for some time, haven't you?"

"About seven years now."

"I came in here a while back with a friend and you helped him. Anyway, it's not important. I understand you have a car just like this one?"

"Yes. That's correct."

"Oh, perhaps you could take our photo now, Mr. Smithe?" JP handed him the camera before he could say no, and stepped near Shannon so he could take the photo. "Smile now, Shannon. This is my big day." JP smiled at the camera. "Take a couple, please. I want to make sure I get a good one."

After the photo session, Smithe handed the camera back. JP reached for the string on it, being careful not to touch the camera. He slipped it back in his pocket.

"So, your car, Mr. Smithe, do you really like the way it handles?"

"Yes, I do indeed. The luxury styling makes me feel like the big man in town." He chuckled. "I guess maybe I am the big man in town." JP did all he could to keep from punching him. How big and important he must feel when he's out hunting for little boys. "You can't go wrong with this baby," Smithe said, patting the roof of the car.

And you do love babies, don't you, JP thought. He took a couple of steps away from Smithe, afraid of what he might do to him if he stood too close. JP looked inside the car again, not saying anything for a few seconds.

Smithe broke the silence. "Are you a rancher, Mr. Torn?"

"Born and bred."

"Think of this as a thoroughbred. You won't be driving some 'Mercedes wannabe.' This car is the real deal. It'll provide you a smooth, classic ride as its aerodynamically sculpted body slices through the country air."

JP didn't know if he could stand to listen to one more word from this man's mouth.

"A thoroughbred, huh? Well, there's nothing like having the real thing," JP said. He turned toward Shannon, for fear his voice would show his hostility if he looked at Smithe. "It's true. You can put lipstick on a pig, but he's still a pig. Ain't that right, ma'am?"

Shannon and Smithe both laughed. Both sounded forced, but the sound coming from Smithe turned his stomach. JP reached in his pocket and pulled out his phone, opened it as if he had a call. "This is JP," he said. He paused. "Okay. Okay. Yes, I'll be right there." He closed the phone, put it back in his pocket. "Sorry, I have an emergency. I'll be back."

Shannon followed him for a few steps. "When can I expect you, Mr. Torn?"

JP raised his hand without turning around and picked up his speed. "I'll call you. Gotta go."

JP walked quickly across the car lot to his pickup. Louie wagged his tail and flipped around as JP opened the door. The dog loved to go for rides and JP took him along whenever the weather permitted, as long as he wouldn't be left too long in the truck by himself. He patted Louie on the head and then picked up Louie's water bottle from the seat. He removed the lid and poured the water into the plastic dish that was attached to the end of it. Louie lapped it up for a second or two and then lost interest. JP turned the bottle back up straight and watched the water flow back inside before he capped it and put it down. He patted Louie again, stepped inside, and drove off a little too quickly. He glanced at Louie. "Thoroughbred," he mumbled. "Like a thoroughbred in a donkey race, I'll beat his ass."

On his way home, JP stopped to see his friend Ernie at the San Diego County Sheriff's Department in Vista. JP wanted to share everything he had gathered about Smithe with Greg Nelson, who fed him information on the Foreman murder case, information that Klakken wouldn't give him. But he knew if he went to Greg with this, he'd have to answer too many questions.

Ernie, on the other hand, wouldn't be so inquisitive.

"I need a favor," JP said to his friend.

"Anything, you know that."

"I need you to check a guy's fingerprints for me."

"Sure, anything you can tell me about him?"

"Not much. He works in Fallbrook, but I don't know if he lives there. He has a connection to a guy who was recently murdered, but I think it's worse than that." JP knew how Ernie would interpret that. "Worse than murder" could only mean children were involved.

Ernie shook his head. "Whatever you need."

JP carefully removed the camera from his pocket by the string. Ernie called for someone to come take it to the lab and have it dusted. "It won't take long," he said. "Then you can take the camera back with you."

They sat and visited for a while until the lab technician returned with the camera.

"I'll let you know as soon as we have something for you," Ernie said.

JP stood to leave. "Thanks, Ernie. And I'll let you know if anything else breaks on my investigation. By the way, have you ever heard of someone with the moniker,Tuffy?"

Ernie thought for a second. "Tuffy. Nope. But I'll ask around."

Back at his house, JP continued the search he had started earlier that morning to find any information he could on Warren Smithe. He hoped it would lead him to Foreman's murder because without Marcus' cooperation it would be very difficult to charge him for his assault on Marcus.

JP researched criminal records online. He made phone calls to Alabama and surrounding states, including Tennessee, Mississippi, and Georgia. He checked high schools and universities in the area searching for Warren Smithe. Due to the time difference, JP mostly left messages. He kept at it until late in the night when he found a school on classmates.com that listed a Warren Smithe in Mississippi.

Chapter 30

JP was back at his computer by six in the morning. Louie sat at his feet waiting for the occasional pat on the head. So far, JP had nothing on Tuffy. However, the previous night JP had obtained a birth date from a record of the California driver's license listed for Warren Smithe. He was born on June 12, 1969, and living in Fallbrook, California. By eight o'clock in the morning he had established that a Warren Smithe with the same birth date had received a Master of Education degree in Elementary Education from Delta State University in Cleveland, Mississippi.

By nine o'clock Ernie had confirmed that the fingerprints belonged to Warren Smithe and the birth date was correct. By ten o'clock JP's research had taken him to the small town of Scooba, Mississippi where Smithe taught in a public elementary school for two years before leaving for a school in Montgomery, Alabama, in 1995. He taught for eight years in a private school in Montgomery where he was officially listed as "resigning under special circumstances." JP couldn't find anything that indicated what the "special circumstances" consisted of, nor did he find any other schools where he had taught.

JP did the math in his head. If he stopped teaching in Montgomery in 2003, that left only a little over a year until he started working at Mercedes-Benz Fallbrook. At best he could have taught one year somewhere else, but if he had, JP couldn't find it. After several conversations with administrators and other teachers in the school districts in both Scooba, Mississippi and Montgomery, Alabama, JP hadn't been able to confirm his suspicions but he was awaiting phone calls from other personnel at both facilities.

The closest he could get was a comment he received from one of the secretaries at the school in Scooba who stated that Smithe had left that school because he was too "friendly" with the students. She wouldn't expound on her statements.

It wasn't long before the phone rang. The call was from the same area code as he had called earlier in Montgomery.

"This is JP Torn. May I help you?"

"Hello." The person spoke softly. "Your name and number were given to me from someone who said you had called earlier regarding Warren Smithe."

"Yes, ma'am. May I ask who I'm speaking to?"

"First, please tell me something."

"What's that?" JP asked.

"I understand you're trying to find out why Mr. Smithe left our school district. Is that correct?"

"Correct."

"Why do you need this information?"

He considered using a cover but decided something close to the truth would work best. "I am an investigator for an attorney who represents a young boy in an abuse case. We know that Mr. Smithe has had contact with this young man. I'm trying to determine to what extent Mr. Smithe may be involved in this case." JP spoke carefully, trying to keep from violating Marcus' confidentiality. He knew he had to tread lightly and hoped he hadn't gone too far. "Did he leave the school district on his own accord?"

"He was asked to resign."

"Do you know why?" JP felt Louie curl up by his ankle and lay his head on his foot.

Several seconds of silence filled the phone. Then she blurted, "He was accused of molesting a young boy, several of them, but only one would give enough information to bring charges against him and he left town."

"Smithe left town?"

"No, the child and his family moved. They snuck out of town. I understand they thought running away was preferable to putting the child through the pain of testifying. He was already having a hard time dealing with the harassment from other students and some of the community members who didn't want to believe him or have him taint the reputation of the school. I think the mother encouraged the move. She feared her husband would kill Smithe if they stayed."

"How do you know all this?"

"I was on the school board. The decision was made to 'just get rid of Smithe and let it all go.' I didn't like it, but I was fighting mostly men on the board and they didn't want the 'stigma' on our school. I was outvoted and they decided to make him an offer. If he would resign, the school board wouldn't take any legal action. Of course, that didn't bind any of the families from doing something, but none of them did. I was furious and frustrated. I should've spoken out and just lost my seat on the board, but I didn't. I fought to get the 'under special circumstances' clause in the official documents, hoping it might trigger questions if he tried to go to another school district. And I went on record to say if I ever heard of another child in trouble with him I wouldn't keep my mouth shut."

"How old was the little boy?"

"Ten or eleven. I think he was in sixth grade."

"So he would be around twenty now?"

"Yes."

"You seem to be pretty connected to the community. Do you know where the family moved?" JP asked

"I have a cousin who was good friends with the boy's mother. She told me they moved to a small town in southern California. Temecal or Temecland or something like that."

"Temecula?" JP said the name slowly and clearly.

"Yeah, that's it, but I don't know if they're still there."

"Could Smithe have known where he went? Perhaps followed him?"

"I don't think so. Why?"

"Because he lives and works only about twenty minutes from Temecula."

"Oh, no." She gasped. And then she added quickly, "He's not teaching again, is he?"

"No, but I'm concerned about the young man and his family." JP didn't want to tell her what he was thinking. If Smithe did kill Foreman, who knows what he might have done to his previous victim and his family.

"Do you really think he might have followed them there? Why would he do that?"

"I don't know, but Smithe may be more dangerous than he appears. I'd like to follow up on the family if you'll be so kind as to give me the names. I'll try to keep you out of it if I can."

The woman gave JP the names of the young boy, his parents, and two older siblings. She also provided descriptions as best she could remember. "And my name is Ada Adams if you ever need me. I'll do what I can to right this wrong."

Chapter 31

Marcus had just started his evening meal when Sabre entered his hospital room. The food on his tray was soft—chicken broth, mashed potatoes, and orange Jell-O sitting next to a container of chocolate milk. The intravenous antibiotics continued to flow into the pic line in his arm.

"I see you're eating. That's a good sign," Sabre said.

"Yes. The doctor said if I eat today I may be able to go home tomorrow."

"That would be wonderful. You look much better today." She looked at the faded yellow and pink line on his neck. The bruising had nearly faded away, but a redness remained where the rope had burned him. Sabre noted that his color was better as well. "You sound good, too. Does it still hurt to talk?"

"Not so much." He took a drink of his chocolate milk and then looked at Sabre with sad eyes. "Am I going to a group home?"

"Why would you think that?"

"Because I heard them talking at Polinsky when I was there about kids who got in too much trouble and so they sent them to group homes. Most of them didn't like it much."

Sabre smiled and touched his hand. "First of all, children from Polinsky aren't sent to group homes for punishment. Sometimes it's the best placement for them. Second, you are not in trouble and you're not going to be punished in any way. We just want to keep you safe. I spoke with your social worker this morning and we all feel it's best if you go home to your grandma's unless you have some reason for not wanting to go there."

A look of confusion drifted across his face and then he said, "I'd like to go there."

"Good. You'll continue to see your doctor and you'll have to go to therapy. Your grandma and Frank both want you to go home and they've even provided an in-home nurse for part of the day so you can stay there. Are you okay with all that?"

He nodded his head in affirmation.

After a second or two Sabre noticed he hadn't eaten anything yet. She said, "You should try to eat some of your food."

Marcus stuck his fork in his mashed potatoes and stirred them around a bit. "When will I be able to live with my mom?"

"I don't know for certain," Sabre said. It was always difficult for her to have to explain to a child why they can't be with a parent. This was worse than usual because Marcus would never be able to live with his father again and Sabre had serious doubts about his mother's recovery. On the other hand, she had to give him hope and some still remained. "Your mother has a lot of programs she has to attend and it'll take some time, but as she gets better you'll be able to spend more and more time with her."

Then as children are so prone to do in these situations, Marcus made the excuses. "I guess that's why she hasn't been here to see me."

Sabre felt her face redden. She was surprised Dave Carr hadn't been able to convince Dana to come back to the hospital and Sabre had been so busy with other cases she hadn't followed up to see if she had been there. "I'm sure that's it," Sabre said.

"She did call me once," Marcus said.

"Has your grandma been here?"

"She comes every day and so does Frank." He reached over to the stand next to his bed and picked up a Game Boy. "They brought me this and it has lots of cool games with it."

"What about Riley? Has he been here?"

"He's usually in school when they come."

Sabre glanced toward his tray. "Eat," she said.

Marcus took a couple of bites of his potatoes and drank some of his chicken broth. Then he ate all his Jell-O and drank his chocolate milk. Sabre visited with him until he finished his food, talking mostly about the games he'd been playing and what levels he had conquered. She still had a sensitive subject to talk to him about and she didn't want to interrupt his meal.

After about ten minutes of just visiting, Sabre took a photo that JP had blown up for her out of her bag. "Marcus, I'm going to show you a couple of photos and I want you to tell me if you recognize this man."

"Okay."

When Sabre handed him the pictures she saw the muscles tighten in his neck and for a second his face flinched. "That's the man in the black Mercedes," he said immediately.

Sabre took the photos back and put them away.

"Thank you. I'm sorry you had to look at those. I know that wasn't easy for you."

"Did he kill my dad?"

"We don't know, but if he did, the police will get him."

"You didn't tell him about me, did you?"

"Of course not. I wouldn't do that. You know, Marcus, if you ever want to tell the police what happened to you so we can have him arrested you just tell me and I'll set it up for you. He should pay for what he did to you."

"But then I'd go to jail."

Sabre shook her head. "No, Marcus. You won't go to jail."

"My dad said I would. And so did Sammy. They told me not to tell anyone or I'd go to jail because I tried to scam him."

Sabre wanted to take him in her arms, hold him tightly, and convince him he was safe. She continued to try to persuade him to believe her and not his father, but he held tightly to the advice his dad had given him. He had so little of his father to cling to and that coupled with his fear of incarceration made it easy to understand why he chose to believe him. She finally let it go.

Sabre gathered up her bag to leave. "I need to get going but I'll see you real soon."

"Will I be going to the funeral on Saturday?"

Sabre found it interesting that he always asked that question, as if he had to go rather than if he could go.

"The doctor said if you're able to go home tomorrow you'll be okay to attend the funeral as long as you feel up to it. Do you want to go?"

"I think so."

Chapter 32

JP drove north with Louie on I-15 past the Fallbrook exit and towards Temecula. He turned off on Highway 74 and drove east, turning whenever Ursula, his GPS, told him to. Sabre had named his GPS and the name had stuck. It was the same name she had given to hers and to Bob's. It had since become a joke that JP spent more time with Ursula than he did them.

The house he was looking for was situated away from the center of town. He turned left onto a road in dire need of new pavement and drove about a mile until Ursula said, "You've reached your destination."

The old, ranch-style house was surrounded by a chain link fence but the gate was open. JP drove inside onto the dirt driveway. The yard consisted of mowed weeds and more dirt, two overgrown pepper trees, and two large eucalyptus trees that offered shade to a picnic table and an old grill. A splash of bright magenta-colored bougainvillea climbed one corner of the fence. Several other dead bougainvillea bushes covered the north side of the fence. A small red tricycle, a plastic bat, and numerous other toys were strewn about the yard.

JP lowered the windows about halfway down on both sides of the truck to let air in for Louie and stepped out. A heavy-set, African-American woman and a golden retriever came out of the house to greet him. The dog ran directly to JP's truck. He stretched his body upward until his paws reached the top of the door and his nose found Louie's.

"Charlie!" the woman yelled, as she walked toward the truck. "I'm sorry. Charlie is just excited to have a visitor." Louie whined to get out. Charlie held his position, his tail wagging.

The next voice JP heard was a deep baritone. "Charlie!" The golden retriever dropped to the ground and ran directly to the tall man standing by the front door. The man's head was shaved clean but he had a goatee and mustache on his face, and his size and his voice commanded respect. Louie continued to whine, scratching at the window to get out. The man walked over to JP, Charlie at his side.

"I can close the gate if you'd like to let your dog out to play with Charlie. He loves other dogs." The man said.

"That would be mighty fine. Louie has been cooped up for more than an hour. I'm sure he'd love to run some."

The man walked over and pushed the gate closed. Charlie stayed at his heels until JP opened the door of the truck and let Louie out. Charlie was there to meet him in three leaps and off they ran around the yard.

"Sorry about all that. May I help you?" the woman asked.

"Are you Mr. and Mrs. Washington?"

"Yes," the man said, reaching out his hand to shake. "My name is Carter. This is my wife Ellie."

JP reciprocated. "I'm JP Torn." Carter stood at least six inches taller than JP and his hand made JP's feel like a child's when he shook it. "I'm an investigator and I'd like to ask you a few questions about something that happened about ten years ago."

Carter looked a little concerned but Ellie said, "Come sit and I'll get us some ice tea."

She directed him and Carter toward the picnic table and she went inside the house. JP and Carter talked about the weather and local sports until she returned. JP felt like he was back in Texas with the southern hospitality he was receiving from these kind people. He had never quite gotten used to the fast-paced, paranoid lifestyle Californians lived. He wasn't sure if it was California or just a large city thing, and he knew there was plenty of reason to be paranoid when a stranger came into your yard, so he understood it but he didn't like it much.

Ellie set three large glasses of ice tea on the table and sat down next to her husband.

"Thank you," JP said and took a drink of the tea. He smiled at her. "It has a taste of mint, like my grandma used to make."

"I knew you were a southern boy the minute I saw you," Ellie said.

"I hate to bring this up, but there's no easy way to say it. I'm investigating a case that has turned up a man named Warren Smithe."

Ellie's facial expression didn't change. It was as if she expected to hear his name, but Carter's gentle eyes suddenly showed hatred in them. Ellie reached over and put her hand on her his.

"Has he hurt someone else?" Carter asked.

"We think so."

Carter slammed his fist on the table. Charlie barked and ran over to the table with Louie close behind. "I should've killed that son of a bitch when I had the chance."

"And let Andre and the girls grow up without a father? You know how that boy needed you and the girls did, too," Ellie said and then turned to face JP. "It hasn't been easy for this family dealing with the pain that man left us, but we've managed. I never could've done it without Carter, though." She looked up at him in pure admiration. "We moved to California and he found a real good union job. All three children graduated from high school and the two girls even went to college, one to community college and the other to the university. The oldest became a hairstylist and our second earned her nursing degree. She works at a hospital in Los Angeles. We even own our home. It still needs a little work, but it's much better than that shack we had in Alabama. Carter and Andre did a lot of work on the house, especially when we first moved in. They painted inside and out and remodeled the kitchen and bathrooms and even added that room over there." She pointed toward the side of the house where the dogs were now playing again. "Andre loved to help his daddy."

Ellie's voice cracked a little every time she said Andre's name. JP wondered if it was because he had brought up the painful memories or if it was something else. She kept talking as if she were afraid to let JP speak. Perhaps she was afraid he might say something that would set Carter off, so JP just listened.

A sound came from the room near the picnic table. Ellie said, "Carter, I hear the baby. Will you please check on him?"

Carter stood up and walked into the house without saying a word.

Ellie spoke softly. "Please don't tell Carter that Smithe's living here. I'm afraid of what he might do."

"You've seen him?"

"Yes, about two years ago. I was at a nursery in Fallbrook. He didn't recognize me, but I knew it was him the minute I saw him. I wanted to scratch his eyes out and beat him with my fists, but instead I just got into my car and drove off. I was so upset I nearly had an accident pulling out of the lot. I wanted to come home and tell Carter but I couldn't. I couldn't tell anyone. I haven't been back to Fallbrook since and I've made darn sure Carter hasn't gone, either."

"You're right. He's been living in Fallbrook for quite a while. I wondered if he followed you out here, but if he hasn't tried to contact you then it's probably just coincidence. You're sure he never tried to get hold of Andre?"

"I'm certain of that," she said emphatically. "What has that devil done this time? Please don't tell me he's working with children again."

"No. He works at the Mercedes-Benz dealership in Fallbrook." JP thought it was best she knew so she could avoid him. "We think he's after young boys and he may even have killed a man. We're still investigating, though, so we can't be sure. But if he has done the things we think he has, I promise you I'm going to get him one way or another and send him to prison where he can spend the next twenty years as some big, mean felon's play toy."

A faint smile crossed her lips that lasted only a split second. It was the first time he saw anything positive on her face since he had brought up Smithe. "I'd like to think he'll pay for his sins in this world, that he'll suffer like my boy did. I suppose that's not a very Christian thing to say, but I can't help it. I do believe the good Lord will make him pay in the hereafter for what he did to my Andre."

"I really don't want any more children to have to endure what your son did. Do you think I could speak to Andre or would it be too painful for him?"

"Oh, Lord. I wish you could. I'm afraid my son...."

Ellie's face looked tired and very distant, and her eyes filled with sadness until Carter walked out carrying a little boy about two years old and interrupted her. The little boy smiled a huge smile when he spotted Ellie. "Momo," he yelled.

Ellie reached out her arms to the little boy, hugging him closely. The child wrapped his arms around her neck and squeezed. She kissed him on his cheek. "This is little Andre, my grandson."

"Hi, Andre," JP said. Andre reached across the table, grabbed JP's hat, and nearly knocked it off his head before Ellie could pull him back. JP sat up straighter, taking the hat out of the baby's range. When Charlie and Louie ran past the table, little Andre lost all interest in JP's hat.

"Chawee," Andre called, squirming to get down.

Ellie handed him back to Carter. "Here, take him to see Charlie."

"Watch Louie," JP said. "He won't hurt him intentionally, but he's still a puppy so he may be a little rough."

Carter nodded, scooped up Andre in his big hands, and flew him like an airplane up and into his arms. Andre giggled as they crossed the yard toward the dogs.

"You were saying about Andre?" JP said.

"Andre had a hard time growing up. He was a sweet, gentle boy, but it always seemed like he was trying to prove how tough he was. He never got into drugs or gangs or anything, but he made sure no one thought he was a 'sissy' either. We made him go to counseling for a while, but he never would talk about what happened to him in Alabama, and I know that's what was really bothering him. He joined the Marine Corps right out of high school. He looked so handsome in his uniform. We were so proud of him." Her voice started to crack and her eyes filled with tears.

JP was afraid to ask, so he just sat there waiting for her to compose herself and finish if she could.

Ellie took a deep breath. "A year ago last February he was sent to Afghanistan. Two weeks later he was killed in the line of duty."

Chapter 33

It had been over a week since Sabre and Bob had gone to Pho's for lunch, and Sabre felt like she was going through withdrawal. Seldom a week went by without at least three visits to their favorite Vietnamese restaurant. Sometimes JP joined them, sometimes not. He didn't much care where he ate but often went with them since it was one of the few times to talk about their cases without constant interruption. Today was one of those days.

Prior to their meal being served they had discussed the possible suspects in the Foreman murder, being careful not to reveal any confidential information from Marcus in front of Bob. They were all trying to solve the criminal case in order to eliminate Bob as a suspect and to that end they were all working together.

"Foreman's funeral is tomorrow," Sabre said. "Are you going?"

"I am," JP said. "I want to see who shows up and watch everyone to see how they act. You can learn a lot at funerals."

"I'm not going," Bob replied. "Leahy strongly suggested that I not go. He's afraid it will appear as if I'm there for Dana. I didn't want to go anyway. I didn't even like the guy. Besides, why should I go to his funeral? I'm pretty sure he won't be going to mine."

JP chuckled. Sabre said, "You're a fruitcake. Let the dead guy rest in peace."

"I hope he's turning over in his grave," Bob said. "He was a jerk. I feel bad for the boys because they lost their father, but truthfully, they're probably better off without them."

"Well, I'm going," Sabre said. "I want to be there for Marcus and Riley. Marcus was released from the hospital today and he's decided he wants to go. So I'm going, too."

"Do you want a ride?" JP asked.

"Thanks, I'd like that."

"Yeah," Bob said. "You wouldn't want to be seen at a funeral without a date."

Sabre and JP just shook their heads and finished eating their meals.

When JP left Pho's he drove to the jail to see if he could talk to Sammy. He had already verified that he was in custody and apparently Ludwik didn't feel it wise to bail him out. Either that or Sammy hadn't bothered to contact him.

Sammy was under no obligation to speak with JP, but he took a chance and stopped in during visiting hours. After signing in and waiting for about twenty minutes, a guard brought Sammy into the room and seated him across from JP.

"Hello, Sammy."

"I don't need to talk to you, you know," Sammy said.

"That's right, you don't. So, why are you here?"

"Curious, mostly. Besides, it's a nice change of pace to get out of the cell and no one else has been here to see me."

For a split second JP felt a little sorry for this lonely, pathetic soul. Then he remembered he had family whom he had alienated long ago—a nice family, in fact, or at least a loving, proud father who tried very hard to make the best life he could for his son. No, Sammy didn't deserve JP's sympathy. He endangered too many children's lives.

"Did you expect someone to come see you?"

"Not really. I called my father, but he said I was on my own. My sister wouldn't even accept the call, so I guess I can't count on her."

"I guess not," JP said.

"I messed up pretty bad this time."

"It's not too late to clean yourself up and make things right with the people you care about. You could start by helping me find someone named Tuffy."

"Tuffy, humph," Sammy said. "I'm Tuffy."

"You're Tuffy?" JP looked at him, face wrinkled in disbelief.

"Sure. I'm Tuffy."

JP chuckled. "I think my friends in the police department would love that bit of information. I know they'd love to get a scumbag like Tuffy off the streets."

"Okay, so I'm not Tuffy. He tells his queens to say that if we're caught. No one knows or sees Tuffy. He operates under the wire. Besides, why would I want to snitch on Tuffy?"

"Because he sells little children to pedophiles."

"That's not what he does. It's all a scam. If the kids do what he says they get away most of the time."

"Most of the time? And when they don't?"

"That's one of the casualties of the business."

JP wanted to jump across the table and shake some sense in him, but since he couldn't do that he tried another line of questioning.

"Do you think Tuffy killed Foreman?"

"Of course not. Why would he do that?"

"Because Tuffy found out that Foreman used his scam and cut him out of the profits."

"Tuffy wouldn't kill my friend George," Sammy said, twitching in his seat.

Either Sammy had a connection with Tuffy or he was up to his usual storytelling. Even Marcus, an eleven-year-old kid, could see through Sammy's stories. Perhaps this was just another one of his fantasies.

"So who is Tuffy?"

"No one knows," Sammy repeated.

"Except you. Right?"

Sammy looked sheepishly at JP, as if he had been caught doing something highly secretive. "So, what if I do know him? I'm not about to help you. Tuffy would kill me."

"Like he did George?"

"I'm telling you he didn't kill George. He wouldn't do that."

"How can you be so sure?"

"Because he knew what George was doing all along. He was alright with it as long as George just used his own kid and didn't try to enlist any of the others."

"I find that hard to believe," JP baited him.

"It's true. I used to run with Tuffy. In fact, it was my idea to pull those jobs in the first place. I'm the one who taught George. Me and Tuffy are like that, man." Sammy crossed his middle finger over his index and displayed it for JP. "We're tight. He was cool about George."

"If you do know Tuffy, I might be able to help you out of this mess. I have a lot of connections with the police department and the DA's office."

"Can you get me out of here?"

"Maybe, but before I call in some markers I need to know that you're telling me the truth."

"For real, man. I knew Tuffy before he was Tuffy."

"Why should I believe you?"

"It don't matter none, 'cause I ain't telling you who he is unless we got a deal worked out, and a darned good one at that or I ain't crossing Tuffy."

"Fair enough. Don't tell me who he is, but tell me this. How does he go about keeping anyone from knowing who he is?"

"He uses a queen bee."

"What's a queen bee?"

"That's what Tuffy calls them. It's the guy who keeps him separated from his drones, his worker bees. Tuffy is the beekeeper so the bees don't really work for him. They only work for the queen. That way, the queen is the only one who knows Tuffy, and most of them don't even know him. None of the drones ever see the beekeeper. Most of them don't even know about him." Then he said proudly. "I was his first queen. Tuffy said that since it was my idea I should have an active part."

"But you don't do it anymore?"

"Naw. It got too risky and I had to tend to my other business so I let Tuffy carry on alone."

JP believed about half of what he heard from Sammy. Trying to sort out which was which was the difficult part. He thought after the last explanation that he probably did know Tuffy because he doubted Sammy could make up the whole "bee" analogy.

"How long has this operation been going on?" JP asked.

"A couple of years."

"How many 'drones' does he have?"

"It depends on how good his queen is. I could handle three or four drones a night, but I don't know what my replacement can do."

JP wrote that off to more puffery. "Does he work the same ones every night?"

"He has a few that work more. If they're good at getting away, they get more work. But you had to be careful because we'd get a lot of repeat customers so the kids needed to be changed."

"So he used the kids to steal money from pedophiles. Does he pull this scam every night?"

"No, mostly on weekends. In the summer there's more weekday action. Lots of visitors to town and all."

Sammy looked at JP as if he had said enough. "So, can you get me out of here? Get my charges dismissed?"

"I'll talk to my friends. I'm not sure I have enough, but I'll see what I can do." JP started to leave.

"Don't take too long. I may change my mind."

JP thought about his visit with Sammy's father and how hard Ludwik had tried to do the right thing raising his kid, or so it seemed. He thought of Carter and Ellie and the pain they went through because of Andre's problems and then losing him to the war. Sometimes he wondered what it would be like to be raising a child. Right now it didn't seem like it was something he wanted to do.

Chapter 34

A small group gathered at the cemetery for George Foreman. It only included his wife and two children, Celia and Frank Davis, JP, Sabre, and Marla, the social worker on the case. Nearly half of the attendees were there because of the fallout from his death. That was not a good testimonial to his life. No church service of any kind was held and Dana insisted on a traditional burial as opposed to cremation. George had not wanted to be cremated. According to Dana, George always figured he would burn enough in hell; he didn't need to add to it before he got there. The funeral director led the short, simple, impersonal service.

He began the service. "The loss of a loved one affects us all in different ways...."

Dana wept for her husband. Riley stared at the coffin but he didn't cry. Marcus cried quietly. Everyone else remained solemn, but no tears accompanied their grief, if in fact they felt any. Sabre didn't believe they did. The majority of the sorrow expressed was not for the body in the casket or even the grieving widow, but for the children because they lost their father.

"We need to accept the sorrow from our loss as a part of life," the officiator continued. Sabre only half listened to his words. She wondered how a man lived forty years and had so few people mourn his death. She knew from what Marla had told her that George didn't have much family. He and his half-sister were raised in foster homes. George hopped from one home to another and eventually lost track of his sibling. His mother spent most of her time in prison and his father was believed to be a prison guard, but it was never confirmed. That explained his family, but had he not been so difficult to get along with he would have developed closer friendships over the years. Sammy seemed to be the closest thing he had to a friend and perhaps he would've attended if he weren't locked up himself.

"George Foreman was a father, a husband, a son. When you think of him, remember the good times," the man continued. The monotone voice did little to keep Sabre from yawning. She hadn't slept well again. The nightmares had become a nightly routine. She covered her mouth and stifled her yawn. JP winked at her, a gesture she took to mean that he understood her boredom.

Sabre wondered if there really were any "good times" in George Foreman's life and for a moment Sabre felt sorry for him, but her feelings soon found their way back to his boys. She remembered her own father's memorial and what comfort it brought her to see the church fill up with hundreds of people who came to pay their last respects. Seeing the crowd at his service made her feel that the world loved him as she did. He had to be a great man if so many people thought so.

Sabre returned to the present when she heard the man ask, "Would anyone like to say a few words?"

An awkward silence filled the already solemn air. No one stepped up to speak about him or on his behalf. There had been so many people who had come forward at her father's service that it took nearly two hours to complete. This one was closer to five minutes. Are people's lives summed up in the length of their memorial service? She knew the boys had never been to a funeral service before. She could only hope that since they didn't have anything to compare it with that they didn't feel what was so blatantly missing at this one. No one celebrated his life and few grieved his death.

"May he rest in peace," the officiator said.

"Amen," was mumbled through the small group.

Everyone stood still for a few moments. No one seemed sure of what to do next. Then Frank put his arm around his wife and they led the two boys away. Within a few steps, Marcus stopped and went back for his mother, who was still standing there staring at the casket. Marcus led her to the car. As soon as Marla left, Sabre and JP began walking toward the parking lot.

"That was dismal," Sabre said.

"Funerals aren't supposed to be fun," JP said.

"Some of them are. I've been to memorial services that were real life celebrations and sure, people cried, but they also laughed and remembered good things. Did you hear any good things said about that man's pathetic life? I can't help but feel a little sorry for him."

"The man was a louse. Those kids deserved more from him."

JP had a way of stating the obvious and Sabre's concern for Foreman fled. "How did your interview with Sammy go yesterday?" Sabre asked.

"It's hard to tell. That boy is more full of wind than a corn-eating horse. He could be just bragging but I think he does know Tuffy. The question is: How well does he know him? He told me how the operation works and he claims he knew Tuffy before Tuffy started this scam. In fact, he likes to take credit for the idea himself."

Sabre raised her eyebrows. "Maybe Sammy is Tuffy."

"I thought about that, but I don't think he's smart enough, to tell you the truth. He gets involved in stuff he has no business in and then brags about it, puffing himself up way beyond reality. I think he's luckier than a leprechaun that he's survived out there this long. One of these days his bragging is going to get him killed."

"So, what now?"

"I'm going to use what he told me and try and find out who Tuffy is. If that doesn't work I'm sure America's Finest and our friendly DA will be glad to take a man like Tuffy off the streets, even if it means making a deal with Sammy."

"Can you do that without betraying Marcus' confidence? He's just not ready to share this with anyone else yet."

"Don't worry, kid. I won't do that. I'm hoping if I can find out who Tuffy is, it'll lead us to Foreman's murderer and then the stuff about the other children will probably come out anyway and Marcus won't have to tell his story, if he doesn't want to. The biggest problem right now is I don't have enough information without Marcus to get anyone's interest."

JP drove Sabre home and returned to his office to see what he could find on the internet about Tuffy. He had very little to go on and after several nonproductive hours he decided to drive back downtown to search the streets again. Several times in the past he had gone undercover as a homeless person and still had the clothes and the face makeup to fit the occasion. He dressed up, drove to a spot near where Marcus had been staying before they were picked up by CPS, and parked his car. From there he followed the route Marcus had indicated he took to where he met Smithe. He wandered around the area for a while, watching people come and go.

When he reached Fifth Street he moved with the crowd through the Gaslamp District until he stopped, sat down on a concrete step, and leaned against the wall of a brick building. A couple of women walked down the sidewalk. As they approached one glanced at him and quickly turned her head, and then they edged their way closer to the street to avoid any contact. Several teenagers and men in suits passed him, all too engrossed in their own conversation to even notice his presence. It was the perfect cover, JP thought. For the most part, he blended into the background. People weren't afraid to talk in front of him and no one ever looked closely enough to identify him. It was as if he were an object rather than a person. He felt about as visible as the cement step he sat on and less important. At least the step had purpose.

A young, skinny boy who appeared to be about nine years old sauntered down the sidewalk past JP. He caught JP's attention because the boy was alone. JP stood up to follow the child when he noticed a man with a baseball cap following the boy. Scraggly, light brown hair escaped from under the back of the man's cap. He stood about five-foot-ten, his weight proportionate to his height. The cap shadowed his face but JP guessed his age to be in the late teens or early twenties. JP followed as the two of them maneuvered their way through the crowd.

Near the end of the block was a restaurant with sidewalk seating. A maitre d' stood outside near a stand that contained a stack of menus. He was taking reservations and seating people from the group that had gathered. For a few seconds the child disappeared into the crowd of people waiting to be seated. When the boy came out the other side, he hurried across the street. The man who appeared to be following him turned to the right, away from the boy, and walked up the street in the direction of Horton Plaza. JP wanted to follow the man in the cap but at this point he wasn't sure if they were even together. He opted for the child since he was too young to be out by himself.

JP had to pick up his speed because the boy moved swiftly along the sidewalk, dashing in and around people. He turned right at the first block and then right again on Fourth Street, circling back to where the man with the cap had headed. When he reached the end of the next street, he crossed it and ducked into the parking garage for Horton Plaza Mall. JP ran across the street and entered the parking facility, but by the time he reached the interior the child had disappeared among the mass of parked cars. The child could've gone to any one of the three levels of parking or out one of the numerous exits onto different streets. He could have even slipped into the mall and out the other side. It was hopeless. He had lost him.

JP walked through the parking structure, watching cars as they left the garage. Across the lot he saw a black car pull out of a spot. JP ran across the lot to try and get close enough to see if the child was in it. Another car came down the ramp and around the corner just as JP stepped out. He dodged to the side, avoiding the car filled with teenagers that moved far too quickly for a parking lot. JP yelled, "Slow down!" Then he dashed across the lot. The black car turned to the right and headed down the exit ramp away from him. JP was too far away to see the passengers. He wasn't even certain what the make of the car was, but he feared it was a Mercedes.

Chapter 35

Sabre slipped on a pair of gray sweat pants with the letters P-I-N-K down the front right leg and a t-shirt that matched. Grabbing the towel from the rack she rubbed her hair, still wet from the shower. It was getting long again. She had decided a few months back to let it grow but now she was considering a short style. It would soon be at a length where she could donate it to a cancer organization. The length now was good because she could pull it back and braid it when she went for her morning runs, but if she had it really short she wouldn't have to worry about keeping it off her face. As she reached for a white, large-toothed comb that lay in her bathroom cabinet, the doorbell rang.

She wondered who was calling on Sunday morning. Expecting to find solicitors or someone disbursing religious paraphernalia, she moved swiftly down the steps with the comb still in her hand and to the door. She peeked through the peephole and the first thing she saw was a black Stetson. Before opening the door, she quickly ran the comb through her hair and dropped the comb in her pocket.

"Good morning. What brings you calling this bright, sunny morning?" She smiled and opened the door wide for JP to enter.

"Hi, kid. You gotta minute? I'd like to go over some things with you."

"Sure. Would you like some coffee?"

"That would be great."

He followed her into the kitchen. "Decaf or regular?"

"Decaf is fine. I've already had more caffeine than I need this morning."

JP took a seat on a bar stool at her island counter. Sabre poured a cup of black coffee, handed it to him, and then added half a cup of hot milk to her own before she sat down next to him.

"So what's up?" she asked.

"I've been doing some research on Tuffy but so far I can't find anything. I think it's time to involve the police."

"How can you do that without violating Marcus' confidence?"

"I'll talk to Gregory Nelson and tell him there's a scam going down using kids and all I have is the street name of 'Tuffy.' And I'll tell him what we know about Smithe's background."

"You can't do that. You heard Tuffy's name from Marcus, as well as the description that led us to Smithe, and Marcus asked us not to tell."

JP raised his voice, something he seldom did, and he never did it when speaking to Sabre. "We can't just do nothing. I saw a little boy last night who may have gotten into Smithe's car. We can't just let that scumbag keep molesting kids."

"I know this is horrible. I haven't been able to sleep since this case started. I have nightmares every night of dead people hanging from the ceiling and ever since you showed me the photo of Smithe, he's become one of the bodies in my dreams. I don't like it any better than you do, but until Marcus gives me the go ahead, I can't...no, we can't say anything."

JP sighed. "So, what am I supposed to do?"

"You need to find something on these guys independent of Marcus."

"The thing that happened to Andre Washington was totally independent of Marcus."

"But what will they do with that? All you can tell them is there's a suspected child molester selling cars in Fallbrook. It happened outside of this department's jurisdiction more than ten years ago, and you have no witnesses. There's nothing they can do."

"But he's a freaking pedophile. And he may be a murderer."

"JP, there are pedophiles living in every neighborhood. You only have to go on the Megan's Law site to see how many there are. And they are only the ones who have been caught and forced to register. There are probably as many who haven't been convicted."

He tipped his hat back. "That's my point."

"And my point is we have an obligation to our client. We cannot defy a confidence. First of all, it violates the Professional Rules of Responsibility and I can be disbarred for doing that. Secondly, and more importantly, I believe whole-heartedly that without that rule of confidentiality, the system wouldn't work. My clients need to be able to tell me anything and know that I will keep their confidence."

"Isn't there some rule about future crimes?"

"Yes, if I know someone is in danger of a future crime that changes things up, but we don't actually know that. And besides that, we may never know if Smithe or Tuffy killed Foreman if the police go after them for something else. It could just scare them off."

JP threw his left hand in the air, almost spilling the coffee in his right. "So, what do I do? I feel about as useless as a screen door in a submarine."

"All you can do is keep digging until you find something we can use. In the meantime, I'll keep talking with Marcus. At some point he may change his mind about what I can tell and what I can't. I expect he wants the police to find the man who killed his father, so you just need to find something that points at Smithe or

Tuffy." Sabre took a drink of her coffee. "By the way, do you know who Klakken has on his list of suspects?"

"There's you."

"Me? Why me?"

"Just because they found him in your office, but you're not a serious suspect."

"I would hope not."

"There's Bob, Dana, Frank, Celia, numerous homeless people who didn't like George, and some drug dealer. I'm pretty sure they're not talking about Sammy."

"And we can add Sammy, Smithe, and Tuffy to that list...and remove Bob and me." Sabre shook her head. "I don't know. I just can't imagine they have anything concrete."

"Apparently not, or they would've made an arrest by now."

Sabre noticed JP's cup was nearly empty. "Do you want more coffee?"

"No. I'm good."

"Is Klakken seriously considering Bob a suspect?" Sabre asked.

JP sighed. "I didn't want to alarm you, but according to my sources, he not only has him on his list, but Bob's quickly moving to the top. Apparently, there was a slip of paper in Foreman's pocket with an address on it."

"Yes, I remember that. The day we found the body, a detective came into the office where we were talking to Klakken and told us about the note, but what does that have to do with Bob?"

"The address is Bob's mother-in-law's house."

"What? That doesn't make any sense. Why would Foreman have the address of Bob's mother-in-law?"

"Beats me, but I'm sure that was the same reaction Klakken had when he saw it. I talked to Bob on the way over here. He doesn't have a clue why Foreman had that address."

"I guess that's all the more reason to find something on Smithe or Tuffy so you can go to Klakken with it."

"I'll give it to Greg. I'd rather not deal with Klakken and besides, he isn't going to take my lead anyway. The man hates me."

"Why is that?" Sabre's brow wrinkled.

"It's not important. What's important is that Klakken is steered in the direction of someone other than Bob."

"Do you think his hatred of you will make him come after Bob?"

"No. He's not like that, but he would delight in proving me wrong or seeing me suffer if a friend of mine were in trouble. If anything, he'll take his time to make sure there are no holes in his investigation before he arrests him. That's probably why he hasn't done it already."

Sabre felt her face flush. Fear for her friend consumed her. She knew she had to do something to lead the police investigation in a different direction. The idea of Bob being a murderer was preposterous and she didn't want to see him spend one minute in jail.

Chapter 36

Sabre and JP waited outside Department Five for a delinquency matter to be called. JP didn't like going to court and consequently only went when he had to, but Sabre needed him this morning to authenticate some photos on a trial that had been continued from last week. They stood near the information desk. Sabre glanced up and saw Dave Carr about ten feet away where he leaned against a counter that jutted out from the wall. He winked at her. She turned her head so he wouldn't see her smile.

"Do you think they'll call us soon?" JP asked.

"It shouldn't be long now. The court officer said there was only one case left on their morning calendar and then they'll call our trial. I still have to do the Foreman case, but Department Four is tied up with some crazy woman. Hopefully, we can do this case first or we may be trailed and you'll have to come back this afternoon." She wrinkled her nose. "I hope that doesn't happen."

"Excuse me," JP said and walked toward the metal detector where he stopped and spoke with a sheriff he knew from when he worked at the department.

Dave Carr walked up as soon as JP left. He motioned his head toward JP. "Who's the cowboy?" he asked.

"That's JP, my private investigator."

"Are you sleeping with him?" Dave asked lightheartedly.

Sabre looked up, surprised at his question, and frowned at him, but her frown quickly turned to a smile at the absurdity of the question. "No. Of course not."

"He wants to."

"He does not," Sabre said.

Dave shook his head, then nodded. "Oh yes, he does. Even worse, I think he may be in love with you."

"That's ridiculous. He isn't in love with me and he doesn't want to sleep with me. We work together. We've been working together for years and he's never once come on to me. He's always been a perfect gentleman."

"I work with you, too, and I want to sleep with you…but then, I'm no gentleman."

"I just don't know what to say to that." She tipped her head to the side and her eyebrows went up. "And not every man thinks like you do."

"Oh, yes they do. It's just that not every man says it." Dave glanced at JP. "But I expect the cowboy is a gentleman, and probably not even the pretentious kind. I watched the way he looked at you. He really cares for you."

"Of course he cares for me. I care for him. We're good friends and we've been through some rough stuff together," she rattled on. "I have lots of men friends. Take Bob Clark for instance. Men and women can be friends, you know."

"I agree. I've seen you and Bob together. He looks at you like he's your brother. He strikes me as the kind of guy who would joke with you about sexual things, but you're confident enough in your relationship that you know he doesn't mean them." Sabre gave him an inquisitive look. He continued. "But not your cowboy. He doesn't tease, does he?" Sabre didn't respond. "He just yearns." Dave stretched out the word "yearns," saying it very slowly and deliberately.

Sabre shook her head. "He doesn't yearn."

Dave nodded knowingly. "He yearns."

"That's crazy. You obtained all that from one short conversation with Bob and a few minutes of observation of JP?"

"Yup. It's all in how they look at you." He paused. "I'm right, aren't I?"

"No. You're not right. Well, you're right about Bob, but not JP. He doesn't want me. He doesn't love me. And he doesn't yearn," Sabre protested. She was sure Dave was wrong.

Dave smirked. "So, if there's nothing between you and the cowboy, what's standing between us and dinner Friday night?"

"The Professional Rules of Responsibility. You've heard of those, right? Terrible conflict of interest."

"Good. We've established a time frame for our first date. As soon as this case is over for one of us, we're going out." Before Sabre could protest he said, "I'll go tell Dana I'm off the case. I'll even forfeit my retainer so she can get another attorney. So, Friday night then?" He turned as if to leave.

Sabre laughed. She knew he was bluffing. Or was he? She didn't really know him that well, but she liked his style. He came across as confident, but not arrogant or pompous. He had a great sense of humor and it had been a while since anyone had made her laugh like he did. "Don't be silly. We need to move this case along. The children need closure."

He turned back. "Okay, then it's a date…the first Friday after I file a substitution of attorney on this case. I'll see you in court." He walked away.

Sabre watched Dave for a second. She found him very attractive but she was both impressed and annoyed by his comments. His flirting fed her ego but she wasn't certain she was ready for anything more than that.

She turned toward the metal detector and focused on JP. He ended his conversation and was walking toward her when a court officer announced their case for Department Five. She looked at him curiously, wondering if there was any truth in what Dave had just said about JP. She tried to reconcile the feelings that came over her, the pleasant thoughts of JP's interest with the uncertainty as to whether or not she wanted them to be true. Then she sighed. Of course she didn't want Dave's comments to be true, and they weren't true, just the ramblings of a curious man.

"Ready?" JP asked, as he walked up.

Sabre felt the calm and comfort his voice and presence brought over her. She was safe, safe from the uncertainty Dave had just provoked. They moved toward the courtroom. JP touched her lightly on her shoulder as he put his arm around her to shield her through the crowd. She tingled at his touch for just a second and then the feeling of familiarity and protectiveness swept over her. Dave was way off base, she thought, not even in the ballpark.

Sabre took a seat alone in the back of Department Four and waited for the Foreman case to be called. JP had left the courthouse as soon as they completed the delinquency case, and Bob was waiting in the hallway for Sabre since he was avoiding any contact with his former client, Dana. Dave Carr walked in and announced he would be setting the case for trial, which prompted the court clerk to look for a trial date. The attorneys all gathered at the defense table with their calendars open. Carr used his phone, but Sabre still liked her paper version. She laid it open on the table as they searched for a date for the trial.

The first date suggested by the clerk created a conflict for County Counsel, the attorney for the

Department of Social Services. The second wouldn't work for Sabre. They settled on a date just a little over a month away. Sabre marked it in her date book. It was on a Tuesday. Carr leaned over toward her with his pen in his hand. "Oh good, it's open," he said, as he drew several circles around the Friday following the trial date.

Sabre glared at him for a second, but didn't say anything.

"Just making sure you don't make other plans," Dave said and smiled a boyish smile.

Chapter 37

JP watched Smithe's black Mercedes pull out of his driveway and onto the highway. This was the third night JP had been staking out his house. So far, Smithe had been to the market, a pizza place, and a video arcade. The night at the video arcade proved to be the toughest because JP didn't dare enter the arcade for fear Smithe would recognize him. JP breathed a little easier when he left the arcade alone. Tonight Smithe took a longer excursion. JP followed him all the way from Fallbrook into downtown San Diego. The streets were fairly crowded for a Wednesday night, but JP was able to keep the car in sight and still keep a safe distance behind him.

Smithe drove down Fourth Street, past Horton Plaza, turned left, and made his way to Fifth Street. He drove slowly, peering out his window. JP knew what Smithe was looking for and it made his blood boil. He followed him three times in a large circle covering several blocks. Smithe then worked his way down Island Street, a quieter, darker street off the main drag. JP dropped back a little, then pulled into a parking spot when he saw Smithe stop and talk with two young girls who looked to be about ten and twelve years old. JP couldn't see their faces so he judged them on size alone. He left the car running and watched.

The creep isn't even fussy about gender, JP thought, as he tried to figure out what he was going to do if the girls got in the car. His first instinct was to pull Smithe out and beat the crap out of him, but he decided to follow instead if it should come to that.

The girls stayed back on the sidewalk. One started to move closer to the car and the shorter girl pulled her back. JP could see Smithe was still leaning toward them when they walked away rather rapidly. Good move, girls, he thought.

Smithe pulled away and JP followed. The Mercedes crossed Fifth Street and JP was ready to follow, but then he spotted the skinny kid he had seen a few nights previously. Apparently, the boy had seen Smithe because when Smithe pulled away he saw the boy raise his middle finger at him and yell, "Asshole."

JP cringed and then opted to follow the boy instead of Smithe, hoping he would lead him to Tuffy, or at least Tuffy's assistant. He wasn't certain if the boy was even working with Tuffy, but the pattern seemed to fit. The boy moved quickly down the street. JP looked around for the man in the cap but didn't seem him.

Several times he lost sight of the boy as he scampered through the clusters of people on the sidewalks. The kid turned onto Third Street. JP cursed the one-way streets downtown as he drove to the next street and turned left. He circled the block and drove back down Fourth Street, hoping he chose the correct direction. The red traffic light gave him time to glance around. This street was not nearly as busy as Fifth except near the Brazilian Café, which he could see from the corner. Just as the light turned green and JP started to pull away, he spotted the skinny boy jaywalking as he dashed across Fourth Street and jumped into a car that appeared to be waiting for him.

JP followed the 1984 silver Nissan as it moved toward Pacific Coast Highway but was unable to get close enough to see the license number without being detected. He kept his distance. About a mile later the car turned right and onto a side street and then into a narrow alley where it stopped. JP passed the alley and then pulled over, far enough forward so he couldn't be seen. He took his gun out from the console, stuck it in his belt on his backside, and then placed a small LED flashlight in his pocket. He quietly closed his door and moved stealthily up the alley on the same side as the parked car, hugging the buildings as he moved along. Total darkness camouflaged him on the first two buildings, but an open space approximately fifteen feet wide stood between him and the next one. He stepped into the street just as the lights from a car lit up the spot where JP stood. He stepped back into the shadows. The freeway above him curved just enough that traffic moving north sent light into the gap. He waited, hoping for the traffic to let up so he could cross without being obvious. He waited in the shadows, watching the Nissan he had followed. He listened. The engine was off and the window was open on the driver's side. JP could hear voices, but he couldn't make out what was being said. He couldn't see the boy, but the arm of the driver rested on the door, a cigarette dangling from his hand. Every so often the driver raised his hand, appearing to be taking a drag of the cigarette.

If it was a "john ," JP figured the boy was relatively safe until the cigarette was finished, but the car was old and beat up and the driver wasn't likely to be someone the kid would've tried to scam. JP glanced from the car to the street above him and back again. For a second, the traffic let up and JP hurried across the open area, apparently undetected since the car didn't move. JP stood still and assessed his plan of attack. He knew he'd have to move quietly and quickly to keep the element of surprise and he assumed the cigarette only had a few more drags on it. Though it was dark, he needed to avoid the path of the car's mirrors. He inched his way closer to the car until he came within twenty feet of the vehicle and dropped down behind a trash can. He could barely see the profile of the driver's face. JP waited.

When the driver flicked the cigarette on the ground, JP stepped out and in four long, quick steps JP was standing next to the man he had seen several nights before tailing the boy. JP shined the flashlight in his face and pointed his gun at him and said, "Get out of the car, slowly. Keep your hands where I can see them." JP looked at the little boy sitting next to him. "Just sit still. I won't hurt you." His voice came out sterner than he had intended. The boy stared defiantly at him but didn't speak.

JP stepped back slightly, allowing room for the door to open. The man began to step out of the car with his arms stretched out and palms facing JP. Just when he had both feet planted on the ground, the passenger door was flung open. JP glanced up for just a second and the man reached out toward JP's arm to fling the gun out of the way. JP grabbed his arm with his left hand, flipped him around, and slammed him against the side of the car in one swift move. "Bad move, punk," JP said, just as the skinny kid ran off down the street into the darkness.

JP took a deep breath and patted him down, checking for weapons. Satisfied he didn't have any, he spun the man around so he could see his face. "Well, if that don't put pepper in the gumbo," JP said. "You ain't nothing but a kid yourself." He looked to be no more than eighteen or nineteen years old, perhaps even younger. JP could feel the kid trembling under his touch. He stood there for a moment just looking at him. Then JP holstered his gun with his right hand while maintaining his hold on him with his left. The kid wiggled and JP quickly shoved his right arm under his chin.

"I'm not a kid. I'm twenty-five years old." he squeaked.

"Yeah, and I'm the pope."

"Are you a cop?"

"No, but you should be wishing I was, kid, because I can make a hornet look cuddly when I'm crossed." JP lightened up on his grip. "What's your name?"

"Who wants to know?"

"You're not too bright, are you?" JP pushed his arm harder on his neck as a reminder and squeezed the kid's arm tighter. "I have a gun; I have you pinned against the car; and I've told you I'm not a cop. This may not be the time to open your ten-gallon mouth. Now this is how this works. I'm going to ask you some questions and my arm here is going to act like a lie detector. Each time you lie to me it's going to push a little harder." The kid was silent. "Now, what's your name?"

"Chris."

"Chris what?"

"McKenzie."

"So, Chris McKenzie, how old are you?"

"Eighteen, but my ID says twenty-five."

"What are you doing with that little boy? You can't find anyone your own age to play with?"

"That's sick. It's not like that."

"So, tell me what's it like then."

Chris paused for a second. "He needed a ride so I picked him up." JP pushed harder on his neck and Chris said, "Okay. We were running a scam."

"What kind of scam?"

"Stealing money from rich guys."

"And just how do you do that?"

"Dillon gets close enough to get their wallet and then he runs."

"How does he get 'close enough?'"

"Sometimes he pickpockets them in a crowd."

"And other times he's lured into their cars?" JP added.

"Are you a john?" Chris asked. JP pushed hard on his neck, more of a reaction than a conscious choice. Then he let up. Chris sighed. "Just askin'."

"I'll do the askin'," JP said. "Who's Tuffy?"

"That's m...me," Chris stuttered.

JP pushed hard. "I know you're not Tuffy. For one thing, you're not old enough and you certainly aren't smart enough. Now, who is he?"

Chris gasped for breath. "I'll tell you what I know."

JP let up. "Start talking."

"I've never met Tuffy. I used to work the streets, like Dillon, with a guy named Sammy. He was my queen. That's what Tuffy called the person in charge. I don't know his last name. When I got too old for the streets I had to stop, but then my grandpa died and I inherited his car so I got a queen position. You have to have a car to be a queen."

"Is Sammy still a queen?"

"No. I don't think he works for Tuffy anymore. I see him once in a while, but I'm pretty sure he's not working with him." Chris was struggling to keep his footing as he stood there pinned to the car.

JP let up a little on his hold so Chris could get his balance. "How many queens are there?"

"Just two of us, I think. There's a guy named Jaleel who's been at it longer than me, but we're not allowed to talk to each other."

"How long have you been doing it?"

"Six months."

"And when you're caught and asked about Tuffy, you're supposed to say it's you, right?"

"Yes, but I didn't think I'd ever be asked, because no one is supposed to know about Tuffy."

"Did you know about Tuffy when you were working out there scamming the rich guys?"

He nodded. "The other kids told stories about him, but no one had ever seen him, just stories that they had heard about the horrible things he would do to kids if they messed up. Everyone was more afraid of Tuffy than they were of the marks or the cops."

"How many kids are working with Tuffy?"

"I have three and I think Jaleel has four. People say Tuffy has groups all over San Diego and in all the big cities across the country."

"But you don't believe it?"

Chris shook his head from side to side, then shrugged. "Could be, I guess."

"If you've never seen Tuffy, how do you deliver his money?"

"It changes all the time. He sends a text of where and when to make a drop."

"Where do you go today?"

"I don't know yet."

"Where's your phone?"

"In my pocket." Chris pointed to the left side of his pants.

JP patted it, making sure that's all that was in there. "Give it to me," JP said.

Chris reached inside his pocket and slowly withdrew his phone. He handed it to JP who took a quick look at the text message folder. "There are no text messages."

"We have to delete them as soon as we get them."

JP dropped the phone in his pocket and reached out his hand. "Give me your keys."

"They're in the car." JP glanced in and saw them hanging from the ignition. He let loose of Chris. "Okay, get lost."

"What?"

"Go."

"What about my car? And my phone?"

JP acted as if he were reaching for his gun. "Go! Run!"

Chris took off in the same direction Dillon had gone earlier. JP reached inside the car and withdrew the keys. Then he took Chris's cell phone out of his pocket and re-checked the text messages. A new one had just been received. "Kettner and Ash, 10:15 p.m. trash." He jotted down the phone number from the text and opened up the contacts, but it was blank. He dialed 9-1-1.

"There's a car in the alley just off Pacific Coast Highway and Juniper. A young boy just ran from the car and an older man was chasing him. I think the boy is in trouble. Please help."

He wiped his fingerprints from the phone, tossed it inside Chris's car, and walked to where he had parked.

It was nearly ten o'clock and JP was only two blocks away from what he assumed was the drop-off for Tuffy's money. He drove slowly to Ash Street and past the corner. A trash can sat near a bench at the bus stop. He continued on until he found a spot where he could watch without being seen. He waited but no one ever came to pick up anything near the trash. He wondered if Tuffy was watching and since Chris had not made a drop, he didn't make a pickup. He looked around to see if he could see where someone might be watching. There was one apartment building that presented as a possibility. Lights were on in twelve of the fifteen rooms and someone could be observing from any one of them. There were cars parked on the street and without going from car to car, JP couldn't be certain there wasn't someone watching from a parked vehicle. There were also several rooftops where a person could hide. There were just too many possibilities.

The more he thought about it, the more he decided Tuffy wasn't expecting a drop. There was probably a code or response for the text required for this very reason. He hoped he hadn't blown the chance of catching him by showing up, but he had been careful. He never stopped near the trash can, and he was well hidden from any observer.

He waited. It was nearly midnight and there was still no Tuffy. By one o'clock JP gave up and went home. He drove to where Chris had parked his car in the alley. It was gone. He would check in the morning to see if it had been towed.

Chapter 38

"This won't take long. I just have to pick up some files and copy a few things for my trial this afternoon. Then we can go to lunch," Bob said to Sabre as they neared his office.

"No problem. We have plenty of time."

Sabre noticed two police cars as they pulled into the parking structure. "I wonder what that's about?"

"As long as it's not about me, they can hang here all they want," Bob said.

Bob parked in the lot. They exited the car and took the elevator up to the second floor. "You know it wouldn't hurt you to take the steps once in a while," Sabre said.

"Nah, that would be way too healthy."

They left the elevator and started across the walkway that looked into the courtyard toward Bob's office. Two policemen were situated near his door. "Bob," Sabre said, "that looks like Klakken inside."

"I've already told them what little I know. I wish they'd leave me alone."

Klakken greeted them as they walked inside the office.

"What can I do for you today, detective?" Bob asked.

"Mr. Clark, you're under arrest for the murder of George Foreman. You have the right to remain silent...."

"I'm not saying a word. Sabre," Bob said. Sabre withdrew her phone and dialed before Bob could finish saying, "Call Leahy."

"I just did." Sabre stepped back a few steps. "Jerry, they just arrested Bob."

"I'll see him at the station in a couple of hours. They'll need to book him before they let me in. It'll take at least that long, probably longer. Just tell him to keep his mouth shut."

"I'll see you there." Sabre hung up the phone and stepped back toward Bob and Klakken. "Bob, Leahy will meet you at the police station. He said not to talk to anyone until he gets there. Think like a lawyer." Sabre followed the detective as he walked Bob out the door. She caught the detective's eye. "Do you really need to take him out in handcuffs?"

"Yes, I really do," he said complacently.

At the police station Jerry spoke with an officer he had encountered many times before. He turned to Sabre and said, "We'll be able to speak with Bob in a few minutes. They'll have him in custody overnight for sure. I'd like to have him arraigned tomorrow morning and out of here, but technically they have seventy-two hours to arraign him. So, if I can't get him on calendar tomorrow, he stays all weekend."

"Will they give him bail?"

"I don't know. It depends on what they charge him with. It's not going to be easy."

Sabre stood up, paced, and sat down again. "This is so preposterous. I can't believe they think he killed Foreman." She felt so angry and choked back tears. She hated to cry but the more she fought the tears, the angrier she became.

"We're going to help him out of this mess. First things first. We need to get him out of here. Everything they have is circumstantial," Jerry stated reassuringly.

"But it was enough to make an arrest and apparently the D.A. thinks it's enough to file charges."

"Mr. Leahy," the officer said, as he walked up to him. "You can see your client now."

Sabre took a deep breath, trying to calm herself as she and Jerry walked down a hallway and into a cubicle where Bob waited for them. "Fine mess you have us in now, Ollie," Bob said, making light of the situation.

"Are you okay?" Sabre asked.

"It's all about the adventure, right?" Bob said.

"Did the police try to question you?" Leahy asked.

"Yeah, but they quit as soon as I invoked my right to counsel. I haven't said a word, not that I really have anything to say."

"Good. Keep it that way. I probably won't be able to get you arraigned until Tuesday, although I'm going to try."

"Any chance of getting bail?"

"I'm not going to lie to you. It won't be easy but there's always a chance. And if we do, it won't be cheap," Leahy said.

"What are we going to do?" Sabre asked.

Bob looked at Sabre. "I need you to cover my trial this afternoon and take care of my calendar tomorrow...and maybe for the next twenty years."

"Stop that," Sabre said. "Jerry's going to get you out of here, aren't you?" She looked at Leahy pleadingly. "Jerry, what can I do?"

"You can find out who really killed Foreman. That would help."

"JP is on it. He has several good candidates." Then she remembered her problem with attorney/client privilege. "We'll find a way."

"A way to what?" Jerry asked.

"A way to figure this out. We'll find out who killed him."

"What other candidates do you have?"

"He's still investigating, but we'll get you something. I promise."

"Sabre, will you do me a favor?" Bob asked.

"Of course. Anything."

"Will you go tell my wife where I am? And try to explain this to her the best you can. I don't want her seeing it on the news or something. She should be at home. If you go right now, you can stop there and still make it to court in time for my trial."

"Do you want me to continue the case?"

"No, just do the trial, if you don't mind. I have a non-offending father who's in custody in Vacaville Prison. He didn't want to be produced and he wants the opposite of whatever the mother wants. He said she's the worst mother he's ever seen. It only took him three kids with her before he figured it out. I think some of it is just from spite, but the reports make Joan Crawford's mother look like a saint."

"I'll take care of it. I don't have anything else on calendar and I'll go see Marilee first."

"Thanks. I know she'll want to come see me so you may want to check on visiting hours before you leave here," Bob said.

"She should be able to come between two and four today," Leahy said to Sabre.

"Are you sure you want her to come here?" Sabre asked.

"You know her. It doesn't matter if I want her to or not. She'll come anyway. But yeah, she's a tough cookie and she'll feel better if she comes and sees me. Maybe I can put her mind at ease a bit. Now, get going or you'll be late."

Chapter 39

JP and Sabre met at The Coffee Bean before court the next morning to strategize a way to help Bob. "You have to talk to Marcus," JP said. "Klakken is going to stop looking now that they've made an arrest."

"I know, and we're the only people in the world who are certain it wasn't Bob who killed Foreman."

"Us and the killer, and we have plenty of suspects."

"Smithe, Tuffy, and Sammy."

"And Chris McKenzie."

"Do you think it could be him?"

"It could, but I'm not sure he even knew Foreman. I suppose he could've been avenging Tuffy's territory. And let's not forget about Dana. We know she lied about having an affair with Bob." JP's usual poker face showed concern. "Right?"

"Right." Sabre looked at JP curiously. "How can you even ask that?"

"Bob is a very good friend of mine and I know for a fact he didn't kill Foreman, but I don't know whether or not he's having an affair with Dana. We never talk about that sort of thing. I may have known him longer than you have but you know him better, so I'm asking."

"You don't talk about that sort of thing because he doesn't do that sort of thing. More importantly, I know Bob well enough to know that if he were going to have an affair it wouldn't be with a client and certainly not someone like Dana Foreman. Bob is a charmer and all the girls like him. He could have an affair with any number of attractive attorneys or social workers or court personnel, and for that he wouldn't risk his marriage. So he sure as hell isn't going to risk his marriage and his license to practice over some loser client. No, Dana is lying and we need to know why."

"Then we'll find out why."

"Do you think Celia or Frank could have done it?" Sabre asked. "They've never liked Foreman and they've had to endure a lot of years with him. Maybe they just reached their limit."

"I don't think Celia has it in her, but Frank certainly does. He seems to be in control, but I think there's something bubbling under the surface with that man. But, I can't see what he would really have to gain by it and I don't think he does anything without a calculated reason in mind. His killing is done in the financial world. Besides, Klakken already investigated both of them and they have alibis."

"That's right. They were home together with Marcus and Riley."

"So what do we do next, boss?" JP asked.

"I need to talk to Marcus about Smithe and Tuffy. We need to get those creeps off the streets one way or another. You could go to Detective Nelson about Sammy and Chris McKenzie, but even if one of them leads back to Smithe or Tuffy we still need Marcus to connect the dots or there's nothing to make them suspects in Foreman's murder."

"So you're saying I need to find something else or Marcus has to come around."

"That's about the size of it, and so far he's been pretty adamant about not wanting me to say anything about the incident with Smithe. If he continues to not allow disclosure, I'll have to respect that and still find a way to help Bob. I'll also see if I can get anything out of Dana's attorney, although that's not likely."

"I wouldn't trust that guy. He's slicker than butter on marble."

Sabre cocked her head to one side and looked at JP. For a split second she remembered what Dave had said about JP wanting her. She swiftly dismissed the thought as ludicrous. "He's a decent guy and a good attorney, which is why he likely won't give me any information," she said. "Do you know if Chris was picked up?"

"I spoke with Greg Nelson last night. He said they impounded the car and they're looking for Chris. They have his cell phone and they may even have him by now."

"Good. Why don't you follow up with Nelson on Chris and see if you can get anything more out of Sammy before he gets out of custody. I'll talk with Marcus, and if we can get anything we can use we'll set up a meeting with Klakken this afternoon."

JP's eyes looked distant for a second. "Sure," he said. Sabre wondered where JP had slipped away. She was pretty certain it had to do with Klakken. She left it alone.

Sabre sat on the edge of Marcus' bed in his room in La Jolla where he beat her in a tense video game of Modern Warfare 3. Sabre didn't expect to win. She was actually quite bad at those games, especially action games. Marcus wasn't an expert either, but he had more experience than she did.

"You're looking real good. How are you feeling?"

"Good. The doctor said I can go back to school on Monday."

"How do you feel about that?"

"I'm ready. I miss my dad. I wish stuff was different."

"What kind of stuff?"

"I wish my dad hadn't been so mean."

"He was mean to you?"

"He was mean to everybody. He yelled a lot and he'd hit me if I didn't do what he wanted. He was nicest when I worked with him."

"Did he hit your mom and Riley?"

"He hit mom a lot, especially when he was drunk. Not Riley so much. Riley knew how to stay out of his way. Riley was always telling me not to talk back to him, but sometimes I couldn't help myself. The words would just come out." Marcus' face changed from distress to sadness. "And now I wish he wasn't dead."

"I'm so sorry," Sabre said. She knew from speaking to his psychiatrist that it was good for Marcus to talk openly. After a discussion with the doctor in very general terms so as not to violate the attorney/client privilege, the doctor had suggested it would be therapeutic if Marcus could help find his father's killer. "Marcus, you may be able to help us find who killed him, you know."

"Do you think my mom did it?"

Sabre sat up a little straighter, surprised by the question. "Do you?"

"No."

"Why do you ask?"

"I hear stuff."

"What kind of stuff?"

"About that attorney she had. But I don't think my mom did it. Did that attorney do it?"

"Do you know what I think? I think it had something to do with the big man in the black Mercedes, the man who beat up your father, and if it was him you can help us with that."

"What would I need to do?"

"You said before you didn't want me to say anything about the man to anyone. I know you were afraid because of some things that happened, so I haven't told anyone, just like you asked. But if the police knew, they could investigate and maybe find your dad's killer."

"Will I have to go to juvenile hall?" His voice was full of fear.

Sabre took his hand. "No, you're not going to be in trouble."

"But I was doing bad stuff, too."

"You were doing what your father made you do. I promise you I will use every bit of fight I have in my body to see that you don't get in trouble. Besides, the police will want to stop that horrible man, not punish you."

Marcus sighed. "Okay, you can tell."

"You are being very brave. When I tell the police they will want to question you, but I'll be with you when you talk to them."

Marcus nodded his head. He looked down at the video game controller he held in his hand. "Do you want to play again?" Marcus asked.

"Sure, but this time I'm going to beat you."

"I don't think so."

Chapter 40

Sammy smiled when JP walked into the cubicle where he waited at the San Diego County Jail. JP felt a little sorry for him again. He was such a pathetic soul. He had to know that JP wasn't there to help him, yet he seemed pleased to see someone, anyone. For a second, JP wondered if he was being played; maybe Sammy was smarter than JP thought. Maybe he really was Tuffy, but who texted Chris with the place and time of the drop? He would've had to have another accomplice or access to a cell phone. JP dismissed the thought as quickly as it came into his mind. Access to a cell phone in custody wasn't that difficult, but Sammy just wasn't that smart.

"Hello, Sammy. How are you doing today?"

"Okay. This isn't the worst place to be and I don't expect to be here too much longer."

"Good for you." JP couldn't see any reason to waste time, so he went straight to the point. "What can you tell me about Chris McKenzie?"

Sammy laughed but it sounded edgy and forced. "Tuffy's latest queen, huh? Have you met him?"

"We had an encounter."

"He's not very good at his job—kind of a mess, actually. He made a much better drone bee than a queen. Did he tell you he was Tuffy?"

"At first."

"But then he squealed like a pig, didn't he?"

"He said a few things."

"I knew that guy was trouble. I told....," he stopped abruptly.

"You told Tuffy not to make Chris a queen?"

"I didn't say that." Sammy said, trying to sound tough.

"Does Chris know who Tuffy is?"

"No." He snickered as if that were ludicrous.

"How do you know? Maybe he has learned who he is since you've been out of commission. You don't work with Tuffy anymore, right? Maybe things are different."

Sammy shook his head. "No way would Tuffy let a numbskull like Chris know anything. He's too risky. He'd squeal in a heartbeat to protect his own skin."

Just like you would, JP thought. He remembered the conversation he and Sammy had had the last time where he was willing to sell Tuffy out for the right price. That's the problem with criminals. There's no real loyalty, which he was very thankful for when he was a police officer.

"What about Tuffy's other queen, Jaleel?"

"Man, Chris really spilled his guts." Sammy took a deep breath and blew it out quickly, making a loud emphatic noise. "I don't know what Jaleel knows, but you wouldn't get anything out of him. Don't even waste your time."

"What does Jaleel look like?" JP asked.

"You're on your own, man. I've said enough."

JP tried a few more questions, but Sammy kept changing the subject. JP threatened to leave several times and Sammy would beg him to stay, promising to answer, but each time Sammy would again avoid the questions. Finally, JP gave up. He had learned a few things that would come in handy for either him or America's finest.

Sabre worked in her office while she waited for JP and Detective Shane Klakken to arrive for the meeting she had scheduled. She picked up the phone to dial Dave Carr to see if she could obtain any information about Dana, but hung up the phone when JP walked in.

"When's Klakken coming?"

"He should be here any minute now."

"Since Marcus gave you permission to talk about Smithe, how do you want to handle this?" JP asked, still standing near the doorway.

"I thought you could just tell Klakken everything you know. You might want to leave out anything that would get you arrested," she said jokingly.

JP didn't laugh or even smile. "It might be better coming from you."

"What is with you two?"

"I just think he'll be more open to hearing the information if it comes from you. I can chime in if need be. Besides, you'll tell him what you want him to know."

"I want him to know enough to look at other suspects and take the heat off of Bob." JP appeared more uncomfortable than she had ever seen him before. "JP, will you please tell me what happened between you and Klakken?"

"It was a long time ago. I was a rookie." They heard the front door open and JP stopped talking. Elaine, Sabre's secretary, soon appeared at Sabre's office door, along with Detective Klakken. JP stepped back so the detective could pass, but before he did JP reached his hand out to him. "Hello, Shane."

Shane shook his hand but he didn't linger. "JP," he said.

Sabre reached across the desk with her right hand extended. "Hello, Detective, nice to see you again. Please have a seat."

Klakken sat down and so did Sabre. JP remained standing against the back wall a few feet from the detective.

"I understand you have some information for me on the Foreman case," Klakken said.

"That's correct." Sabre said. "I believe we have a great deal of information that will interest you. As you know, I represent the children in the Foreman dependency case. Marcus has had a pretty rough time and is suffering from depression over the loss of his father and other things that have happened to him in the past year or so. George Foreman ran a scam on the streets and he used his son, Marcus, to pull it off."

"What kind of scam?"

"He would use his son for bait for rich guys looking for young kids."

"He was pimping out his own kid?" Klakken said. Sabre could hear the disgust in his usual, even-keeled tone.

"Yes, but the plan was to take the money and then Marcus would run, but I think on at least one occasion he wasn't able to get away. I'll be glad to set up a time so you can talk to him, but I promised him I'd be there when you did."

"But now that Foreman is dead he can't run the scam anymore, so what does this have to do with his murder?"

"You're aware that Foreman was beat up a few days before he was killed, right?"

"Yes."

"The guy who did that was a mark who was ripped off, but it wasn't the mark's first encounter with Marcus. They had tried the scam on this guy once before, but it failed. I'm not sure exactly what happened because Marcus was reluctant to talk about it, but the man was mad enough the second time to slam Foreman around. He may have even been mad enough to kill him."

"And you know who this mark is?"

"Yes, JP was able to track him down."

JP handed Klakken a piece of paper with Smithe's information. "His name is Warren Smithe. He lives in Fallbrook and works for the Mercedes dealer there. He received a teaching credential in Mississippi, where he taught elementary school for two years until he left under suspicious circumstances. He then taught for eight more years before he was asked to leave because he molested a child."

"Does he have a record?" Klakken asked, without looking at JP.

"No," JP said. "The child's family left town to avoid the humiliation. They refused to testify. No one else would come forward, either, although it was suspected that there were many others." JP didn't see any reason to tell Klakken that the family moved within twenty minutes of the molester. Interrogating them wasn't likely to help at this point and that family had been through enough already.

Klakken looked directly at Sabre. "And you think Smithe killed Foreman?"

"I think it's worth looking into, but that's not all," Sabre said. "There's someone who calls himself Tuffy who has been working this same type of scam with a group of homeless kids. It's been going on for years. Tuffy has a hierarchy set up so he doesn't deal directly with the kids. He calls the kids his drones and he has his queen bees do what Foreman was doing. Then the queen bees drop off the money collected in different places each time."

"And you know who Tuffy is?"

"No, but we know he has at least two queens, Chris McKenzie and Jaleel. We don't have a last name for him. Either of them could have killed Foreman."

"Because he was in Tuffy's territory?"

"Yes, and the connection between Foreman and Tuffy is a guy named Ludwik Bernard Sampulski. He goes by Sammy. He's in custody right now awaiting a preliminary hearing on some drug charges." Klakken didn't say anything so Sabre continued. "Sammy was a friend of Foreman's and we think he was an old friend of Tuffy's. We know Sammy worked with Tuffy recently as one of his queen bees. He then taught Foreman the scam and they used it with Marcus as their bait."

When Sabre stopped talking, Klakken said, "Anything else?"

"JP?" Sabre asked.

JP shook his head.

"That about covers it," Sabre said.

Klakken stood up. "If you can give me the information you have on each one of these guys, I'll turn it over to our sex crimes unit."

JP stepped forward from the wall he was leaning against, putting him within two feet of the detective. "Damn it, Klakken. Every one of these guys had a reason to see Foreman dead."

"We already have the man who killed Foreman," he said calmly. "I believe he's a friend of yours."

JP's face turned red with anger. He took a quick, short breath. "Don't do this, Shane. You have the wrong guy."

Sabre saw the look in JP's eyes and was afraid of what he might do. She had never seen that look before. She handed Klakken a sheet of paper that JP had drawn up for her earlier. It listed each one of the possible murder suspects, their descriptions, and any other details that might be helpful to the police. "Here is the information you need," she said in her attorney voice. Then she added pleadingly, "You have a reputation for doing the right thing and you're a diligent, smart cop. Please find the guy who really killed Foreman."

Klakken reached out his hand to her, shook it, and said, "Thank you." He left without looking at JP.

Chapter 41

In less than an hour after Klakken left Sabre's office, she received a phone call from the sex crimes unit. They made an appointment to meet with Marcus at his home. Sabre arrived at Frank Davis' home first and explained to Marcus that there were two detectives coming to talk to him about Smithe. Sabre was with Marcus in his room when the two detectives, a man and a woman, were brought in by Frank.

Sabre approached them and introduced herself.

The woman, a short African-American with big beautiful, round eyes and a reassuring smile said, "I'm Detective Marcia Jones. This is my partner, Olen Williams."

"Nice to meet you." Sabre turned to the boy sitting on the end of his bed. "This is Marcus Foreman. He has been so brave through this whole ordeal."

"Nice to meet you, Marcus," Marcia said, taking the lead. Olen took out a note pad and jotted down notes as Marcia interviewed Marcus. After explaining why she was there, Marcia questioned Marcus about Smithe. Sabre was impressed with the detective's approach and her questions. Marcus opened up to her and told her everything he had told Sabre.

"How many times did you see the big man in the black Mercedes?"

"I only saw him twice. The time I told you about and once about a week earlier."

"Tell me about the first time," Marcia said.

"I was walking down the street and he pulled over and started talking to me."

"He just happened to pick you out of a crowd?"

Marcus shook his head. "My dad had been watching him. He said the man was looking at all the little boys on the street. The man kept driving around the block and my dad approached him and talked to him."

"Were you with your dad when he did that?" Marcia asked.

"No. I'm not sure what exactly my dad told him, but my dad told me the man would be looking for me. Then my dad sent me out by myself when the man circled back. It worked 'cuz he pulled over and said something to me."

"What did he say?"

"He asked me what I was doing on the streets by myself."

"I said I didn't have a place to live and I was looking for somewhere to sleep. Then he said, 'I can help you.' And I said, 'I just need some money.'"

"Did he offer you money?" Marcia asked.

"Yes. So I asked him how much money he had and he said, 'Lots.'"

"Then what happened?"

"Then he took out his wallet and showed me. He had three or four hundred dollar bills in his wallet. I wanted to grab the wallet and run, but he had both hands on it. He told me to get in the car and he would give me money. So, I got in the car and he drove off."

"Where did he go?"

"He drove to a street off of Pacific Coast Highway. I'm not exactly sure where, but it was dark and quiet. There was no one around."

"What happened then?" Marcus squirmed. "I know this is difficult. Just take your time."

"He touched my wiener and he opened his pants and made me touch his," he blurted out.

Sabre cringed before she realized it. She turned her hot, red face away for a few seconds and tried to calm down for Marcus' sake. She couldn't let him see her concern for fear he would stop talking. He was doing so well and she could see how hard it was for him.

"Did he do anything else?" Marcia asked.

"He made me rub him fast, but then he took over and jacked off. I pulled my hand away and I started to cry. When he was done, he told me not to cry. He said I did just fine and I would do better next time. I wanted to throw up."

"Did he give you the money?"

"Not at first. He drove me part way back to where he picked me up. Then he stopped and took out his wallet. He gave me $100 and said I would get $200 next time if I did a good job."

Sabre sighed, louder than she intended to. Marcus looked at her. "You're so brave," she said. "I'm so proud of you."

"I wasn't brave. I was really scared."

"It's okay to be scared and you should have been," Sabre said, touching him lightly on the shoulder. She started to say that Smithe could have really hurt him; then she realized he had really hurt him. As many times as she had to deal with this sort of thing she never could get used to it. It always made her feel as if someone tied her stomach in a huge knot and just twisted.

Marcia spoke up. "That's true, Marcus, and I think what your attorney is saying is that you are being very brave to tell us what happened. I agree with her. I know this isn't easy."

Marcus nodded his head, but didn't speak.

"You saw the man again after that, correct?"

"Yes, the night my dad got beat up."

"What happened that time?"

"The man drove up to me again on the street just like the first time and he asked me to go with him again. I made him show me his wallet to see if he still had money before I would get in the car. He grumbled something about having plenty of money but he took it out and opened it up."

"Did you get in the car again?" Marcia asked.

"No. This time when he opened his wallet and showed me the money, I stabbed his hand with a little jackknife and he dropped the wallet. I grabbed it and started to run, but I tripped over the curb. He jumped out of the car and grabbed me by the neck and pulled me against him. My face hit him in the stomach. He held me so tight I could hardly breathe. I still had the knife in my hand and so I stabbed him in the gut with it. He let loose a little bit and I kicked him in the shin, ducked under his arm, and ran off. He ran after me, but I gained on him when I ran around some parked cars in a lot. I don't think he could see me but I could see him 'cuz he was so big. Then I made the mistake of running toward my dad who was a couple of blocks away, and the guy must have recognized my dad because he chased him when I dodged behind a building."

"That's when your dad got beat up?" Sabre asked.

"The last I saw, the guy was chasing him. I ran around for a while before I went back to where we were sleeping. When I got there, Dad was already asleep. The next morning Riley told me Dad had gotten beat up, so the guy must have caught him."

"Did your father ever tell you who beat him up?" Marcia asked.

"No. I only saw Dad a couple of times after that because Social Services picked us up. When I saw him there was always a social worker or someone with us so Dad wouldn't talk about it."

Sabre said. "He only had two visits after that and they were supervised."

Marcia took a notebook out of her pocket and glanced at her own notes. "What can you tell me about a guy named Sammy?"

"We were with Sammy earlier that night...."

"Which night?"

"The last time I saw the big guy—the night I stabbed him. Sammy was supposed to be there with the car when I got the wallet, but he didn't show. That's why my dad was on foot. He should have been in Sammy's car."

"How well do you know Sammy?"

"He's my dad's best friend. I saw him a lot. He taught my dad the scam and we made a lot of money." A confused pride came through in his voice. "Before that, we mostly just stole stuff. Sammy was teaching me how to pick pockets, too, but I wasn't very good at it."

"Your attorney mentioned someone named Tuffy. Did you ever meet him?"

"No. I just heard about him."

"What did you hear?"

"I heard he did the scams like my dad did but he had lots of kids working with him."

"Where did you hear that?"

"I heard Sammy telling my dad about him. He said no one ever saw Tuffy. He was too smart for that."

"Did you ever meet any of those kids?"

"Not that I know of. None of the kids talked about what they were doing."

Marcia thanked Marcus for his help and told him he had been very brave. He looked at her with his brow lowered. "Did you have something else to add, Marcus?" she asked.

"Will this help find my dad's killer?"

Marcia glanced at Sabre, who said quickly, "The police are doing everything they can to make sure they find the right guy. I'm sure this will help."

Olen, the thin, quiet detective who had been taking notes stepped forward. He had said very little during the interview. He looked Marcus straight in the eye. "Young man, I promise you that we will use everything you gave us to put this man away and we will give all the information to the detectives who are working on your dad's murder. I'm sure it will be very helpful."

Chapter 42

"How are you holding up, brother?" JP asked. Sabre and JP sat across from Bob in a little cubicle separated by glass. Bob's eyes drooped.

"Just getting a little R and R."

"You don't look like you're resting," Sabre said. "Did you get any sleep last night?"

"Not so much. This isn't exactly a five-star hotel. I'm sure you know Leahy couldn't get the arraignment set until Monday so I'm stuck here for the weekend…at least."

"Is there anything we can get for you?" JP asked.

"A #124 from Pho's would be great. Can you smuggle it in for me?"

"I'll see what I can do," JP said seriously.

"We have other suspects for Foreman's murder—good suspects—and we've turned the information over to Detective Klakken, so I'm sure something will break soon."

"Thanks, Leahy told me what you did. He also said if we go to trial he'll be able to use the information about the other suspects to create reasonable doubt. I hate to think this will go that far."

Sabre forced a smile. "It won't. We're going to find the real killer and get you out of here. We're not giving up until we do."

"Hey, the good news is that this ought to take care of my smoking habit. Cigarettes aren't as easy to get in here as you might think. Besides that, I've met some very interesting people, mostly repeat offenders. They really hate this part of the process. Most of them want their trials over with so they can get back to their 'long-term, government-funded vacation.' They say it's a lot better in prison because they can work and meet up with old friends. So see, I have something to look forward to."

"But you don't have any friends there, just clients you've obviously failed to help. You'll have to make new friends," JP joked.

"Stop it, you two." Sabre said. She looked at Bob. "You're not going to prison."

"I know. I have faith. Not in the system. It obviously doesn't work very well, but I know you two will find a way to solve this." Bob's face took on a more serious look. "How is Marilee holding up?"

"She's doing okay and Corey just thinks you're away on business."

"Yeah, she told me that's what she told him. She tried to be strong when she came to visit me, but I worry about her."

"I talked to her earlier today, and I'll go see her tomorrow. She'll be okay."

"And my trial yesterday?"

"We settled it and I picked up your calendar from your office. I'll see that everything is covered. There are plenty of people willing to help me if I need it. You just concentrate on keeping your spirits up. And not smoking is a good thing," Sabre said.

They visited a while longer. Bob continued to joke about what he had to look forward to and Sabre repeatedly told Bob they would find the killer. Conversation seemed strained by the surroundings. From the first moment when Sabre and Bob met, conversation was easy. Never in the six years she had known him had they struggled to communicate, but this was awkward. It made it more awkward to leave, but Sabre hoped the next time would be easier.

JP and Sabre left the San Diego County Jail a little after six and walked to where JP had parked his truck. JP opened the passenger door for Sabre. When they started to drive off JP said, "Would you like to get some dinner?"

Sabre's first reaction was to decline, but she decided a quiet dinner with a good friend might be just what she needed, although she was pretty certain it would be spent discussing the case. She and JP seldom talked about anything else. She realized just how little she knew about him, starting with what happened with Klakken so many years ago. Perhaps she could change that tonight.

"I'd like that," she said. "How about The Fish Market? It's close and it shouldn't be too busy yet." Sabre cocked her head and looked at JP. "Do you like fish?"

"The Fish Market is perfect."

The long lines at the restaurant hadn't formed yet, and JP and Sabre were seated next to the window looking out at the water with a great view of the setting sun. The pink sky melted into the deep blue sea, erasing the line where the water stopped and the sky took over.

"What was life like for you growing up?" Sabre asked.

"About the same as everybody else, I suspect. Some good times, some bad. Why do you ask?"

"I recently realized how little I know about you. I mean, I know you're a good, honest person and you're exceptionally good at your job, but I know little about your personal life."

"There's not much to know. I spent my childhood in Texas. I was a cop for twenty years in California. I was married once. It didn't work. But you already knew all that."

Sabre shook her head. She wanted to know what his life was like in Texas, his experiences as a cop, and why his marriage didn't last, but she knew he wasn't going to go into detail even with a great deal of prodding. And right now she was concerned about Bob. "Do you know what Bob's going through? I guess what I'm asking is, have you ever spent a night behind bars?"

"I spent more than one night behind a bar and many a night in a bar," he said lightheartedly. Sabre looked worried and JP must have noticed because he added, "Yes, I did spend a night in jail once. I was in a fight in a small town in Texas when I was nineteen years old. Frankly, I was scared to death, as I suspect Bob is even though he tries to make light of the whole situation. I probably shouldn't say that because I'm sure most of his act is to make you feel better, but I also know it doesn't help. You've always been straight with me and I promised you the same. You know as well as I do that we need to find who killed Foreman because no one else is as vested in this as we are."

"You mean Klakken isn't going to do it?"

"Klakken is a good cop and if he thinks he has the wrong guy in custody he'll work hard to find the truth."

"But?" Sabre asked.

"But he may be convinced Bob is guilty. In which case, he isn't going to do me any favors."

"Why is that? What happened between you two?"

JP peered into Sabre's eyes. His gaze pulled at her like a magnet, leaving a fluttering feeling in her stomach. She thought about his strong yet gentle demeanor and it made her want to reach out to him, but instead, she looked away. Then she heard him say. "It's not important. Klakken will follow up if anything leads him in another direction. And that Olen Williams you talked about, didn't you say he seemed determine to help Marcus find his father's killer?"

"Yes, he told me he would do what he could."

"So there. We have America's finest working on it and I'm not done looking. If I have to go half way through hell in gasoline pants, I will until I find who killed Foreman."

The corner of Sabre's mouth went up. She reached over and squeezed his hand. "Thanks," she said. Sabre let go to answer her ringing phone. "Sabre Brown." She listened. "Okay, thank you. I appreciate the information. She touched the face of the phone hanging up the call.

"What is it?" JP asked.

"That was the detective who questioned Marcus earlier, Marcia Jones. They have Smithe in custody. They've charged him with P.C. 288."

"So, just the child molestation? Not murder?"

"Not murder. Smithe is no longer a suspect. Apparently, he was at some training program in New Jersey when Foreman was killed."

Chapter 43

The three-year-old girl in a white sundress with little red ladybugs flung her arms in the air, waving her hands as she dodged through the hanging bodies. She tried to scream, but nothing came out. She couldn't find the door and everywhere she turned there were feet kicking her in the head from another dead, dangling body. Her eyes searched for her father. He would save her. He always saved her. She screamed again until sound finally emanated from her mouth. "Ahhh!" Sabre screamed, waking herself up from another terrifying, realistic nightmare. The dreams seemed to be getting worse and the faces clearer.

Her body shook as she stepped from the bed while glancing at the clock that read 4:53 a.m. She drew herself a bath and poured melon bubble bath in the water. She slipped into the bubbles and took deep breaths, summoning herself to relax. She felt better, but the dream still haunted her. She sometimes would shift from being an older girl to a young girl, but she always wore the same sundress and was always in the same little, yellow house with dead people hanging from the rafters. And her father always rescued her unless she woke up too soon. That's the only part of the dream she wanted to relive—the part where she saw her father again as a strong, loving man protecting her from the evil world. Why was it so real?

Then she remembered her mother running out of a white house that was in front of the yellow one in her nightmare. Sabre suddenly knew it was a memory, not a part of the dream. Her mother reached for Sabre to take her from her father, but Sabre wouldn't let go. Her mother was crying and caressing her. But that wasn't part of her dream; Sabre always woke up when her father saved her. There was no dream after that. So why was she remembering her mother taking her from her father after she left the yellow house? Where did that memory come from?

Sabre stayed in the soothing bubbles until they were all gone and the water was tepid. Then she dressed, ate a small bowl of steel cut oatmeal with cranberries and walnuts, and took a hot cup of tea out onto the front deck to watch the birds. At 8:30 she decided to check on Marilee. She stopped at Spouts on her way and bought a carton of fresh strawberries and a bottle of Merlot, two of Marilee's favorites.

She visited for nearly an hour with Marilee, most of which was spent reassuring her that they would find who did this and it would all work out. Sabre thought if she said it often enough she would soon believe it herself. Most of the time she remained optimistic, but her optimism had faded when Smithe's alibi held up and he was ruled out as a murder suspect. That was a blow. She thought him to be the most likely suspect, but there were still three other very likely candidates and even if Klakken wasn't investigating, Olen Williams was.

Confident that Marilee was okay, Sabre got in her car and called her mother to let her know she was on her way to visit her. She listened to the entire new Scotty McCreery CD and half of her old Carrie Underwood CD before she reached her mother's house. The sun was shining and the traffic was light, which would normally put a smile on her face. But not today. Today she felt anxious and a little guilty. Her mother was always telling her to come home to visit but Sabre's schedule was so full. Something always came up that kept her from going on a regular basis. She knew if her father were there she would've made it a greater priority.

It's not that she didn't love her mother. She did. They just were never as close as she and her father had been. She could never quite figure out why but she always felt like she blamed her mother for something or for everything. When things didn't go right as a teenager, it was always her mother who received the brunt of her anger. It was different when her brother, Ron, was around. He was a mama's boy and Sabre's best friend. Ron always kept the peace between Sabre and her mother. Now that Ron was gone, her mother probably needed her more than ever.

Sabre justified her lack of visits because her mother kept a very busy schedule with bridge games and volunteer work. She had a hectic schedule like Sabre's. The older Sabre became, the more she wondered if there was truth in what her father and Ron both claimed for so many years—that Sabre and her mother didn't get along because they were too much alike.

Sabre walked in the house to the sound of a whistling teapot and the smell of homemade zucchini bread.

"Ahh, the smells of home," Sabre said, hugging her mother.

"It's so nice to have you here. Would you like some tea?" Her red lips formed the words that came straight from her heart.

"Tea would be good."

The attractive, sixty-one-year-old woman moved gracefully across the kitchen in her light yellow, cotton dress. Her yellow tourmaline earrings hung like teardrops just below her earlobes. Sabre liked that her mother always looked so perfect. Her mother always said a woman wasn't finished until she had on her lipstick and earrings. She was such a lady.

They sat down at the small kitchen table by the sliding glass door that looked out to a well-manicured back yard. The roses and the bougainvillea surrounding the patch of green grass brought the yard to life. "So, how have you been, darling?"

"Busy. I have a case that is pretty tough right now. I represent an eleven-year-old boy who tried to commit suicide."

Her mother shook her head. "I don't know how you do it, honey. You see so much suffering among those little children."

"Mom." Sabre hesitated. "Can I ask you something?"

"Of course."

"Did we ever live in a white house with a little, yellow house behind it?"

Her mother looked surprised. "Yes, we did, but I can't imagine you would remember that. You were not even four years old. Why do you ask?"

"Because I've been seeing it in my dreams."

"What are you dreaming about?"

"They're not really dreams. They're nightmares, actually. I'm wearing a white dress with red ladybugs."

Her mother stood up and went to the oven and removed the zucchini bread. She removed the bread from the pan and sliced it, laying the perfect slices on a serving plate. Sabre sat in silence, even though her mother was only a few feet away. When she set the bread and two small dessert plates on the table Sabre continued, "The dream is always the same. I open the door and walk into the little, yellow house and...."

"Help yourself, dear," her mother interrupted her.

Sabre put a slice of bread on her plate and picked up a fork, but she didn't start to eat. Her mother's face grew pale and she looked as if she might cry. "Mom, I see dead bodies hanging from the rafters," she blurted.

Clang! Her mother's fork hit the floor as her hand covered her mouth. "Oh, honey, I'm sorry. You were so young. We thought what happened would fade from your memory, and you never asked about it so we never said anything."

"It was real?" Sabre asked incredulously. It had seemed so real but she didn't really want to believe it. Now her mom had confirmed it.

"You saw a body, not bodies. It was your Uncle Bill. He hanged himself."

"Why? How?"

"Oh, Sabre. I'm so sorry."

Sabre reached for her mother's hand. "Mom, you don't need to be sorry. "

The tears were rolling down her mother's face. "But I do, honey. I do need to be sorry. I didn't protect you from him."

"In my dream, Daddy comes and gets me. He swoops me up and takes me outside. But then I remember your coming out of the big, white house and you look so scared and that wasn't in my dream."

"Do you remember anything else about your Uncle Bill?"

Sabre shook her head. "I didn't even know I had an Uncle Bill. Do you have any photos of him?"

"Not anymore. We destroyed them all."

"So that I wouldn't remember what I saw."

"Yes, we didn't want you to suffer from those horrible memories."

Sabre looked at the distant, scared look on her mother's face. "There's more, isn't there?"

Her mother took a deep breath. "Bill was not a very nice man. He was my brother and I loved him growing up. He was such a sweet little boy. He left home before he graduated from high school. One day he just took off. He wrote to me a couple of times from Japan after he joined the navy. After he was discharged he moved around for a while and ended up in Florida, where he lived for about ten years. He married a woman with two little girls and a year later they were divorced. He had nowhere to go and so he came to stay with us. We had a guest house on our property—a small, yellow house where he stayed for a couple of weeks. I had no idea what he was like when he came here because it had been nearly twenty years since I had seen him. When he left home he was still a boy and he came back to me a very troubled man."

Sabre grew more and more uncomfortable as her mother spoke. She began to see where the conversation was going, but she had to know. "Why did he hang himself?"

"It was nearly dinner time and I sent you out to tell your uncle he had about fifteen minutes. When you didn't come back right away, your father went to see if you got lost along the way. He found you in the bedroom with Bill and he had his pants open. I don't think anything happened to you, but we never knew for sure. Your dad grabbed you up and ran out threatening to kill Bill."

"Oh, no. Did Daddy kill him?"

"No, but he came inside and got his gun. I was hysterical. I screamed at him to put the gun away. You were screaming. I wanted to take care of you, but I had to stop your father from killing Bill. Trust me, I didn't care about Bill. I just didn't want your father to go to prison over him. I yelled at you to go to your room and you took off." Tears ran down her mother's face as she spoke and her face burned red with anger.

"What did Daddy do?"

"I couldn't stop him. He even pushed me out of the way. Your father had never laid a hand on me in anger or on anyone else I know of, but he was filled with rage. He kept yelling about how he was going to kill him. He ran out the back door and I went to your room looking for you, but you weren't there. I looked out the window and saw you running after your father toward the guest house. I ran downstairs but by the time I got there you were already in the house. The next thing I saw was your father carrying you out. Bill had hanged himself before your father had the chance to shoot him, but unfortunately you saw him hanging."

Sabre stood up and walked to her mother. She knelt down and hugged her. Her mother just kept crying and saying, "I'm sorry, Sabee. I'm so sorry." Her mom hadn't used that pet name for her since she was about nine when Sabre asserted she was too old for such a baby name.

"Don't cry, Mom. It's okay. It's not your fault," Sabre said, as she fought the tears herself. Sabre wasn't concerned for herself, but rather for the years her mother had suffered with this agonizing secret.

Her mom sniffled, pulled back from their embrace, and looked down at her. She stroked her hair like she did when Sabre was little. "My strong, brave, little girl. You've grown into a magnificent woman."

"Thanks to you, Mom. Everyone always said I'm a lot like you."

"No, my Sabee, you are your father. You have his strength, his intelligence, and his ambition. And just like him, you spend your life helping people less fortunate than you."

"So do you, Mom. Look at all the volunteer work you do. You help people every day."

"Honey, I volunteer because I'm bored. Sure, it does some good, but for your father it was a lifestyle, just as it is for you."

Sabre tried to smile. "Thank you, Mom, for telling me. I know it wasn't easy. And I think it'll be good for me. Now that I know, maybe the nightmares will stop."

"That client of yours, the little boy who tried to commit suicide, did he try to hang himself?"

Sabre nodded. "Yes. I'm the one who found him."

"And that's probably what triggered your memory and it came out in your dreams."

"I expect so, but now I can deal with it. I'll be able to sleep again." She decided not to tell her mother that she now had a recollection of what happened in that bedroom.

Chapter 44

Sabre's drive home seemed longer than usual. The events her mother had shared with her bounced around in her head. She wondered how much influence they had in shaping her life. She often questioned why she chose to work with abused children. Perhaps this explained it. She only knew she was more determined than ever to help them now and to stop creeps like Smithe and Tuffy.

She drove toward her home, but she didn't really want to be alone tonight. She needed someone who made her feel safe, someone like Bob or JP. She knew Bob would make light of it and find some way to make her laugh, but even if she could see him he didn't need her problems right now. He had enough of his own. JP would be perfect. She wouldn't even have to share what happened. His presence would be enough. She felt a certain comfort just thinking about him. She picked up her phone and said, "JP." The phone dialed his number. It rang four times but he didn't pick up. "Just checking in," Sabre said. "Please call when you get a chance."

Sabre was about ten miles from home when her phone rang. She pushed the button and spoke into her microphone. Expecting JP, she said, "Thanks for calling back."

"Always my pleasure, gorgeous," Dave Carr said when she answered. "I see you called me yesterday. Sorry I took so long to get back to you."

"No problem. It wasn't urgent. I just wanted to talk to you about Dana."

"Okay. Let's meet right now for a drink."

That wasn't exactly what Sabre had in mind, but it sounded like a good idea right at the moment. "Name the place, but nothing fancy. I'm slumming it today and I don't feel much like going home to clean up." She thought about her mother and how she would've been wearing earrings and lipstick. Sabre had neither. Wherever they went tonight, jeans, a t-shirt, and sandals would have to do.

"How about the Firehouse Café in Pacific Beach? Maybe we can even catch a sunset."

"See you in about twenty minutes." As soon as Sabre hung up the phone she thought it was a bad idea. She picked up her phone to call back, but decided one drink wouldn't hurt.

The traffic on Garnet and the search for a parking spot slowed Sabre's arrival to nearly half an hour. Maybe he won't wait, she thought. She entered the café and glanced around, not really expecting to see him downstairs. The view of the sunset and the ocean was much better from the top level. She no sooner stepped off the last step upstairs when she heard her name called. Dave Carr was seated at the bar that faced the ocean. He waved at her and then stood up when she approached.

"Have a seat. What can I get you?"

"I'll have a Midori Margarita."

Dave signaled for the bartender, ordered the margarita and a Coors Light, and then sat down next to Sabre. "I'm glad you came."

She looked at him sternly. "This is not a date."

"It's close enough," he smiled.

"Don't make me regret this," she said.

He winked at her. "I promise you won't."

"I need to talk to you about Dana."

Dave looked at the time on his phone. "Three minutes and twenty-four seconds."

"What?"

"I had a wager with myself. I gave you less than five minutes to start talking shop. You were way under, so I win."

She laughed. "The wager was with yourself. You win either way."

"But I'm a winner because I made you laugh and you look pretty stressed."

"It's been a rough day, and thank you for the drink. It's just what I need." She took a sip of her margarita. "But that doesn't get you off the hook. I still have some questions about your client."

"Any I'll be able to answer?"

"Probably not."

"But yet you're here." A devilish smirk passed his lips. "Okay, let's get the shop talk over with and then we can just relax. What's your question?"

Sabre sighed. He was impossible and incredibly witty, traits she appreciated in a man. "Look, I'm absolutely certain Bob didn't kill Foreman and I'm equally certain Bob wasn't having an affair with Dana. Does she still maintain they were?"

"I'm afraid so."

"Does she understand that could implicate her in the murder as well?"

"I've explained all that to her."

"So why would she lie about it?" Sabre asked.

"Exactly. Why would she?"

"At first, I thought she was running a scam on Bob and thinking she could sue him or blackmail him, but that doesn't make sense if he goes to prison. Besides, why would anyone go after a juvenile dependency attorney? We're probably the lowest paid attorneys around."

"Easy access, maybe. You guys are always setting yourself up for problems, given the way you go out on a limb to help your clients. Bob drove her to the hospital. He delivered papers to her house."

"Are you saying she's setting him up for some scam?"

He shook his head. "No. I'm not saying that at all. I don't know whether Bob killed my client's husband or not. I, like you, don't want to see an innocent man convicted of any crime, least of all murder." He placed his hand on her arm, looked her directly in the eye, and in the most serious tone Sabre ever heard him speak said, "I'm not saying my client has told me anything. I'm not saying I know who killed George Foreman. I'm just saying that if you are convinced Bob and Dana weren't having an affair, you need to ask yourself why she would say they were. Why would she lie?"

"Because she's a druggie and druggie's lie."

"Think outside the box."

She gave him a puzzled look. "Okay."

He smiled at her. "Can we stop with the shop talk now? I'd like to start our date before we miss the sunset."

Sabre's voice rose, getting the attention of the other six people in the bar. "We're not on a date."

Dave looked out into the small bar at the small crowd, lifted his beer bottle to them, nodded, and mouthed, "We're on a date."

Chapter 45

Sabre met JP at the court for Bob's arraignment. Jerry Leahy informed them just before they entered that the DA had charged him with second degree murder. They all knew that gave Bob a better chance of getting bail. Sabre was aware that most murder defendants don't get bail, especially if the charges contain what they call "special circumstances."

Sabre was sitting next to Marilee and heard her gasp when they brought Bob in for the arraignment. He was attached by chains to four other prisoners. They shuffled in and the two sheriffs directed them to a bench behind a glass wall to the left of the defense table. Sabre knew what to expect and should have prepared Marilee for this unnerving sight. She squeezed her hand.

The court heard several cases before Bob's was called. Finally the court clerk said, "In the case of Robert A. Clark."

Jerry stood up and introduced himself. The DA argued against bail and Jerry argued Bob's connections to the community, his family ties, and his lack of any previous record. The judge listened to both sides and made his order. "Bail is granted in the amount of four million dollars."

"Thank you, Your Honor," Jerry said.

Sabre breathed a sigh of relief that bail had been set, although she was frustrated at the amount. At ten percent Bob would have to come up with $400,000. She wasn't certain what equity Bob had in his house but she knew it wasn't that much and he didn't have a lot of cash in the bank.

Jerry walked back to where Sabre and JP were sitting. "Come with me. They're taking Bob to an interview room so we can talk with him."

Jerry looked at Bob's wife. "Marilee, it'll be a little crowded, but you're welcome to come with us if you'd like."

"No, thank you. I need to pick Corey up at school. I'll see him later."

Sabre, JP, and Jerry walked over to the Central Jail and took the elevator to the fourth floor. They traversed several hallways until they came to the window and signed in. Then they passed through a door that locked behind them into a small area. A control person buzzed them in and the second locked door opened. They passed the visiting area for the public. Sabre peaked in. There were four cubicles. The inmates were behind glass where the visitors couldn't pass them anything. Alongside those rooms was another series of four cubicles for the attorneys and other professionals to visit with their clients.

Sabre said, "I noticed these rooms have bars instead of glass like the public visitation rooms have. That's different than juvenile court."

"There are many times when we have to give our clients some paperwork or obtain a letter or something from them. It makes it a lot easier."

They passed the first three cubicles and entered into a room with a door at the far end. The five-by-six-foot room was a little crowded with all three of them in it and two chairs. On the other side of the bars was about the same amount of space. It contained a small, attached bench and a door. The walls were all bare. They were only in there a few minutes when Bob was brought into the room.

He smiled at the group. "You look like a cage full of monkeys."

Jerry chuckled. "It's all about perspective. So, we have the bail set, but it will cost you $400,000. Do you want me to call a bail bondsman?"

"Heck no. That's Corey's college education."

Sabre hadn't even considered that Bob wouldn't post the bail. "Bob, I'll help you. I have some money saved."

"I have a little, too, Bob. You're welcome to it," JP said.

Bob shook his head. "No. I appreciate it, but I'm not willing to waste that kind of money. You three just need to find a way to get me out of here for good."

"Are you sure?" Jerry asked.

"Yes, I'm sure. Thanks, Jerry, for trying. Maybe if it had been a million I would have considered it, but it's just too much. I don't have it, and even if I did, I wouldn't be willing to pay that much to the surety company."

"It's your choice," Jerry said. "I've got to run." He turned to Sabre and JP. "Are you two staying a while?"

"Yes," Sabre said. "We were going to do some brainstorming at my office, but we'll do it here instead. We need Bob's help."

"I'll walk out with you, Jerry. I need to retrieve some things from the car." JP opened the door and Jerry followed him out.

JP returned with a whiteboard that he propped up on an easel in the tight area behind the two chairs in the cubicle, positioning it so Bob could see it through the bars. The board contained all the suspects for George Foreman's murder listed in JP's perfect handwriting. Another spot had all the facts about which they still had questions.

Sabre added a few comments to the board and then sat down and stared at the board. The answer had to be somewhere on there, unless the killer was someone else they hadn't considered who had a grudge against Foreman. She couldn't think about that right now. She had to concentrate on what they had. She thought about what Dave Carr had said Saturday night about Dana.

She looked at JP. "Why do you think Dana lied about having an affair with Bob?" she asked.

"Because she's a stupid, lying bitch," Bob answered.

"Obviously, but what did she have to gain from saying that?"

JP shook his head. "Let's back up a little and start with the missing keys." He directed his question at Bob. "Since you never found your keys and the killer didn't break in, he or she must have used your keys. Who had access to them?"

Bob thought for a minute. "I know I had them when I met with Dana and George in your office because I used the key to open the door. And I used it to lock up when I left so it wasn't taken then. I think the last time I remember having my keys was the Wednesday before Foreman was killed. I met with Dana that afternoon in my office."

"Was George with her?" JP asked.

"No. She was alone."

"So, the only one connected to Foreman who could have taken your keys was Dana, right?" JP said, as he wrote "Bob's Keys" on the whiteboard under her name. "Let's assume for now she took the keys. What other evidence doesn't make sense?"

"Why Foreman had the address of Bob's mother-in-law in his pocket."

"Do you think he could have been following Dana or me?" Bob asked.

"Why do you ask?" JP said.

"Because I gave Dana a ride to her parenting class that same day my keys disappeared, but I stopped at my mother-in-law's house on the way to drop something off for Marilee."

JP scowled at Bob. "You what? You never told me that."

"I forgot I even did it until right now. I didn't go inside. I just put the bag on the porch and left."

"It looks like George was following one of you," JP said. "He must have jotted down the address to use later. Let me guess: You left a cigarette butt behind there as well."

Bob shook his head. "No, I don't think so."

"Well, he picked up one of your butts somewhere and saved it to use later," JP said.

"To blackmail Bob," Sabre added. "Which means he was probably working with Dana on a scam. Foreman was either following them because he didn't trust her or was just helping to gather material. And then he was killed before they pulled off the scam."

"Which means either Dana killed him or someone who had nothing to do with their little plan intervened," JP said.

"So why would Dana tell the police we were having an affair?" Bob asked.

"Either she decided to go ahead with the plan without George or she was trying to draw attention away from someone," JP said. Then. catching the expression on Sabre's face he added, "Herself, most likely."

Sabre rolled her eyes at JP. "That wasn't too smart of her," Sabre said. "That could implicate her even more."

"I wouldn't rule that out. She's not that bright," Bob said.

JP walked back to the board and pointed at the names. "Let's look at our other suspects. I think the most likely candidate is Tuffy."

"But we don't even know who he is," Bob said.

"True, but I spoke with Nelson this morning and he said they're putting pressure on Chris and on Sammy. Hopefully, one of them will crack. Oh, and the sex crimes unit picked up Jaleel last night, but he lawyered up right away."

"Does anyone think Jaleel might have done it?" Sabre asked.

"No, in fact, he had a good alibi, but they've charged him with corruption of a minor, larceny, receiving stolen property, and numerous other things. They've picked up at least two kids who were working with Jaleel." JP pointed at a name on the board. "And there's Sammy. I think he'll deal if they give him a decent offer. With all that, there's a good chance someone will lead them to Tuffy. They're best shot is probably Chris, but so far they haven't found him. Jaleel won't tell them anything beyond his name. The good news is the sex unit wants Tuffy as badly as we do, so they'll keep on it."

Sabre looked back at the board. "What about Celia or Frank?"

"Celia is pretty weak and someone smacked Foreman pretty hard with an hourglass," JP said. "It could be Frank, I guess, but why would he do it? He didn't like Foreman, but he's nothing if he isn't a business man. He would've made a calculated decision and I doubt if he thought Foreman's life was worth much."

"So, we're down to Tuffy, Chris, Sammy, Dana, and some random person that George ticked off somehow as he skated through life," Sabre said.

"And that list could be endless. It sounds like Foreman had a pint brain and a ten-gallon mouth. I expect he left a lot of angry people in his wake."

"But enough to kill him?" Sabre asked.

"A few. When I spoke with Nelson he said they had looked at everyone they could come up with, especially in the drug world, but they came up empty handed."

They continued up and down the list until they finally took the board down and folded up the easel.

"I'm sorry we don't have anything more concrete," Sabre said to Bob.

"I know you two will come up with something. Just keep me posted. And take care of my family."

"Won't Marilee be expecting you to come home today since bail was ordered?"

"No. We've already discussed this. She doesn't like it, but she's going along with it, at least for now. She's coming back to visit me after dinner."

Sabre pushed the buzzer on the intercom system. "We're finished with Robert Clark."

"Okay, someone will be right there. Please wait until he's excused."

A uniformed officer entered through the back door and frisked Bob, making sure nothing inappropriate had been passed to him. Then they buzzed Sabre and JP through the two sets of locked doors.

As soon as they were out of the jail, Sabre said. "Okay, spill. What were you thinking earlier? Who do you think Dana was covering for?"

"Maybe I should check it out first," JP said.

"You think she was covering for Marcus, don't you?"

JP put his hand on her shoulder. "Think about it. Marcus had a love/hate relationship with his dad. He didn't like the way Foreman treated his mother or himself. Foreman put him out there on the streets to get molested. Marcus tried to kill himself and then he wasn't sure he even wanted to attend his dad's funeral. The kid has a lot of guilt and turmoil. What if he did it?"

"But he was home with Frank and Celia."

"He's a street kid. You don't think he could figure out a way to sneak out?"

"But how did he get all the way to my office? That's at least fifteen miles away."

"I don't know, but I think we need to consider it."

"And just what do I do with that information if we find it's true? I can't sell my own client down the river."

"We'll deal with that when we know for sure."

Chapter 46

Marla Miller, the social worker, took Marcus to Sabre's office right after school the next day. She dropped him off and left. Sabre had agreed to take him back to La Jolla when they were finished.

JP walked in carrying a box of hamburgers and fries from In-N-Out. "Would you like a hamburger, Marcus?"

"Sure," he said. JP handed him a double-double and some fries.

"Thanks," Marcus said.

"Sabre?" JP asked.

"No, I'm good." Sabre walked to the copy room, took two sodas out of the refrigerator, and gave them to the boys.

Sabre sat behind her desk directly across from JP and Marcus. She asked Marcus about his return to school, his therapy sessions, and life at home. He appeared to be adjusting fairly well. He liked his therapist and he seemed more relaxed than he had in the past.

She hated the thought of talking to him about his father's murder. She had to do it, though, for his sake if nothing else. If he did kill his father, she knew he'd have to deal with it or he would constantly be at risk for suicide. Her dilemma was what she would do with the information. She had taken an oath to not reveal a client's confidence and yet she couldn't let Bob go to prison for murder. It wasn't only that she would lose her license to practice or that her client would get convicted. She really believed in the system, a system that protected the attorney-client privilege.

When Marcus finished his hamburger, Sabre said, "Marcus, I want you to think back to the day before your father was killed. It would've been a Thursday. What did you do that day?" Sabre and JP had agreed earlier that Sabre would ask the questions. She knew Marcus better and thought he'd be more comfortable with her. JP was to chime in if she missed anything.

"I went to school. I had detention that day because I got in trouble in class."

"What about after school?" Sabre asked.

"My mom came to visit but she didn't stay very long. She was really mad at my dad."

"Do you know what she was angry about?"

"I don't know. She just said he always messed things up and she wasn't going to let him mess things up anymore." Marcus fiddled with his french fries and then stuck one in his mouth.

"Do you know what she meant by that?"

Marcus swallowed his food. "She said she was going to get some money and get us back. She said all it took to keep your kids was to have money."

"Did anyone else hear her say those things?"

"No, we were in my room, just the two of us."

"Where was everyone else?"

"Frank wasn't home and Grandma had one of her headaches and was lying down."

"Where was Riley?" Sabre asked.

"Riley saw her when she first came in, but he told her he didn't want to see her when she was drunk."

"Was she drunk?"

He looked a little embarrassed. "I don't know. I think so."

"What happened after your mom left?" Sabre asked.

"I played video games in my room until Frank came home and made dinner. After we ate, we cleaned off the table and loaded the dishwasher like we always do."

"Does Frank usually make dinner?" JP asked.

Marcus nodded. "Most of the time. And he helps clean up. Grandma has a lot of headaches and Frank says he likes to cook. He's teaching me."

"What did you do after dinner?" Sabre asked.

Marcus thought for a second. "Same as always. Frank and Grandma watched TV and me and Riley went to our rooms. Riley always has homework. I'm glad I don't have that much."

"Did you see anyone before you went to bed?"

"Frank came up and told us to go to bed about nine-thirty. That was it."

"Marcus, have you ever sneaked out of your grandma's house at night?"

"No," he answered without hesitation. "I've thought about it a few times, but I don't know the alarm code and if I set the alarm off Frank would be furious. He says he'll give it to me when I'm Riley's age and responsible. Besides, he says I'm too young to be home alone anyway, so why do I need it."

"I'm going to ask you a tough question," Sabre said, "but I need you to tell me the truth. Do you think you can do that?"

Marcus nodded. Sabre wanted to give him the "confidentiality speech" assuring him that anything he said would be kept in confidence. But was she going to keep his confidence? She was conflicted in her own mind as to what she would do with the information and she just couldn't get that speech to come out.

"Do you know who killed your dad?"

Marcus squirmed in his chair. "Was it my mom?"

"Why would you ask that?"

"Because she was so mad at him."

Chapter 47

JP and Detective Olen Williams sat at a small table at Winchell's Donuts on Rosecrans. The table held JP's coffee and in front of Olen was a large cup of black coffee and a plate with two donuts. JP wondered how Olen stayed so thin.

"I wish we had a Dunkin' Donuts around here, but Winchell's is good too," Olen said. I don't go for all this fancy coffee and bagels crap. Give me a good old-fashioned glazed or cake donut any day."

"I'm with you on the coffee. I haven't joined the Starbucks fan club." JP smiled. "By the way, thanks for meeting with me this morning."

Olen wolfed down his first donut. "No problem. Do you really think your friend is innocent?"

"I'm as sure as night follows day."

"I know that attorney, Ms. Brown, believes in him, too. I followed up on everyone we have questioned so far in this child sex ring, and I'm sorry to say you may need to start looking elsewhere. We just took Jaleel and Sammy out of the lineup. They were both in the police station all night the night of the murder. There was a ruckus downtown at a bar and there were a whole lot of people brought in for questioning. Jaleel and Sammy were two of them. As it turned out, they weren't involved, but neither of them could have killed Foreman."

"So that leaves Chris and Tuffy."

"Chris's cousin says he was with him all night, which may or may not be true. His cousin is a little older and seems pretty responsible, but he could be covering for him. And as for Tuffy, we still don't know who he is. We've offered Sammy and Jaleel pretty good deals but neither of them are talking."

"Have you found Chris yet?"

"No, which makes him more suspect. We'll find him and he'll pay for his crimes. Do you think he would deal with us?"

"Oh, I think he'd give Tuffy up in a heartbeat to avoid going to prison, but I doubt if he has ever met him or ever heard his real name. Did you get anything from his cell phone?"

"Not really. We know they buy the disposable phones, but we haven't found any calls that lead us to Tuffy. The text messages come from a computer. We've traced the IP address to wireless accounts like Starbucks, McDonalds, and other WiFi connections."

"And you have no other leads on Tuffy?"

"Nope. We're hitting walls everywhere we go. He's like a phantom and as good as he is at eluding us, he could very well be your killer. I really want that scumbag off the streets. He can go to prison and be somebody's bitch and see how he likes it."

JP was frustrated that they had lost so many of their likely suspects. After the conversation with Marcus yesterday, he was pretty certain he didn't do it based on the way he responded when asked if he knew who killed his dad. Also, there's no way he could've sneaked out of Frank's house without setting off the alarm. When JP dropped Marcus off at his house, he confirmed with Frank that Marcus didn't know the code.

He was glad Marcus was no longer on their list, not only for the kid's sake but for Sabre's as well. But the more suspects they eliminated, the more Bob looked guilty. That left Dana, Chris, and Tuffy. He had nowhere to go on Tuffy; he just had to count on Olen to find him. For that matter, he couldn't think of anything else he could do about Dana. He couldn't even talk to her, but he could talk to Riley. He called Sabre to get the go ahead and then drove to see Riley.

Riley was in his art class, which was just about to break. JP approached him before he left the class. "Can you talk a minute?"

"Yes," he said, picking up his drawing pad.

JP managed a quick glance at a drawing of a tarantula with full detail of his face and body. "Wow, that's really good. Did you do that?"

"Yeah."

"Can I see some of the others?" JP asked.

Riley tucked the pad under his arm. "They're really not that good. That was the best one."

"No problem," JP said, as they walked out of the classroom together.

Riley directed him to a bench near the art department. "We can talk here."

"I need to ask you about the night before your father died. I understand your mother came to see you. Is that correct?"

"Yeah."

"Did you talk to her?"

"Just for a minute."

JP knew Riley wouldn't be very talkative. He never was, but he was hoping to get a little more than he was getting. "Tell me what happened that night, starting from the time your mom arrived at your house."

"Not much happened. Mom came in and gave me a hug before she went to see Marcus. She spent most of her time with him. I was in my room doing homework when she left. Then we ate dinner and I went back to my room."

"Had your mother been drinking?" JP asked.

Riley shrugged but didn't respond at first. JP waited. Finally, Riley said, "I think I smelled alcohol on her." Riley stood up, "Can I go now? I need to get to class."

JP knew it was hard for Riley to talk about either of his parents. He seemed to want to put everything behind him and move forward. JP didn't really blame him. That's exactly what he would've done if he were in his shoes. Riley was doing well in school, had made a lot of friends, and generally seemed to fit in well at his grandma's house. It was interesting how the boys had reacted so differently to the same situation, but poor Marcus was so troubled. JP wondered how much this kid had endured when his father was alive. He was pretty certain it was a lot more than they knew about.

JP drove back to his house. Louie, JP's beagle, came running up to him. He reached down and petted him. Louie ran around in circles, jumping up and down against JP's legs. JP took a few steps into the house and Louie ran off, grabbed his pink flamingo, and brought it back to JP. Louie's head was flipping from side to side, the pink flamingo dangling from his mouth. When Louie tired of that game, he ran and retrieved another item he had been chewing on and dropped it at JP's feet.

JP picked up the bedraggled, shredded piece of nylon that was once a leash.

"Louie, what did you do?"

Louie just wagged his tail.

"You silly boy. I can't take you for walks with that piece of string." JP playfully batted him around a few times, picked up his file on the Foreman case, and he and Louie went out in the backyard. He threw a Frisbee for Louie, who ran and caught it in the air. After about thirty throws JP laid the Frisbee down and Louie looked up at him with big, sad eyes.

JP took a seat in a lounge chair and opened the file. He started reading from the beginning of the case. He combed through the social study and every report he had written for Sabre, as well as the summaries Sabre had provided. He compared her notes to his, looking for discrepancies in the case.

He reached down to Louie, gently scratched the dog's head, and said, "Well, butter my butt and call me a biscuit, Louie. I know how to find out who Tuffy is."

Chapter 48

Ludwik Bernard Sampulski welcomed JP into his home and offered him tea. JP declined the tea but sat with him at his table while the old man drank his.

"I'm sure you didn't come by just to visit, young man. Is Sammy out of jail yet?"

"No, he's still in custody. There've been more charges filed on him. Pretty bad charges, I'm afraid."

"Such a waste of a good mind. He's brilliant, you know?"

For a minute JP thought Ludwik was talking about someone else. The Sammy he had met didn't strike him as brilliant. In fact, he found him to be about as bright as a burnt-out light bulb in a dark room with no windows.

"He could have been a doctor if he'd wanted to be. He never had to study and he was an avid reader. There's not a classic that boy hadn't read by the time he was in middle school. He would get nearly perfect scores on his state tests at school, but he was so lazy." He sighed. "And so troubled."

"He was that smart?"

"He was, but you'd never know it now. And now he sits in jail and not even for something he used his mind for. He called me when he was arrested. Collect, of course. I accepted the call and I talked to him, but I refused to help him. I don't know if it was the right thing to do or not, but at some point a boy has to become a man and handle his own problems."

"I think you did the right thing, Ludwik. He's been doing some pretty bad things. He's been selling marijuana to young kids."

"Oh, no! I've begged him over and over again to not use drugs. And to sell them to kids! That's horrible."

"It's worse than that. He was running some scams using kids to help him make money. He told me he started doing it with a guy named Tuffy. Have you ever met anyone with that name or did Sammy every mention him?"

He shook his head from side to side. "I don't believe so."

"I'm here to ask for your help and I need it desperately. Here's the problem we're dealing with: I have a very good friend who has been charged with murder. He's innocent. I know that, and I can't bear to see him spend the rest of his life in prison for a crime he didn't commit. He has a wife and young child and he's a good man who made the mistake of helping the wrong person."

Ludwik listened. His face filled with compassion as JP made his plea.

"The man who was murdered also ran scams with Sammy. The dead man had been using his own eleven-year-old son to distort money from men who wanted time with little boys."

"Do you think Sammy murdered someone?"

"No, I don't," JP answered quickly. "But there's a good chance Tuffy did. The problem is that your son is the only person who knows who Tuffy is, and he won't talk. I'd like to look in Sammy's room and see if anything helps me figure out who Tuffy really is."

Ludwik didn't answer right away. He had a faraway look in his eyes as if he were remembering a better time, perhaps a time when Sammy was an innocent child.

"Ludwik, I'm sure your heart must go out to Sammy, but you are more than a father. You are also a good, compassionate man with a strong sense of justice. I'm certain you don't want to see an innocent man convicted of murder."

Ludwik stood up and walked over to the shelf where the Mason jar sat, the jar that contained the dirt he had retrieved when he first set foot on American soil. He sat back down and opened the jar. With his right hand he reached in and took out a little dirt and placed it in his left palm. With his right index finger and thumb he rubbed it around gently and deliberately as if it were flakes of gold.

"From the moment I picked this dirt up I wanted to take it to Poland and place it on my father's grave so he could have a little piece of the America he so wanted to be a part of. But over the years I think I needed this dirt more than he did. It brought me through many tough times. When I had hard decisions to make or when I wanted to give up or felt sorry for myself, I would hold a little dirt in my hand and think of my father. Every time I look at this dirt I'm reminded how lucky I am to be a free man, to have opportunities so many people don't have, and to be able to make choices, the very things my father wanted for me. The things I wanted for my son. My father would boast of one day coming to America. He dreamed of the land where there was 'liberty and justice for all.' He would say, 'Son, when we go to America we will embrace its laws and customs and we will become good American citizens.' He believed as I do that with freedom comes great responsibility. It doesn't mean we are free to hurt people and my son has hurt so many people. I'm glad my father isn't here to see what his grandson, his namesake, has become."

Ludwik poured the dirt back in the jar and carefully brushed the few remaining grains in as well. "I will help you get justice."

"You need to know that what I find may not be good for Sammy."

"It will be good for Sammy to take responsibility for his actions." He stood up. "Come with me. I don't know if you'll find anything, but I'll show you his room."

They walked down the short hallway and into a small bedroom. The bed was neatly made but the desk had papers and junk piled next to the computer. Video games were stacked haphazardly on shelves and on the small table next to the bed.

"I apologize for the mess. I fix his bed when he leaves and pick up his clothes but the rest of his stuff I just leave alone." He pointed to the desk. "There's his computer."

"Thanks," JP said. "Do you know if he has a laptop?"

"He had one, but I don't know if he still does. The last few times he has been home I don't think he had it with him. In fact, I think a lot of times he comes home it's just to use the computer. He wanted to take it with him, but I told him no. I guess I thought he wouldn't come home at all if the computer wasn't here. Each time I hope he has grown up, but then things like this happen and I wonder if he'll ever grow up." Ludwik stepped toward the door. "Take whatever time you need," he said and walked out.

JP looked at the items piled on his dresser: game cards, old copies of Fight magazine, super hero comics, a comb, video games, and Zig Zag roll-your-own papers. He opened each drawer and found only clothes. The small closet was jammed with shoes, action toys, and two bongs. From the closet rod hung a long pea coat and a windbreaker, a pair of dress pants, a white dress shirt, a black hoodie, and numerous t-shirts. Several of the t-shirts contained the Tapout logo. The hoodie had "The Ultimate Fighter" logo across the front.

JP moved to the computer. Sammy must have expected to return sooner or he was just careless because his email program was still open. JP rummaged through his emails looking for some sign of Tuffy, but no clue emerged. JP knew his way around the computer but he was no expert and certainly no hacker. All he could do was check what was in plain sight. He looked at Sammy's history. It listed martial arts and video game websites, particularly The Ultimate Fighter. The only other thing in his recent history was his MySpace account. He clicked it on; Sammy's username and password had been saved so the program opened right up. His home page was covered with martial arts graphics. The man was obsessed. His list of friends all seemed to be "warrior" related. Sammy bragged on his posts about his prowess as a fighter, telling in great detail about his experiences in the ring. JP chuckled. What a dreamer Sammy was. He was no more a fighter than the Pillsbury Dough Boy.

JP jotted down a few names that could have some remote connection to Tuffy. He rifled through the rest of the items on the desk, but came up empty handed. He left the room feeling disappointed that his idea hadn't paid off.

As JP entered the kitchen, Ludwik must have read his face. "You found nothing."

"Nope. I appreciate your letting me take a look, though." JP pulled his card from his pocket. "Please, if you think of anything that pertains to Tuffy, let me know."

JP returned to his office, typed a report regarding his trip to Sammy's father's house, and emailed a copy to Sabre. Then he printed out a copy and slipped it in his file. He picked up the folder, tucked it under his arm, and left for the pet store to get a new leash for Louie. As he neared Sabre's office, which was only a few blocks from the pet store, he saw her car was parked in the lot. Deciding to stop and see her first, he pulled into the lot and went inside.

"Hi, JP. I was just printing out your report," Sabre said.

"There's not much in there. I really thought I might find out something from Ludwik but I'm afraid I struck out."

Sabre glanced over the report. Then she looked up and smiled at JP. "Oh, but I think you did."

JP raised one eyebrow. "What?"

"Remember how Marcus said Sammy bragged about how he was going to be an Ultimate Fighter champion?"

"Yes. He has t-shirts, video games, magazines, and his computer is filled with mixed martial art material. The guy's obsessed."

"Exactly. I didn't think of it until I saw it in writing, but look at this." She pointed to the report and read, "The Ultimate Fighter. T-U-F."

"Tuf. Tuffy. Sammy is Tuffy."

"I think so."

"I didn't think he was smart enough, but his dad said he's brilliant. Maybe that's true," JP said. "And that would explain why he hasn't made a deal with the DA. His little drug charge is nothing compared to the sex crimes and scams he's been pulling. He can't tell them he's Tuffy."

The "ah-ha moment" look on Sabre's faced was replaced with one of disappointment and frustration. "You know what that means?"

"Yes. If Sammy is Tuffy, we just lost our most likely suspect for Foreman's murder. We know Sammy didn't do it because he was in police custody that night."

Chapter 49

"I'm sorry Frank and Marcus aren't home," Celia said, as she let Sabre in. "They just left. Frank promised to take Marcus to dinner as a reward for being so good about going to his programs. Then Marcus has a group therapy session and Frank will just wait for him. I expect they'll be gone about three hours." Since Frank was normally the host in this home, Celia must have felt obligated to explain.

"That's okay. It's really Riley I came to see this evening," Sabre said.

They walked toward the stairs. "It's so nice to see Riley studying. He wants to do well in school. We're very proud of him," Celia said.

"Does he spend a lot of time on his homework?"

"Yes, he's very motivated. He's not at all like he used to be. The only thing he was ever interested in before was cars."

"Cars?"

"Yes, he'd talk about what kind of car he was going to get when he started driving, not that his father would have helped him buy one. He knows the make, model, and year of every car on the road."

"Really?"

"Yes. He still talks about them some, but not like he used to. Frank and I promised him a car when he graduates from high school if he has good grades and is accepted into college. He seems determined to get there."

"Good for him, and that's very generous of you and Frank."

"He's a good boy in spite of the life he's had to endure." Celia stopped at the foot of the stairs. "It's the first door on your left at the top of the stairs."

Celia remained at the bottom of the steps as Sabre started up. The purpose of Sabre's visit was to see Riley this time. Up until now Marcus had led them to many suspects, but perhaps Riley knew something that he didn't even know he knew. Sabre was running out of options and she had to do something to help Bob.

She knocked on Riley's door. Unlike most kids his age, instead of just yelling "come in" he actually came to the door and opened it. She thanked him for being a gentleman, after which she wondered if the door had been locked. Either way he was very polite when he invited her inside.

"Your grandma said you were doing homework. Do you have a lot?"

"Yes, especially in my World History class."

His book lay open on his desk next to his computer. "What are you working on?"

"We have to write a paper on a World War II battle. I was assigned the Battle of Okinawa."

"Wow! My grandfather fought in that battle. He was wounded there, and he received the Purple Heart. His papers read 'for wounds received while in action against the enemy.' He was very proud of that medal."

"How was he wounded?"

"He never said exactly. He didn't give too many details, but I know he lost his foot. He had a prosthesis."

"I've been reading about it, and a lot of people died in The Battle of Okinawa, both American and Japanese. And a lot of ships and aircraft were lost."

Sabre was pleased that Riley was speaking in more than one-word responses, as he usually did when she talked to him. "Yes, they did," she said. "And even more were wounded." Riley looked over at his computer. "Well, enough about the war. I'm sure you need to get back to your paper so I'll try to make this quick."

"Okay."

"Riley, I know that Marcus spent a lot of time working the streets with your father. Did you ever go out with him?"

Riley intertwined his fingers together in front of him, pushing his hands back and forth and making his fingers pop. "Just once."

"What did you do that time?"

He shrugged. "Nothing, really."

"Do you know what your father did when he went to 'work,' as he called it?"

"Not really."

"Can you tell me exactly what happened the time you went out?"

Riley hesitated as he moved his laced hands back and forth. "He wanted me to talk to this man and steal his wallet, but I wouldn't."

"Did he get angry?"

"Yes."

"What happened next?" Sabre was once again frustrated with his short answers but she continued.

"He hit me and I ran home."

"Riley, did he ever hit your mother?"

He nodded, still wiggling his hands in a nervous gesture. "My mom didn't kill him." His voice sounded cold.

"I'm not suggesting she did, but why do you say that?" Sabre asked.

"Marcus thinks she did."

"Why is that?"

"I don't know."

"Did your dad ever hit Marcus?"

"All the time."

"Did Marcus ever tell you what he was doing when he went to work with your dad?"

"Not really."

When Sabre paused, Riley said, "Can I get back to my paper now?"

"One more thing: Do you know if Marcus has ever sneaked out of the house at night?"

"Not that I know of." Sabre noticed a sketchpad lying on Riley's bed. The front covering was filled with drawings. "JP said you draw exceptionally well." She nodded her head in the direction of the sketchpad. "Nice work. Is that yours?"

"Yeah." He picked it up and pulled it up to his chest so she could no longer see the cover.

"It's okay. You don't need to share your drawings with me. Some artists are very private about their work. And you are definitely an artist."

"Thank you," Riley said.

Sabre talked to him a little bit more about his paper. He seemed to be the most comfortable with that topic and she wanted to leave him in a better frame of mind. She also asked him about living in La Jolla with his grandma. He appeared to be quite content there and not real anxious to go back to his mother. The one thing that was so obvious to Sabre was that Riley didn't smile a lot. He showed little emotion of any kind in comparison with Marcus, who had extreme highs and lows. Marcus was either laughing and joking or very disturbed; sometimes he exhibited anger or sadness or even depression. Riley, on the other hand, was very even tempered. He smiled politely when appropriate, but he didn't show his emotions, at least not to Sabre. Sabre found it astonishing that two boys raised in the same environment had reacted so differently.

Sabre stopped to talk with Celia a bit before she left.

"He seems happy here," Celia said. "Will he be able to stay?"

"That depends a lot on your daughter. If Dana can complete her programs and stay clean and sober, she has a good chance of getting the boys back in her care. Of course, she'll have to have housing."

"If she would stay clean she could live with us, and I'd like that very much," Celia said. "Marcus is doing better and Riley has just blossomed since he's been here. He's doing so well in school."

"He definitely appears to be benefiting from this placement," Sabre said. "And he's quite the artist."

Celia looked surprised. "He doesn't usually show people his artwork."

"He didn't. I saw his sketchpad lying on his bed. There were drawings on the front of it. I saw enough to tell that he's remarkable."

"He truly is. I've kept him in sketchpads over the years. When he was about seven I saw how good he was and started buying the notebooks for him. Back then he would show me what he had drawn whenever he'd come to visit. He would draw in them nearly every day, especially when something unusual happened in his life. They were like a diary to him."

"When did he stop showing them to you?"

"Three or four years ago. Dana said his dad would make fun of him and tell him it was stupid. George even threw a couple of them away. After that, Riley started hiding his sketchpads. I was pretty angry at George for making him feel bad about such a talent. I was afraid he would stop drawing so I gave him supplies when George wasn't around. Besides, his drawings kept me informed as to what was going on in the boys' lives. I'm ashamed to say it, but I would sneak a peak whenever I got a chance so I could see if everything was okay at home. He even put the date on each page when he drew something so I always knew the time frame. Like I said, it was as good as reading a diary."

"Have you seen any of his recent work?" Sabre asked.

"No. After he moved in I figured I didn't need to do that anymore, especially since he's doing so well. I've tried to respect his privacy in this house. He's had so little of it."

Chapter 50

"Hey, kid," JP said, as he stepped into Sabre's office. He stopped in the doorway and leaned against the rim of the door. "You need to lock your door when you're here alone, especially after dark."

Sabre looked up and smiled. "You're right. I got busy and didn't realize how late it was." They had agreed to meet and hammer through this case once again, but she was always pleased to see him. "What do you have for me?"

"I just spoke with Detective Olen Williams and unfortunately, he confirmed that Sammy and Tuffy are one and the same."

"Dang, I was so hoping we were wrong. I guess that moves Dana to the top of our suspect list."

"Yes, and I think Riley knows a lot more than he's telling," Sabre said.

JP sat down in the chair across the desk from Sabre. "Do you think he knows who killed his father?"

"He was very quick to say his mother didn't do it, which makes me think he knows more."

"It's his mother," JP said. "Don't you think it's normal for him to defend her?"

"It was more than that. There was something different in his voice."

"Different how?"

"Kind of cold and almost calculating."

"Maybe he was angry that you suggested his mother may have killed his father."

"But I didn't suggest that. I just asked him if his father ever hit her. And he said that Marcus thinks his mom killed Foreman."

"Has Marcus ever told you that?"

"No. He asked me if she did, but he never implied that he thought so."

"So, let's focus on Dana. What can we do? What do we need to know?"

"I need to get Riley to show me his sketchpad."

"What?"

"Celia says Riley's sketchpad is like a diary. He draws whatever happens in his life. I need to see the events of the last few weeks before Foreman's death. Maybe it'll tell us something."

"That's not going to be easy," JP said. "Riley is very protective of his artwork. He snatched it up real fast when I tried to look that day at school."

"I know. He did that to me, too."

"So what's your plan?" JP asked.

Sabre pursed her lips and wiggled them back and forth. "I don't know. I don't actually have a plan yet. I was hoping you had an idea."

"Well, I could break into the house and steal it, but when the alarm goes off and I get caught, you'll have to bail me out of jail. That's if Frank doesn't shoot me first."

"You have another idea?" Sabra asked.

"He either has to let you see it or you have to trick him into showing it to you. Or you can look without his knowing it. Which way would you like to go? And keep in mind that if you go with the first choice and it doesn't work, the other two are probably out because he'll be onto you."

"Of course, I'd like him to just show it to me, but...." Sabre threw her hands in the air. "I can't believe I'm even talking about doing something like this."

"Why? Is it unethical?"

"Yes. No. I don't know, but it sure doesn't feel right."

"Saving an innocent man's life feels right to me," JP grumbled.

"You're right. I need to find a way to see the sketchpad and if it leads us to Dana we'll find a way to disclose it. My first obligation is to protect my minor client. At some point I'll need to take sides on whether Riley and Marcus return to live with their mother. And if she's a murderer that certainly would factor into my decision." Sabre sighed. Perhaps she was just rationalizing, but she had convinced herself that she needed to see Riley's sketchpad. After all, she really didn't want those boys living with a murderer. "I don't think I can trick him into showing it to me. So, how do I see it without his knowing about it?"

"Is Riley still home alone with Celia?"

Sabre looked at the time on her phone. "Marcus' therapy session started about ten minutes ago and if we factor driving time back from therapy, they should be home in about an hour."

"Then let's go. We're going back to see Riley. You need to think of something to ask him that you forgot to ask earlier. I'll take care of the rest."

Sabre was reluctant. Talking about it was bad enough. Now that they were actually considering deceiving Riley so they could see his drawings, she wasn't so sure it was a good idea after all. "You think?" she said.

"I think." JP stood up. "Let's go."

JP led her out the back door and to his car. "I'll drive."

"Of course you will."

Once on the road, JP said, "And when we get there, you need to limp."

"Limp?"

"Yes, we'll tell Celia you sprained your ankle after you left here. Just don't tell her you did it on her property. She may be afraid you're going to sue her," he said jokingly.

"So, I've sprained my ankle and so I can't walk up the stairs and Riley will have to come down to see me."

"That's the plan. And I'll take care of the rest."

Sabre was getting more and more nervous by the time they reached the Davis house. When she stepped out of the car and started to walk up to the front door, JP reminded her to limp in case someone looked out.

"Oh, wait," JP said. Sabre stopped and JP returned to his car and retrieved a video game from his trunk.

"What's that?" Sabre asked.

"A present for Marcus. Did you figure out what to ask Riley?"

"Yes," Sabre said and rang the doorbell.

When Celia opened the door Sabre thought she smelled a whiff of alcohol on her breath. Sabre spoke quickly, "I'm so sorry to bother you, but I need to speak to Riley again for just a moment. Would that be okay?"

"Of course, please come in."

"Hello, Celia," JP said.

"Is Marcus home yet?" Sabre asked.

"No, another half hour or so, I should think."

Celia opened the door wide as they entered. Sabre's limp prompted Celia to look down at Sabre's foot and ask, "What happened?"

"I just sprained my ankle. On the step at my office," she added quickly. "That's why JP drove me here."

"I'm sorry."

"I'm sure it'll be okay in a day or so," Sabre said.

Celia started to lead them toward the stairs. JP spoke up. "Perhaps Riley could come down here so Sabre doesn't have to climb the stairs." He stepped around both Sabre and Celia. "In fact, I'd be glad to go get him." He raised the video game he had been carrying. "Besides, I have this game for Marcus. I'll drop it in his room while I'm up there."

"Thank you," Celia said.

JP bounded up the steps and Sabre said, "I'll wait here for Riley. I'm sorry to interrupt your evening like this. I don't mean to be a bother."

"It's no bother. I was just watching a movie in my room."

Riley started down the steps. "Here he is now," Sabre said.

Celia pointed to an area just off the living room. "You can meet in the sunroom if that's okay."

"That would be perfect, and you can get back to your movie. I'll only be a minute and Riley can see us out." Sabre had a feeling Celia was anxious to get back to her nightcap. She made a mental note that she'd have to look into her drinking. She was starting to see a pattern that may have to be addressed, but for now she still felt this was the best placement for the boys.

Celia walked away as Riley led Sabre to the sunroom. "Did you finish your paper on The Battle of Okinawa?"

"Almost. I'm working on the conclusion."

Sabre continued to talk about the paper as she stalled for time. She didn't know how long it would take JP and she didn't have many questions to ask about the case. She also knew she would receive short answers, so the longer she could talk about Okinawa the more time she could give JP.

Upstairs, JP dropped the video game in Marcus' room while Riley descended the steps and then JP went into Riley's room. He picked up the sketchpad lying on the bed and opened it up. It only had four pages filled, and the last one was from yesterday. It contained a drawing of the tarantula JP had seen at school in the biology lab, a soccer player, and a teenage girl with a sad, painful look on her face. All the drawings appeared to be about school activities and perhaps Riley had a love interest. The very last entry was a car smashed into a tree with two bodies on the ground. JP wondered if Riley had witnessed a car accident.

JP looked around the room for more sketchbooks. There was nothing on the shelves or on the desk. He opened the top two drawers on the side of the desk. The third one, a larger drawer built to hold file folders, was locked. JP looked around the desk for a key, trying to be careful to not change the placement of the papers and things on his desk. It wasn't there. He pulled open the middle drawer directly under the computer. It contained pens and numerous other writing tools, but there was no key. He feared Riley had the key on him. He thought about trying to pick the lock, but even if he was successful he would have to re-lock it so Riley wouldn't know someone had been in the drawer.

He walked with swift feet to Riley's dresser. Nothing sat on the top of it. He opened the drawers and glanced quickly through them. He saw nothing but clothes, and there weren't many of those. As he walked back to the desk, he spotted a lanyard on the floor near the chair. It had three keys on it. One looked like a house key. He tried the second one in the drawer, but it didn't work. The third key opened the drawer.

The drawer held four sketchpads. He took them out and laid them on the desk. The first one he picked up had dates from over a year ago. The second one ended about a week ago. Bingo! That's the one he needed. He took out his iPhone and snapped pictures of each page, moving quickly through the pad without really looking at the drawings, but occasionally checking the dates. Suddenly, one drawing caught his eye. He gasped.

"Oh, no," he said under his breath. He paused for a second and then started clicking again. He was about two weeks beyond when Foreman had been killed when he heard some male voices downstairs. Marcus and Frank were home and JP expected Marcus upstairs any minute. JP clicked a few more times and then shoved the phone into his pocket and closed up the sketchpad. He returned the pads to their original order and placed them in the drawer. He heard Marcus running up the stairs. He locked the drawer, dropped the lanyard on the floor where he found it, and walked to the door. Peeking out, he saw no one in the hallway. He stepped out and closed the door behind him just as Marcus dashed out of the bathroom.

"Hi, Marcus, did you see what I brought you?"

"No, what?" he asked, grinning from ear to ear. He was so easily excitable, JP was glad he brought the game.

"I put it in your room." Marcus dashed into his room followed by JP. He immediately spotted the game sitting on his bed.

"Wow, Black Ops. This is such a cool game."

"I'm glad you like it. I don't have time tonight, but maybe we can play it together sometime."

Marcus darted to his computer, placed the video in the drive, and started it up. He was focused. JP patted him on the shoulder, left the room, and walked downstairs. Frank greeted him as he started toward the sunroom.

"Good evening, Frank."

Sabre appeared with Riley, who had a somewhat quizzical look on his face when he saw Frank. "Is your homework done?" Frank asked.

"Almost," Riley said. He then told Frank goodnight and bounded up the steps two at a time.

JP stared down at Sabre's foot and she rolled her eyes. She wasn't limping. Frank was standing where he wouldn't have seen her walk yet. She just hoped Riley hadn't noticed. Frank turned around and noticed her walk.

"What happened?"

"Just a little sprain," Sabre said. "We'll get out of your way here. Sorry about the intrusion," Sabre said.

"It's no problem," Frank said. "We're getting used to it. There are social workers and such coming and going all the time here. We've been told it'll settle down eventually."

Once inside the car, Sabre took a deep breath. "I almost blew it. Sorry."

"You were fine." JP handed her the phone. "But you're not going to like what you see. Look at the drawing on the date Foreman was killed."

Sabre clicked on the photos. When she reached that drawing, her hand flew up to her mouth. "Oh, my God!"

Chapter 51

Sabre's desk was covered with copies of the drawings that JP had taken of Riley's sketchpad. Sabre held the one from the day that Foreman's body was found. It was a detailed drawing of the murder weapon.

"That's my brother's hourglass. It has the same exact Victorian design. Riley has never been in my office and that's the only way he could have known what it looked like." She looked up at JP who stood across the desk from her. "Has there been anything released in the media? A picture of it perhaps?"

"The type of weapon wasn't ever mentioned. Detective Nelson and I were just talking about that yesterday. And this hourglass drawing can't be a coincidence."

Sabre clutched the picture to her chest. "Do you think Riley killed his father?" she said in a quiet, strangely calm voice.

"He could've sneaked out that night. He does know the alarm codes," JP said.

"But how did he get to my office?"

JP pointed to a drawing on the desk of a 1989 Acura. "Do you know what kind of car that is?"

"No, but I can barely tell a VW Beetle from a Cadillac."

"It's Sammy's car. Do you remember that Riley told me he didn't know what kind of car Sammy drove? Well, he knew it well enough to draw it."

"His grandma told me there isn't a car on the road that Riley doesn't know," Sabre said.

"So, he lied to me about that. Why do you suppose he did that?" But before Sabre could answer, JP added, "Because he had something to hide. He didn't want us to know that he was in Sammy's car the night his father was killed."

"But Sammy couldn't have driven him. He was at the police station all night."

"So someone else drove Sammy's car. There must've been something Sammy wanted from Riley and he made a deal with him. When he couldn't leave the police station, he sent someone else."

"Like who?"

"I haven't figured that out yet. Maybe it's in the drawings. What is the date on the drawing of the car?"

"It was six days before the murder."

"So whatever was going on must have started at least by then." JP came around the desk and stood next to Sabre. His arm touched hers as he leaned forward. Sabre looked up at him, her face inches away from his. She felt his breath on her face and it made her uneasy. She turned quickly away.

"Look at the sketches just before and just after Foreman's death," she said. "We have a woman crying and although her mouth and nose are covered by her hands, she sure looks like Riley's mother. Look at her eyes, her hair, and her body. Her shirt is torn and hanging off her shoulder. The next one is a street scene with homeless people and bottles of alcohol and drug paraphernalia everywhere. Both of the drawings are dark, even sinister."

JP picked up a third drawing. "But look at this one. It's James Bond surrounded by all kinds of spy gadgets and he's smiling and cheerful. In the background is the 1989 Acura with 007 across the side."

"Do you think it means something or did he just see a James Bond movie that day and decide to draw it?" Sabre asked.

"And put Sammy's car in the background?"

"The next picture is the hourglass, all by itself except for its shadow. And that's followed by one that looks like hell."

"Why?" JP leaned over her shoulder to get a better look at the drawing. "What's wrong with it?"

"No, I mean it looks like a picture of hell with flames and demons."

JP pointed to two figures, one taller than the other, enveloped by flames. "Who do you suppose they are?"

"I'm afraid to guess," Sabre said. "And after that, on a Sunday, is a family sitting at the dining room table. It looks like Frank's dining room and there are two boys, a man, and a woman eating dinner. On Monday he drew his biology lab, and on Tuesday there is no drawing." Sabre picked up the next picture slowly. She felt a shiver through her body as she looked at the young boy hanging from a rope. "This is Wednesday, the day Marcus tried to kill himself." She laid the picture down. "Grandma was right. It's like reading a diary. He's drawing all the things that had an effect on him that day."

JP pointed to the next three. They were all drawings of Frank's house with a man, a woman, and one boy in them. "These only have one boy which makes sense because Marcus was in the hospital."

Four more dates were missing and then there were two drawings of school activities. She set those aside. "This one is Foreman in a coffin, but his bruised face and cuts aren't covered with makeup. That's interesting because that's not how Foreman looked in the coffin. Why would he not have the makeup on him?" Sabre said. "The people behind the coffin all have their backs to it. That makes a curious statement."

"I guess that's his way of saying no one cared about his father."

The last picture was in the sunroom at Frank's house with a teenage boy and two women, one with gray hair. They were all smiling.

JP stood there in silence studying the progression of the drawings, occasionally picking up one to examine it more closely.

"What does it all mean?" she asked.

JP shook his head. "I don't know, but we're going to figure it out."

"It's not going to matter much if Riley is the one who killed his father. I won't be able to do anything with that information." Sabre threw her hands in the air, expressing her frustration. "That would be the ultimate betrayal. My job is to protect my minor client. How would I be protecting him if I help send him to prison?"

"Sabre, I know you, and I know you can't let Bob take the blame."

Sabre's hand shook as she picked up another picture. JP reached for her hand, took the drawing, and laid it down. Then he put his arm around her and pulled her into his arms, giving her a strong, safe hug. She laid her head against his shoulder for just a few seconds. She wanted to stay there forever in his safe, loving arms. For one moment in time the rest of the world didn't matter. But it did matter. Reality mattered and she alone could make it right. Hiding in the security blanket JP wrapped her in didn't change anything and that, too, would fade away. It always did. Sabre gave him a quick squeeze and pulled away.

"Okay, let's figure this out," Sabre said. "Then we'll find a way to make it right. We have to."

They lined the pictures up in order of date again. JP picked up the one of Riley's mother crying. "Here's what I think. Dana is upset and Riley wants to find out why. Or maybe his father hurt his mom and that's why his mother is crying. Either way it makes Riley angry and so he made some deal with Sammy to take him to see his father or at least use his car. Riley followed his dad to your office. Why Foreman went there, we don't know, but Riley and his father have a confrontation and Riley picks up the hourglass and hits his father over the head."

"He may have been protecting himself," Sabre said. "It could be self defense. Or whoever was driving Sammy's car may have killed him."

"That's true, but Riley ended up with the hourglass because there is no way he could've put that kind of detail in the drawing if he didn't have it for an extended length of time."

"So, either Riley killed him or he certainly knows who did. And who would he protect besides his mother?"

"Which leads us back to Dana."

Chapter 52

Sabre sat on her sofa with Riley's drawings spread out on the coffee table. The grandfather clock chimed four times. She had slept restlessly for about four hours. When she had another nightmare, she got up and went downstairs. Only this time it wasn't her usual dream. In fact, she hadn't had that one since she returned from the visit with her mother.

This time she dreamed of the objects in Riley's drawings. Something about them nagged at her, but she couldn't put her finger on it. She still agreed with the scenario she and JP had figured out earlier and she was pleased that it led back to Dana, leaving Riley with a possible out, but she felt like there was more. She picked up the drawings for the two weeks prior to Foreman's death and dissected each drawing several times. She was missing something.

She laid that bunch down and picked up the rest of them. The drawings with the family were like Rockwell's—a clean, bright, happy family together—but the others were dark, disturbing ones, like the one with Marcus hanging from the rope. She studied it, even though it made her stomach hurt. Something was wrong. She went through the drawings again and again. Just as the clock chimed five times, Sabre screamed, "Oh, no!" She laid the pictures out again, picking up the family pictures to inspect each one carefully.

She jumped up, picked up her phone, and called JP.

"Good morning, kid," he said.

"I think Riley tried to kill Marcus," Sabre said frantically.

"Calm down. Why do you think that?"

"Because Riley drew that sketch before Marcus hanged himself. Look at the pictures."

"Okay. I have them in front of me," JP said. "But it is dated the same day as the attempted suicide."

"But when would he have drawn it? He went to the hospital with Frank and Celia. He was there a good part of the night. But more importantly, look at what Marcus is wearing. You know how anal Riley is about details. He would have drawn him in the clothes he was wearing, but he didn't. He drew him in Alvarado Hospital issue, the way Marcus was dressed the last time Riley saw him before he drew the picture."

"Maybe."

"And another thing. Marcus is never in another family picture. It makes sense that he's not there while he was in the hospital, but Riley never puts him back into the drawings."

"So, what do we do next, boss?"

"I'm going to see Riley."

"Not alone, you're not."

"I'll be fine."

"Sabre, don't argue with me," he said in his sternest voice. "I'm going with you. He's only fourteen, but he may have already killed one person and tried to kill another."

"Okay. I'll meet you at the school around 7:00. We can catch him just before he goes into class. Then I can go the courthouse and you can go on your way."

Riley was a little annoyed at being questioned again. He protested that he would be late for class. Sabre assured him she'd be quick, although she was still uncertain as to exactly what she was going to say. Sabre had made arrangements with the office to use an empty classroom so they could have some privacy. She sat down at a student table across from Riley. JP remained standing and positioned himself at the end of the table between them.

"Look, Riley, I'm your attorney and I'm on your side, but some things have come to light and I need some answers so I can best represent you."

"Like what?"

"I know who killed your father." She looked him directly in the eyes. "And so do you. Do you want to tell me about it?"

"No," Riley said.

"I also know about Marcus." Riley didn't respond. "Do you hate your brother?"

"He does nothing but cause trouble. Always has."

"Enough that you wanted him dead?"

"Even if I did, you can't tell anyone," Riley said in an arrogant tone, one Sabre had never heard him use before.

"What you tell me is confidential," Sabre said. JP swallowed and shuffled his feet.

"I didn't murder my father. I promise you that." Riley's voice was quiet and sad. "But If I did kill George, he deserved it. He was always hurting my mother. He would've killed her if someone hadn't killed him first." His eyes narrowed and a threatening look came over his face. "No one hurts my mother and gets away with it."

"Riley, did you hang Marcus?"

"No. He did that himself."

"Did you encourage him?"

"He does whatever I tell him to do. He's such a baby."

"You need help, Riley. Let me take you somewhere where you can get help."

"No. I know what I need. I need my mother to come home and live with me. You can do that. You can bring her home. Tell the court to send her home. Just my mom and grandma and me. That's all I need. It won't be long now."

"What do you mean by that?"

"Nothing," Riley said.

"You should talk to someone...."

Riley interrupted. "I don't need to talk to anyone. I haven't done anything wrong. And you can't tell anyone." He stood up. "I'm going to class."

"Riley," Sabre pleaded, as he bolted out the door.

"That little punk!" JP said after Riley left. "He's sick."

"He needs psychiatric help and he needs it quickly," Sabre said. "And I still have the same dilemma. Riley's right, I can't tell anyone."

"Do you believe him, about not killing his father?"

Sabre shook her head. "I don't know."

Chapter 53

Sabre left Riley's school and had driven about ten minutes in the direction of the courthouse when she remembered the last drawing Riley did of the family. It contained two women and a boy, and then she thought of the accident Riley drew. That was it, she thought.

She pulled off the road before she entered the freeway and called Frank. He didn't answer his cell or the home phone. She started back toward Frank's house, which was only a few blocks from Riley's school.

Sabre called JP. "I think Riley tried to kill Frank and Marcus."

"Because?"

"The last picture of the family has two women and a boy. If that boy is Riley, which I expect it is, the women must be his mom and grandma."

"And there is no Frank in the picture, and I bet he drives a Jaguar."

"The car accident Riley drew was of a Jaguar and there were two bodies on the ground: one child and one adult male," Sabre said. "And you should have seen the look on Riley's face when Frank came home last night. I don't think he expected him to return."

"And remember Riley said, 'it won't be long now.' He must have something else planned."

"We need to warn Frank."

"I called and left a message telling him not to drive his car. I'm heading over there right now before he takes

Marcus to school. It's about that time. And I'm calling Klakken."

"Are you sure?" JP asked.

"This is a future crime, not something he's already done. It doesn't fall under any privilege," Sabre said. "I have to go. I'm almost there. I'll call you when I leave Frank's house. Oh, and could you try to call Frank again?"

"Sure."

Sabre hung up and just before she pulled into the Davis' driveway, she called the cell number Klakken had given her and left a message. "This is Attorney Sabre Brown. I have some information on Foreman's murder. I also have reason to believe that Frank Davis may be in danger. I'm going there now. Please call me as soon as possible."

As Sabre pulled into the circular driveway she noticed the garage door was open. Two cars were parked inside: a cream color Cadillac and a silver Jaguar. She breathed a sigh of relief. She wasn't too late. She walked quickly up to the front door and rang the bell. The door opened and suddenly Sabre was yanked inside, a gun to her head.

JP tried calling Frank a couple of times but no one answered. Then he tried Sabre again and when she didn't answer he exited the next off ramp and reentered the freeway, heading back the way he came. He called the school and discovered Riley had not shown up for class this morning. JP broke the speed limit as he moved rapidly north on Interstate 5 until he exited onto the La Jolla Parkway off ramp. He followed it until it dumped into Torrey Pines Rd. He was only a few blocks away from Frank's house.

Riley's eyes combined hate and fear as he held an unsteady 9 mm gun near Sabre's face. Frank, Celia, and

Marcus were lined up on the green designer sofa in the living room. A young man around eighteen or nineteen years old held them in place with a shotgun. Sabre didn't recognize him.

"Sit down," Riley said, nodding toward a green chair near the sofa.

Sabre looked at the group of hostages as she sat down. Marcus' face was white with fear. Celia looked as if she were about to pass out. Frank looked like a caged tiger ready to pounce at first chance. He was always in control, always the one calling the shots; Sabre feared he would do something foolish and they may all be killed.

"Watch them, or kill them, or whatever you're going to do," the older boy said. "No. Don't kill them yet. We need to leave as soon as the shots are fired and I need to finish getting the stuff out of the safe." He picked up a bag from the floor near his feet. "Let's take the Jaguar. I've always wanted a Jag."

Riley looked at him, dumbfounded. "We can't take the Jag, you idiot."

The young man chuckled. "Oh, that's right. I forgot. A person could get killed in that car." He walked off hastily down the hallway.

"How did you get into the safe, Riley?" Frank asked.

"When I was little I would see Grandma open the safe. I guess you never changed the combination," Riley said. Frank shot Celia an exasperated look, but she didn't seem to notice.

JP parked at the bottom of the circular driveway and walked up the side of the yard closest to the garage. The shades were closed on the front window. Moving carefully through the garage he made his way to the door, gun in hand. He very slowly turned the handle, but the door was locked. He left the garage and walked around to the back and hoisted himself up onto the deck where he could inch his way along the wall to the partially open sliding glass door of the sunroom. Standing back where he couldn't be seen, he peered around the corner. From there he could see the living room where Frank, Celia, and Marcus were huddled together on the green sofa and Sabre in the chair next to them. Standing in front of them, with his back to JP, was Riley with a gun pointed directly at Frank's head. JP could hear most of what was being said.

"Riley, you don't want to do this," Sabre said.

"I have to," Riley said. "You don't understand."

"But I do understand. I know you want to live in this house with your mother and your grandmother. You want life to be simple and you want to be loved. But you are loved by many people. You don't have to do this."

"My mom and grandma are the only ones who love me."

"Then let your grandma go. You don't want to hurt her. Look at her, Riley. She's so frightened." Riley glanced at his grandmother, who was trembling. "Your family won't be complete without her. You better let her go before she's accidentally hurt."

"I can't. She'll call the cops."

"Please, Riley," Celia said, leaning forward toward Riley. "Let Marcus go."

Sabre shook her head at Celia and said, "No, Celia."

But Celia kept talking. "He's just a little boy. Let him go."

Riley's face was red with anger as he whipped the gun toward Marcus and pointed it at his head. "No, Grandma. Don't you try to protect him. He's just trouble to you. I'm your good boy, not Marcus."

Celia pulled back against the sofa, her hand tightly grabbing Marcus' arm.

Sabre glanced around the room trying to figure out what to do. She knew the young man helping Riley would return soon. He could already be watching them since Sabre couldn't see the hallway from where she sat. The doorbell rang just as she started to plead again with Riley.

"Who is that?" Riley said to no one in particular.

"It's probably the police," Frank said. "I expect the house is surrounded by now."

Sabre wondered if he really believed that or if he was bluffing. Either way she wasn't sure it was the right move. Riley was very fidgety and she was afraid he could do anything at this point.

"You lied to me," Riley said, looking at Sabre. "You called the cops on your own client."

"No, I didn't, Riley. I haven't told them anything. Look, I can still help you. Please let me help you."

"You don't want to help me."

"Yes, I do. Riley, you don't need to do this. There are other ways."

Riley ignored her and said to Celia. "Grandma, answer the door." He yanked Marcus off the sofa and pointed the gun at the side of his head. "If it's the cops, make them go away or I'll kill Marcus."

Sabre fixed her eyes on Marcus, trying to make him feel a little safer. He was trembling. She wanted so badly to get him out of Riley's clutches. She wanted to trade places with Marcus, but she feared even the suggestion would set Riley off.

The doorbell rang again.

"Go," Riley said to his grandma.

JP was about to back off the deck and call 9-1-1 when he heard the doorbell ring. He waited. When Celia stood up and walked to the door, JP inched the door open and slipped inside. He positioned himself behind a wicker armoire which blocked him only from Riley and Marcus as long as Riley's back was turned. He caught Sabre's eye and she quickly glanced away. Riley had his eyes on his grandma.

Celia opened the door.

"M…may I help you?"

"I'm Detective Shane Klakken, San Diego Homicide. Is Frank Davis home?"

JP spotted Riley's accomplice, Chris McKenzie, standing in the hallway near the stairs. JP pointed his gun at Chris just as Chris raised his gun and aimed it at Klakken. JP yelled, "Klakken, watch out!" Chris fired his gun and so did JP. Klakken hit the ground, pulling Celia down with him.

Riley pushed Marcus down and turned his gun on Sabre.

"You liar! You called the police!" His hand trembled as he waved the gun at her.

"No, I didn't," Sabre said firmly.

Chris lay at the bottom of the stairs in a pool of blood. JP kicked Chris' gun away as he passed him. JP and Klakken moved swiftly across the floor toward Riley, guns drawn. They both stopped when Riley yelled, "Stop or I'll shoot her." His gun pointed at Sabre's head.

Klakken stood several steps behind the chair where Sabre was seated. JP stood to his left. Riley was only a few feet from Sabre and Frank.

"Put the gun down, son," Klakken said. "It's over."

"No. It's not over. Someone has to die for hurting my mother. They all hurt my mother."

"Someone has already died," Klakken said. "Your father is dead. Isn't that enough?"

Riley started to cry. A blend of raging man and little boy emerged as the sadness and anger spread through his voice. "I didn't mean to kill him. I was so mad and when he laughed at me and called my mom a 'stupid bitch' I just picked up the hourglass and hit him. Then Chris said…."

JP slowly moved closer to Riley as he spoke.

"Riley," Sabre said, as she slowly stood up. She could hear sirens. Help was on the way. "Don't say anything more. Let me help you."

He looked at her with pleading eyes.

"I can help you. Your father's death was an accident. It's not too late if you stop this right now."

"I didn't kill my father," Riley said. A sudden rage crept back into his eyes. He started to move the gun away from Sabre but still held it at the same level.

Klakken took a step closer. "That's it, son. Put the gun down."

But Riley's hand stopped when the gun reached Frank, but he didn't look at him. Keeping his eyes on JP and Klakken, Riley said, "Tell them, Frank. I didn't kill my father, did I?"

JP inched his way closer to Riley. He was within about three feet when Riley yelled, "Stop!" Then Riley turned abruptly back to Frank. "Tell them, Frank."

"Come on, son. Put it down," Klakken said. "Listen to your attorney. She can help you. Hear the sirens. This place will be filled with cops in a minute. There's no way out."

For several seconds no one said anything. The only sound was Marcus softly whimpering on the floor and the sirens getting closer.

"Tell them what you did," Riley yelled at Frank.

Frank's brow wrinkled. "I don't know what you're talking about."

"Oh, yes you do. Tell them." Riley shook the gun at him.

"What's he talking about?" Klakken asked. "Frank, do you know who killed Foreman?"

"He did." Frank nodded his head toward Riley. "He just said he did and that he didn't mean to. He's talking crazy now." A stern look came over Frank's face. "Riley, put the gun down before someone else gets hurt. I'll help you through this. Everything will be alright. I can help you."

"Just like you helped my mom," Riley said bitterly.

Sabre could hear the police vehicles pulling up to the house.

"Riley," Frank said in a softer voice. "Please, put the gun down. The police are surrounding the house. It's over."

"I killed George alright, but I didn't kill my father," Riley said, accentuating the last word and furiously looking at Klakken. "Foreman wasn't my father." He swung his head back toward Frank. "Tell them, Frank. Tell them." The gun shook as he aimed it lower on Frank's body. "What's the matter? Are you afraid of your own son, Frank?"

Frank remained calm. "Riley, listen to your attorney. We'll both help you. It's over."

Riley glared at him for one second and then said, "You're right. It's over." In one swift move Riley aimed at Frank's crotch and pulled the trigger. JP lunged at Riley and pushed him to the floor. The gun fell from Riley's hand and clanged as it hit the tile.

Frank yelped and doubled up. Blood flowed from his body onto the expensive green sofa. Police rushed in and with Klakken giving directions, they handcuffed Riley. JP swooped Marcus up off the floor where he lay whimpering. Then with Marcus in one arm, JP wrapped his free arm around Sabre and escorted them both outside.

Chapter 54

Sabre and JP waited until Riley was ushered into the police car and hauled away. Then she called Marla, the social worker, and gave an accounting of the events that had just taken place.

"I'll be right there. Should I plan on picking up Marcus?" Marla said.

"You may have to. He should probably go to Polinsky for the night. His grandma said he could sleep downstairs in the guest bedroom next to her room tonight and she assured me she'd keep an eye on him, but she's not in very good shape herself."

"And you don't think he's at risk for suicide?"

"He never tried to commit suicide," Sabre informed her. "Riley made him do it."

"How?"

"Marcus told me he was very afraid of his brother. Riley would threaten him all the time and he always came through with his threats. This time he told him he wanted to draw him hanging for a school assignment. When Marcus refused, Riley said he'd kill his grandma if he didn't do it. He also assured Marcus that he wouldn't get hurt. He just wanted to see what it looked like and it would only be for a second. Then he'd save him. He promised he wouldn't let him die."

"That's horrible. But why did Riley want Marcus dead?" Marla said. "Was he jealous of Marcus? That doesn't really make sense because Riley appeared to get way more attention than Marcus did. It annoyed me the way Dana would refer to Riley as her 'good son.'"

"I think Riley wanted anyone out of the way that hurt his mother. That meant Frank, George, and Marcus all had to go. His mind has gotten pretty twisted. I'm just hoping the psychiatrists can sort it out and help him."

"Me, too. Thanks for calling, Sabre. I'll see that Marcus is safe tonight."

Sabre hung up just as Klakken walked up to JP. Klakken extended his hand to JP, who reached out and shook it. "Thanks for saving my life," Klakken said.

"I'm glad I was here," JP said. Klakken let go of JP's hand and started to turn away when JP spoke. "I'm sorry, Shane. I'm really sorry for everything."

Klakken looked back at him, nodded his head, and walked away.

JP's face showed sorrow and anguish as he watched Klakken leave. Sabre could see as he choked back the words that he wanted to say more, but he either couldn't find the right words to say or there just weren't any.

He put his arm around Sabre's shoulder and led her toward their cars. "Let's go. I'm taking you home. I'll pick up your car later and bring it to you."

"I have to go to court. And I'm okay to drive."

"I'd rather you didn't. Look at you. You're trembling. I have to give you this: You were steady as a rock while Riley held that gun on you, but now you're about as frazzled as a cow's hide under a branding iron. Please, let me drive you."

Sabre started to acquiesce but changed her mind. "Really, I'm okay. I need my car this morning, but could you please call Jerry Leahy and tell him what happened? Maybe he can get a hearing set today and get Bob's charges dropped."

"Sure." He turned and stepped toward his car.

"JP?" Sabre called after him.

He looked back. "Yes."

"Can I buy you a drink tonight?"

"You bet."

Sabre hurried back to court, where she completed her morning calendar as well as Bob's. She was still pretty shaken by the events, but she was feeling much better by the time her calendar was concluded. Then she set up a special hearing for later that day on the Foreman case to inform the court of what had happened and to be relieved as Riley's counsel. The court could decide whether or not to have her continue representing Marcus.

Sabre called the other attorneys on the case to let them know about the special she had set and then drove to Pho's to get an order to go. With her order of rice paper rolls and a number 124 she drove to the courthouse downtown for Bob's hearing. She received a call from JP just as she parked her car.

"All charges were dropped," JP said. "They're working on his release right now. It won't be long."

"I'll meet you out front in a few minutes."

Sabre walked to the front steps of the courthouse and sat down on a concrete wall. She set her food order on the wall next to her and she waited. It was finally over. Bob would get his life back. But her heart went out to both Riley and Marcus. Their lives were forever changed. She could only hope that Dana would get her life together and make a home for Marcus and that Riley would get the help he needed to make him whole again.

Only about five minutes had passed when the courthouse door flew open and Sabre saw Bob and JP walk toward her. She dashed up the steps and hugged Bob. He hugged her back and then took a deep breath.

"What a great feeling—sucking that smoggy air into my lungs," Bob said.

"At least there's room for it now that you haven't been smoking," Sabre said. Then she threw an accusing look at Bob. "You haven't been smoking, have you?"

He shook his head. "No. Cigarettes weren't too readily available...at least not for me. I didn't know how to work the system like some of the regulars."

"Good. At least that's something."

"Yes, that's something," Bob said.

Sabre held the plastic bag up from Pho's. "Smell," she said. "Oh, that's right, you don't have a sense of smell. Well, I knew you'd be in a hurry to get home to Marilee and Corey so I brought you lunch from Pho's." She handed him the bag.

"Thanks, both of you."

"Ready?" JP asked. Bob nodded. JP turned to Sabre. "How about if I meet you back at the juvenile court after I drop Bob off? You said you had a hearing, right?"

"Sure. That'll work."

Sabre sat on the bench outside of Courtroom Four talking to Dave Carr as they waited for the special to be called.

"Dana confessed to the police that she lied about the affair with your friend, Bob Clark," Dave said. "She and George were initially going to try to extort money from him. Then when Foreman died she didn't see any reason not to continue with the lie."

"Didn't she realize that it made Bob look more guilty?"

"I don't think she thought it through. I'm just glad I didn't know any differently. That must have really haunted you to have to keep your client's confidence while your friend sat in jail."

"It wasn't easy," Sabre said.

"I'm sure you'll be pleased to know they bandaged Frank up and placed him under arrest. He's still in the hospital, but he's handcuffed to his bed."

"So, what Riley said was true?"

"According to Dana, Frank molested her from the time she was about twelve years old until she left his house with George and Riley. The DNA will tell for certain, but Dana says there's no doubt who the father is. She claimed she wasn't even sleeping with George when she got pregnant." Then Dave smirked. "Riley had a pretty good aim. He hit Frank where it hurt the most."

"What do you mean?"

"Let's just say, Frank won't have the balls to do that again."

Sabre looked up and saw JP standing in the hallway near Department Four. She smiled at him. He stayed there and Sabre knew he was being respectful of her private conversation. She stood up and said, "Excuse me a minute."

She walked over to speak to JP, certain that she felt Dave's eyes follow her across the floor.

"We're next," Sabre said.

"I'll wait outside. I just wanted you to know I was here." Without even looking at Dave, he said, "I don't like that guy." And he walked out.

Sabre couldn't help seeing the shrewd look on Dave's face as she walked back to the bench where he sat. The usual smiling eyes were replaced with more serious ones. Then he sighed and smiled and the playful look returned. He gently picked up Sabre's hand. "I really like you, Sabre. And you know I'd like to get to know you better." He paused.

Sabre waited. She didn't know where he was going with this and she was a little distracted by the setting.

Dave stood up, still holding her hand. "When you're over the cowboy, let me know." He brought her hand up to his lips, kissed it quickly and gently, and then let go and walked into Department Four.

Chapter 55

The waitress delivered a Corona and a Midori Margarita to the tall bar table where Sabre and JP were standing. JP paid for the drinks.

"Hey, this is my treat," Sabre said.

"Next time," JP said, but Sabre knew it would be the same the next time. He never let her pay when it was just the two of them.

Sabre raised her glass. "To Bob," she said.

"To Bob." He clinked his beer bottle against her margarita. They each drank from their respective drinks. "So, what's going to happen to Riley and Marcus?"

"It's hard to say. Riley will be charged but hopefully they'll try him as a minor, not an adult, but either way they have to be able to see how troubled he is. And I'm hoping Dana can get her act together and regain custody of Marcus. If his grandmother doesn't get her drinking problem under control, Marcus won't be able to stay there. At the hearing this afternoon, they both seemed committed to making things better for him, but only time will tell."

"I hope so," JP said.

"Some parents make growing up so difficult for their children," Sabre said.

"And some kids make growing up difficult for their parents. My parents were good and sometimes I was such a pain in the ass; one of my brothers was even worse. And look at Sammy's dad, Ludwik Bernard Sampulski. He spent his whole life trying to make things better for his family and look how Sammy turned out. By the way, Ludwik called me today. He's taking a trip and he asked me to check on Sammy while he's gone, just to make sure he has books to read and stuff like that."

"You must have made quite an impression on the old man." Sabre looked at JP admiringly. "Where's he going?"

"He's returning to Poland with a canister of dirt. He scooped it up off the ground when he first arrived in America. He has saved it all these years and now he's taking it home to sprinkle on his father's grave."

Sabre didn't even know what to say to that. They sat in silence for a few minutes, then Sabre raised her glass again and said, "To Ludwik Bernard Sampulski."

"To Ludwik," JP repeated.

The waitress came by with another order of drinks. JP paid again over Sabre's protests.

Sabre thanked him. She took a sip of her margarita and then looked into the eyes of a man she had such respect and genuine affection for and wondered why it made her so uncomfortable to think about changing their relationship in any way, not that he wanted to. But did she? Each drink brought her closer to saying something to him. Their eyes held each other in silence. The silence made Sabre squirm. Finally, she said, "What happened with you and Klakken?"

At first JP didn't answer and he appeared very distant. He sighed. "We were rookies and I was young and foolish and a whole lot wilder. Some would even describe me as 'cocky.' The uniform made me more attractive with the ladies and I took advantage of it. I never dated any one girl too long. When they started getting too close I would back off."

Sabre was surprised to hear this side of JP. She had known him several years now and all she ever saw was a stable, caring man. His charm was in his ruggedness and his laid-back attitude, but although he was extremely handsome and all the women found him charming, she never quite pegged him as a ladies' man.

JP continued. "Then at a big Christmas party I met this one woman who was as beautiful as rain in west Texas and twice as mysterious. I fell hard and fast, too hard and too fast. It was a whirlwind romance of hotel rendezvous and secret meetings in dark places. She never invited me to her house and she never even told me her last name. I could have found out who she was had I put my mind to it, but at that age the mystery was part of the intrigue." JP paused.

"And then you found out she was connected to Klakken somehow," Sabre said, anticipating what was to come.

"Yes, she was his wife and he loved her very much. He idolized her. You could tell by the way he talked about her at the station, but I had never seen her with him and I didn't know she was married to him. Klakken and I weren't partners or anything so I wasn't that close to him, but the other guys said that she was all he ever talked about."

"Oh no. He found out, I take it."

"That wasn't the worst part." JP swallowed. "We were meeting one night at a shady hotel, a place that rented by the hour. I know it sounds cheesy, but she always picked the hotels and they were always on the cheap side. I appreciated it because I had only been on the force about a year and I wasn't making a lot of money. But for her, I think it was more about the secrecy and the adventure. We would share a six-pack of beer and she always had a cigarette when we were done, although she said she never smoked any other time. It was like something out of an old noir movie."

JP stopped talking for a minute. He finished off his Corona and ordered another round before he started to speak again.

"I usually arrived at the hotel first, paid for the room, and waited inside. That's the way she wanted it. But that night I was running late and I arrived just as she pulled up. I probably would have noticed I was being followed if I hadn't been frustrated that I was late. And I was anxious to get there and see her. Anyway, I drove up right next to her and got out of the car. She took two steps toward me when a car flew up close to us. I saw the gun sticking out of the window and I flung myself at her to knock her out of the way. But it was too late. There she lay, sprawled on pavement in a pool of blood, her beautiful face blown to bits."

"Oh, my!" Sabre shuddered.

JP sat in silence.

Sabre said, "Did they catch the guy who did it?"

"Oh, yeah. It turned out to be some punk-ass kid trying to make a name for himself in the gangbanger world. The bullet was meant for me because it would have changed his status if he killed a cop. He's still doing time in Soledad State Prison. But it was all over the news, local and national."

"National? Why?"

"Because it turned out the shooter was the illegitimate son of some congressman from one of the southern states." JP's eyes dropped down. "Klakken not only lost the love of his life that night, but he was further humiliated by the circumstances of her death. He didn't want to blame her, so I received the brunt of his anger...not that I didn't deserve it. I did. I should've found out who she was. I was an arrogant kid back then, but I'd like to think I wouldn't have been with her had I known."

JP looked at Sabre with a strange emptiness in his eyes. This strong, private man had just made himself so vulnerable to her. She suddenly felt the urge to hold him, to comfort him, even to kiss him. She quickly realized how inappropriate the latter would be and she grew frustrated with herself. It must have been the alcohol. She wasn't used to drinking and her third margarita glass was nearly empty. It felt good to let loose after all that had happened the past few weeks—the Foreman case, the nightmares, and Bob's arrest. She hadn't realized until now just how much had piled up. Sabre didn't think she was drunk, but she definitely had had too much to drive. That much she knew. She felt lightheaded and her lips were beginning to feel numb. Words were harder to pronounce, but she felt the need to console JP. She reached over with her right hand and touched his arm. He placed his hand on top of hers and his expression softened.

"JP," she said, with some difficulty. "Why haven't you and I…why is it…?" She reached up to his head with her left hand and gently stroked the side of his face. She teetered to the side and he reached out and steadied her. His face was so close that his breath felt warm on her cheek.

JP pulled back just slightly and his eyes smiled again when he spoke. "You are something special, Sabre. Probably too special for me, and as much as I'd like to have this conversation right now, I think you've had a little too much of the ignorant oil." He loosened his hold on her.

Sabre tried to steady herself but she had little control. JP reached his arm around her. "We better go," he said.

Sabre smiled at him as they walked out. "Tomorrow," she said. "We'll talk tomorrow."

"Tomorrow," he repeated.

ABOUT THE AUTHOR

Teresa Burrell has dedicated her life to helping children and their families. As an attorney, Ms. Burrell has spent countless hours working pro bono in the family court system. She continues to advocate children's issues and write novels, many of which are inspired by actual legal cases.

Teresa Burrell is available at www.teresaburrell.com.
Like her page on Facebook at
www.facebook.com/theadvocateseries

Please send an email to Teresa and let her know what you thought of THE ADVOCATE'S DILEMMA. She would love to hear from you. She can be reached at: teresa@teresaburrell.com

Made in the USA
Charleston, SC
06 January 2013